Praise for Walter Keady's previous novels

Keady will leave readers of Irish fiction eager for a sequel

– Publishers Weekly

Keady is a true storyteller, with an absolute command of the English language

– St. Petersburg Times

Keady will win the hearts of readers with his charming tale

– Irish America Magazine

Keady is a refreshing new voice in Irish fiction

– Library Journal

The great strength of this novel is that it is not afraid to ask big questions

– The Philadelphia Enquirer

You have to love the title character of Walter Keady's second novel

– The New York Times

A gem-like celebration of life

– Dallas Morning News

This novel will connect Irish-Americans with their heritage

– Booklist

Sweet and funny, with a touch of tartness – an apple pie of a book

– Orlando Sentinel

Keady ... has cleverly, subtly, captured the warm nostalgic spirit of rural Ireland

– Boston Sunday Herald

THE SILENCE OF GOD

by

WALTER KEADY

To my friend Eamon, ever encouraging me along

Walter 12/8/16

Castletree Books

New York

Published by *Castletree Books*

To

The Wheeler Family

Acknowledgments

My thanks to my special friends, the members of *Taconic Writers* – Elaine Andersen, Cary Auerbach, Paul Callagy, Josephine Hausam, Ed Lieberthal, Elton Renfroe, Virginia Reynolds, Nanette Stone – for listening to and critiquing the novel.

I would also like to say thanks to David Cole Wheeler for his wonderful cover design.

And I am grateful to my wife Jennifer for her ever generous support.

DEIRDRE

The day Ignatius Lally walked into her office in Clyard, Deirdre McCarthy admitted later to her sister Eavan, was the most significant day of her life. She had actually seen him arrive at the novitiate the previous afternoon, though she had thought nothing of it at the time. She was passing the entrance on her way home from work when a car coming from the opposite direction waited for her to go by before turning in. She had glanced at the driver; a smasher, she noted casually in passing, though not a familiar face. But when he came into her office next day with Father Norton she remembered him immediately as the handsome man in the car. Norton himself was a rather dour fellow. Though they got along reasonably well, the relationship between herself and the retiring novice master had always been a bit strained. As she explained to Eavan more than once in their phone conversations, the man didn't seem to know what on God's earth to make of women, and he oscillated between the sulky and the patronizing in her presence. So she was thrilled when he said Father Lally would be taking over from him. And though she politely refrained from shouting "whoopee!" she shook the handsome priest's hand with a good deal more warmth than the protocol for greeting a new boss required. And that was the start of a relationship that blossomed on her part in the space of just a single month into the lust she later admitted to Eavan. Not that she gave Father Lally any indication of the fires that were scorching her knickers. On the surface it was *yes Father* this and *no Father* that, till Father said one day, "call me Ignatius, Deirdre."

"I worship the ground he walks on," she told her sister a couple of weeks later in her convent-cultivated accent. But Father Lally seemed not to have been affected at all by the heat she was generating for him. He stepped into the dour one's shoes without missing a step, had her explain how the fund-raising system worked, said it was quite clear she knew how to handle it without any help from him and, to prove he meant it, gave her an immediate raise in salary, something his predecessor had always been miserly about doing.

When Ignatius visited the office, which he did for about an hour every Monday morning, she'd give him a brief report on her work before adroitly turning the conversation around to himself and pumping him discreetly for every scrap of information she could dig out about his life and his thoughts. If she couldn't get to know him carnally, which was what she'd really like, at least she could have intimate acquaintance with the rest of him. She learned about his growing up dirt poor, as he put it, on a Mayo farm. About his father, a decent man but an alcoholic whose vice sent him early to his grave. And about his mother, a hard-working woman, God bless her, but a harridan to husband and children alike; still to the good, he admitted, smiling ruefully, and still ruling the roost on the farm, where his youngest brother Dan had a family now and was making a good business out of the land. The rest of his seven siblings were scattered over the globe like sailors gone to sea, some in England and America, one in Madagascar of all places, and one in Singapore.

But it was Ignatius himself Deirdre wanted to know about and she probed his experience in Brazil under pretext of it helping her organize the Missionary Fund-raiser. In that way she became familiar with the *favelas* of Sao Paulo, and the *communidades de base,* and the liberation theology that was frowned on by Rome but embraced by those who dealt with the reality of destitution amid plenty; and their despair of ever changing the status quo. And she watched him expound his beliefs as those brown eyes lit up, and dreamed that his passion for justice might some day become passion for her.

Just after the Christmas and New Year holidays, then, it seemed the most natural thing in the world for her to say to him one Monday as he was taking his leave, "would you ever like to come over for dinner with the family on Sunday?" It wasn't that she particularly wanted him to meet her family, or vice versa, but she couldn't very well ask him for a candlelight tête-à-tête, which was what she'd really have liked. However, when he said he'd love to come to dinner she was terrified, and worried for the rest of the work-day about whether Padhraig, her husband, would be mad at her for asking him.

Her friends in Dublin had said eighteen years earlier that she was starkers when, fresh out of the University, she had gotten engaged to Padhraig McCarthy. Not only was he eight years older, he was a bloody cow doctor. Worse still, she had only known him a few months: a friend of a cousin she had gone to a rock concert with had brought him along, more from pity than interest she later admitted, and the two had struck up a relationship. It wasn't the case that Padhraig had gone out of his way to chat her up in a hurry or anything; on the contrary it was his taciturnity that had intrigued Deirdre, who loved to talk herself and wondered what deep waters must flow beneath an exterior so silent. Anyway, the upshot was that she married the vet six months later and went to live with him in a back of beyond hole in the wall called Clyard, down in County Tipperary.

Sadly, like many a marriage, the union turned out to be less than ideal. Her husband's deep-flowing waters contained more sludge of grudges against mankind than rich philosophical ore. The same waters were also thickly laced with a dark patriarchal silt. When Eavan put it to her that had this latter trait come to light before the exchange of *I do*'s, she might not have walked down the aisle with him in the first place, Deirdre had to admit that she most likely would not. "Though to tell you the truth, Eavan, I probably married him because deep down he resembled father, the nicest of men in many ways but also a stickler for obedience to authority, especially his own."

And for fifteen years she had struggled to reconcile her growing independence of thought, heavily influenced by the wildfire raising of women's consciousness all over the country, with her role as mother and housekeeper and nurturer of her domineering husband. And she might, she admitted to Eavan, have gone on that way for the rest of her life without ever taking decisive action to assert her own personal rights, if it weren't for that casual remark thrown off by Padhraig one evening in the middle of dinner. Fiona, the eldest child, fourteen years old at the time, forever Daddy's pet and forever at odds with her mother, had pseudo-innocently asked a loaded question: "are you in favor of divorce, Daddy?" It was the week before the second national referendum. "Mrs. Langan says everyone ought to have a well-thought out opinion on the subject." Fiona's English teacher was an outspoken proponent of women's causes.

"Does she now?" And when Padhraig McCarthy finished chewing he sucked in air twice and expelled it with force each time before answering the question. "Well you can tell Mrs. Langan that your father does indeed have a well-thought out opinion on the subject, And you can tell her what it is, too: a woman belongs to her husband from the day she marries him and she has no earthly right to go trying to get away from her duty to him." He stabbed an emotional slice of potato before adding, "and women like Mary Langan have no right to be putting their ridiculous notions in other women's heads."

There was nothing novel about her husband's position on divorce, or on women for that matter, Deirdre admitted to herself afterwards. He had taken a clear stand against the dissolution of marriage during the first referendum in 1986 and was equally outspoken when the issue was raised again ten years later. What *was* novel was her own reaction to her husband's statement. While she would rail among her women friends against the subjugation of her sex by patriarchal men she had never been able to acknowledge that included in that generic injustice was her own particular subjugation by patriarchal Padhraig McCarthy. But the instant he uttered the phrase *a woman belongs to her husband*, her eyes were opened and she saw wifely obedience for the tyranny that it was, and she could never be the same again. And immediately, like a woman reborn, she spoke up in a way that she had never challenged her spouse before, especially in front of the children.

"The days of slavery are gone," she said, quietly but firmly, addressing her eldest daughter. "Nobody owns anybody any more. And most certainly husbands do not own their wives. So you can tell Mrs. Langan that your mother, too, has a well-thought-out position on divorce. And it is that when a marriage breaks down to the point where the spouses can no longer live together in peace and harmony then divorce ought to be an available option." Flushed with that effort, she picked up her fork and resumed her dinner.

Fiona giggled nervously and looked at her father. "What do you think of that, Daddy?"

Padhraig chewed on in silence for a bit. Then, also addressing his daughter, he said, "your mother has a right to her opinions, too." And, after pausing for effect, he added, "especially when she's wrong." His smile told the children that it was perfectly all right to laugh at their mother.

Which invitation to ridicule gave rise to the spurt of adrenalin that assured continued life to Deirdre's new-born independence. *How dare he!* And though she said nothing at that moment, his days, as she told Eavan later, were over as master of her soul or lord of her body. Her behavior thereafter, while remaining outwardly compliant for the most part, became inwardly more and more independent. That translated into devious, inconsistent, untruthful, and a host of additional modes of thought and action of which she was in no way proud but which she felt were necessary for the good of her mental and physical health, the care of her children, and even the survival of her mediocre marriage.

Asking Father Lally to dinner without first getting her husband's agreement was an indication of how far she had advanced towards freedom in the past three years. From the beginning of their marriage Padhraig had attempted to exercise a strong control over her social life, choosing the people with whom they would associate and discouraging her from seeing certain of her existing friends whom he regarded as bad influence or a threat to the utter devotion he must have from his wife. These included not only old flames but also several of her women friends from Dublin days whom he labeled trendy feminists and whose moral character he thought quite deplorable. She got around this prohibition by visiting Eavan in Dublin, a religious duty she piously told him, since her sister was single and needed the social and spiritual consolation of her company. While there, she and Eavan would entertain those friends and acquaintances whom her husband considered unsuitable for a wife and mother.

She was surprised, then, when on informing Padhraig that the new novice master about whom she had already told him much, was coming to dinner on Sunday, he merely said, "I'm looking forward to meeting him."

"You're going to like him. He's a nice man," she added casually, almost too casually.

Ignatius Lally was disappointed at the intellectual potential displayed by four of his five young charges. The novitiate class of '98-'99 was not laced with *la creme de la creme* of Saint Fursa's, as it had been in his own days. However, what the young men lacked in brains they made up for in piety, as he said more than once to his assistant Master, Noel Corrigan. So pious were a few of them that the same Corrigan sometimes grumbled that they were "too bloody holy for my taste," after he had to pry them from chapel benches at bedtime or persuade them to wear socks in the coldest days of winter.

The quality of their piety occasionally disturbed Ignatius. The fervor that had been drummed into himself in novitiate and seminary he had honed and tuned and mellowed in the liberal religious climate of Brazil. That experience, he felt, had cleansed him of the dross of casuistry and scruples. Compassion for the poor who surrounded him in the favelas had replaced concern for impractical nuances of theology. The besetting sin of Brazil was the failure of the power elite to mitigate the poverty of the masses, he lectured his Lord, not the lasciviousness of *carnaval*. His God had agreed, and made not a syllable of fuss either when Ignatius repudiated infallibility, both papal and ecclesiastical, in conversations with his fellow priests.

His novices, on the other hand, with the exception of their one intellectual, Sean Moylan, were a narrow-minded intolerant lot in the matter of legal observance. Priggish was a word he'd rather not use in their regard, *but priggish they are,* he complained to his God. They represented, in their immature thinking, the most conservative attitudes of the country in matters theological and social, parroting no doubt the beliefs of their parents and teachers. He repeatedly encouraged them to think for themselves and solicited their very own thought-out opinions on all class subjects. "The world you'll be working in," he told them in conference one evening shortly after Christmas, "is a world in change. And even the church herself must reflect that change if she is to survive."

Up went the hand of ruddy-faced Richard Walsh. "But doesn't the pope tell us, Father, that it's the world that must change, not the church; that the church teaches eternal truths? At least that's what my dad was always drumming into us at home," he added.

"Indeed, Richard." They were sitting in comfortable chairs and sofas in what had once been Mr. Darley's drawing room. "The fundamental truths of Christianity are of course eternal, but their application often can, and sometimes must, be modified to meet the particular needs of time and place and circumstances."

"Could you give us an example?" Richard had established himself early on as a persistent defender of the status quo.

"I'll give you a couple from the past." They weren't ready yet to face present-day controversies like abortion and homosexuality that were still open sores in this once conservative Catholic country. "It's not too long since the church condemned what it called usury. Today, the world's economy depends on the practice, and the church itself gets much of its financial support from the money market." When he looked around, three brows were furrowed, as if he had just uttered incomprehensible gibberish. "Another more recent example: from the mid-nineteenth century on, Protestant scholars have been developing methodologies such as textual and literary criticism, as well as archeological diggings, for studying the Bible, thereby making great advances in understanding the text. Catholic scholars, however, were forbidden to use those methods until the nineteen forties."

The furrowed brows remained furrowed. Annoyed, he added, "just a few years ago the present pope said that slavery was intrinsically and always evil. Yet the Church condoned slavery in the past; even popes owned slaves."

"So what do you think of contraception, Father?" Sean Moylan, the clever one, the mask of innocence on his baby face cloaking the undoubted malice of the question.

"Good question, Sean." He'd rather not deal with it yet, but since it had been raised ... "Tell me what *you* think of it?" Which brought a snigger from Richard Walsh; Noel Corrigan had informed him that only the strict rules of novitiate behavior had kept those two from coming to blows on more than one occasion.

"Richard here says it has turned the world into Sodom and Gomorrah, but I think it's cool." Sean swung around and winked at Walsh.

"But the pope has condemned it, hasn't he?" Kevin Harper almost shouted at Moylan. A paleface blond with deep blue eyes, Kevin had the look of a cherub and the mind of a sieve; Ignatius had more or less decided to send him away for lack of intellectual acumen.

"Several popes have condemned it," he acknowledged. "On the other hand, the church is the people of God, isn't it?" He paused for reaction. Heads nodded slowly and hesitantly, as if fearing the consequence of assent. "And it would appear that the people of God, or at least the great majority of them – even in this country – have decided that contraception *is* okay. So who is right, the pope or the people of God?"

"Ah Jeez! I'm really confused now," Brian Lenihan moaned. But Ignatius left them without a solution. "This is the world and the church you must live with," he said forcefully. "There aren't clear answers to everything, and as priests you're going to have to make up your own minds on a lot of very thorny questions."

"They're going to have to learn to think for themselves," he told his Assistant on several occasions when they discussed the progress of their charges. He knew well that Corrigan, who was only a few years ordained and had no pastoral experience, was himself inclined to hew to strictest orthodoxy.

PADHRAIG

Padhraig McCarthy didn't bother to tell his wife that he already knew Father Lally. The very first time she had mentioned the man's name he knew it had to be him. Who else could it be? Naeshie Lally, his one-time friend at Saint Fursa's had gone off to be a priest with the Congregation of World Missionaries. Hadn't he himself almost gone with him! His confessor had suggested several times during his senior year that he join their ranks. He had on occasion since regretted that he hadn't; he'd be a bishop in Brazil by now. And it would have been a better job than sticking his hand up the arses of cows, that was for sure. On the other hand, he'd have had to do without sex. Or would he? More and more it was coming to light that the clergy had been managing to combine sex with celibacy; having their cake and eating it, as it were. Not that married sex was all it was cracked up to be – at least not for him. Deirdre, despite her youth and beauty when he married her, had turned out a bit of a disappointment in that respect. She'd gone from a kind of girlish aggression in the sack – which used to put him off his stride – to a sort of resigned passivity after she had the babies. And, once the youngest, Cathal, was born no more pregnancies occurred. He suspected that she was taking the pill without telling him; but although he challenged her several times, pointing out that birth control was immoral and against Catholic teaching, even quoting the sacred words of Pope Paul the Sixth that "every act of love must be open to the possibility of life," damn the bit of good it ever did. Matters had gotten even worse in the past couple of years: for though she never directly denied him access, she made him aware every time that the favor was hers for the giving and that she gave only when she chose.

So now he was tempted to look elsewhere, though the opportunities weren't too great in a place like Clyard without everyone knowing what you were up to, especially when you were a public figure, as he was. However, his sexual needs had become so urgent lately that he was even looking at daughter Fiona. The clergy would say it was wrong of course, but then the clergy said everything that gave pleasure was wrong. The law said it was wrong, too. Fair dues to that. But the fellows in the Old Testament did it, and God didn't seem to mind, did He? And the tradition in Ireland was strong, too, and it was old, and the old people were never that far wrong about things, were they? Didn't his own father do it with Ida? And his mother knew about it, too, and she never said a word. Not that he'd want Deirdre to know about himself and Fiona if they ever got going: God alone knew what she might do, especially in her present frame of mind. She had changed so much in the past couple of years: all that women's lib stuff had affected her, especially after the divorce referendum with its endless spouting from the liberal media. Wife-swapping sodomites, the lot of them.

One of these days he really was going to go for Fiona. She'd let him, too, he'd bet: anything to please her Daddy. Just turned seventeen and gorgeous, with her long legs and well-developed breasts; looking more and more like his sister Ida. God! Ida was great. Always laughing and up to every sort of devilment. The two of them used to do everything together, Ida the eldest and himself next, and the younger ones not able to keep up with them. They'd start the milking at exactly the same time and almost pull the teats off the cows trying to be first to finish. And race each other back to school on their bikes. And dodge into town on a Saturday to buy sweets or ice cream and then race home before the old man missed them.

A big man, his father, who terrorized his family with his leather belt and his tongue. "The ten commandments are not to be made little of," he'd shout from the head of the kitchen table whenever one of them was caught infracting any of those fearsome rules that governed the life and death and eternal destiny of all mankind. And he'd pound the table with the side of his huge fist and glare at each of his seven children in turn and not exclude his wife, Julia, who sat on his right. Then he'd follow up each time with more or less the same harsh sermon on the law of God. After which he'd order the malefactor of the moment to leave the table and report to the hay shed where he or she would receive condign punishment from his leather belt as soon as he had finished his meal. An unforgiving man, Finbarr McCarthy, where the law of God was concerned. No excuse was ever known to have been accepted: if you were caught – and the evidence of guilt need not be strong – you were punished. And this was only the merest foretaste, he'd tell the suffering miscreant as he meted out justice, of the punishment Almighty God would inflict on the wicked in the life to come. Padhraig would never forget the spring afternoon the father spotted himself and Ida coming out of the ice cream shop in town when they were supposed to be out the fields at home watching for new-born lambs. It was the worst strapping he ever got from the old man, and he had many a walloping to compare it with. He was first to the hay shed, where he received a dozen ferocious belts across the bare backside. He limped out the back field, alternately rubbing and stretching to diminish the pain, and when Ida joined him after her session he asked her how many she got. "None this time," she said bleakly, "but he did other things to me." He pressed her to tell him what, but she cried and wouldn't say. It was only in recent years that it had dawned on him what the old man had been up to.

But although the youthful Padhraig had resented his father's uncompromising administration of justice and was glad to escape to boarding school at the age of thirteen, the mature Padhraig didn't behave so differently when his own turn came to be paterfamilias. His father had inculcated in him a fearful love of a demanding God, and Padhraig retained that relationship across the years. He modeled his behavior towards wife and children on the attitude of the Eternal Father to His earthly children. He read and reread the phrases and doctrines that portrayed his God as the conditional lover and implacable judge. *Let women be subject to their husbands,* Saint Paul said; *because the husband is head of the wife. And let the wife fear her husband,* the great apostle said, too. So Padhraig ruled his family as absolute master, while treating them with the benevolence of his Lord as long as each knew her or his place. The children must be firmly disciplined, he constantly admonished his tolerant wife; not for this family that laissez faire sloughing off of parental duty that nowadays passed for enlightened upbringing. Even corporal punishment must not be ruled out; his father had severely chastised *him* in his youth, and was he any the worse for it? Here, however, he listened to Deirdre's caution about the law and society becoming increasingly intolerant of anything that smacked of child abuse. If there was one thing he didn't want, it was any kind of a brush with the law. So, unlike his father, he hardly ever used the belt. Instead, he found insult and ridicule of the obstreperous to be equally effective and even more to his liking. It had the merit, too, of resembling the fiery words of the Old testament God to ancient sinning Hebrews.

He had tried to tame Deirdre, too, and though he was never quite sure if she had fully accepted him as her divinely appointed lord and master, she had extended at least outward compliance to his wishes; until this new independence of hers had put his home life into serious turmoil. At least, he consoled himself, he didn't have to worry about her fidelity. In the first years of their marriage, when she was still a ravishing beauty, he had suffered agonizing torments from jealousy. But when he analyzed his condition and realized that his anguish stemmed from her relationships with friends of single days – both male and female – he cut her off from those connections. As a result he could safely say that for years now he had rarely been plagued by the green-eyed monster.

Unlike Deirdre's husband, Ignatius failed to connect the name of Padhraig McCarthy with his erstwhile friend from Saint Fursa's. So he was totally surprised when the big man who opened the door to him that Sunday afternoon said, "Naeshie Lally! By God you haven't changed a bit."

"Padhraig!" Though McCarthy had gotten considerably heavier, even slightly jowled, since their days at Saint Fursa's, recognition came almost instantly from somewhere in the recesses of Ignatius's memory. How could he forget that shock of unruly yellow-brown hair and the fierce dark eyes under incongruous blond eyebrows.

"Well, what do you know?" The powerful squeeze of the big man's handshake was almost painful. "I figured it had to be you the first time she mentioned your name."

"You two know each other?" The look of surprise on Deirdre's face was comical as she offered Ignatius her hand.

"Come on in and take the weight off your feet." McCarthy disappeared in the door of the front room, ignoring his wife's question.

"We were at school together," Ignatius explained as he followed. "Small world isn't it?"

"Twenty-nine years I haven't seen you." Padhraig stood by the sideboard, a bottle of Bushmills in his hand, and not a trace in either voice or look that he harbored any rancor over that last year at school. "You'll have a drop?"

"I'll see to the dinner then," Deirdre said quietly. "I'm sure you two will have a lot to talk about." And she closed the door behind her.

He'd have preferred her to stay. Neither he nor Padhraig would want to dredge up those painful last-term memories of their schooldays. But he soon found out that he was wrong on that count. As McCarthy handed him a drink he asked casually, "is old Tommy Tiger still to the good?"

"Ah no, he died a couple of years ago." Father Thomas 'the Tiger' O'Reilly had been the rugby trainer at Saint Fursa's.

"Make yourself comfortable, why don't you?" McCarthy motioned him to an armchair. "You know, I never forgave the bugger." He shook his head and there was vehemence in his voice. "And I still won't, even if he's dead itself." He plunked heavily onto the sofa. "That's the way I am."

"He did you wrong, all right, I'd say," Ignatius said soothingly, though he didn't really believe it. "But it's water long since under the bridge, I suppose." He raised his glass: *"slainte*!" It was a long time to carry a grudge, but that was the Padhraig McCarthy he remembered. Funny he hadn't made the connection when Deirdre mentioned her husband's name.

The Clyard vet tasted his whiskey. "He had no right to do it."

"No," Ignatius agreed. "He hadn't." But *will you let it rest, you elephant*, was what he was thinking. It was twenty-nine years ago, for God's sake, since Tommy the Tiger had moved Padhraig McCarthy from outhalf to left wing on Saint Fursa's senior rugby team and replaced him with Ignatius Lally. McCarthy had been livid, which was understandable at the time: he had been cock-of-the-walk, the college's best rugby player in almost everyone's opinion, and fully expecting a Leinster cap that year. But the Tiger had accused him of not playing a team game: of running when he should be passing, of not doing his fair share of tackling, and especially – and this was the real reason, everyone said – of not following his trainer's instructions. Anyway, McCarthy, in high dudgeon, had refused to play any more. What was worse, he held a grudge against Ignatius, which he refused to drop even when they were saying their final goodbyes after doing the Leaving Certificate examinations.

"'Tis I'd have got that Leinster cap, and not you." Padhraig glowered into his glass.

"You would have," Ignatius said. "So you're a vet, I

understand?"

"I am." Ignatius thought he detected a trace of hostility when McCarthy glanced across at him, but it was replaced by an immediate grin. "I like cows; they don't talk back at you." And he launched into a monologue on the technicalities of being doctor to sick animals. Deirdre announced dinner from the doorway. "If you're ready so, we'll eat."

"You're hungry, I suppose," McCarthy said, without looking at her. "I never knew a priest that wasn't." Deirdre's bacon and cabbage changed Ignatius's perspective on that staple dinner of his growing-up years when the cabbage would be overcooked and greasy and the bacon salty and fat; this meat was lean, with just the slightest flavoring of salt, while the cabbage was fresh and cooked *al dente*. Padhraig talked Tipperary hurling, with many interruptions from Cathal, a rather sulky looking thirteen-year old, and occasional comment from Ignatius just to keep the conversation going. Deirdre herself was quite subdued, almost a different person from the ebullient talker in the fund-raising office. She hardly spoke, other than to ensure that everyone was properly taken care of. Several times during the meal Ignatius caught Fiona, the eldest, looking at him with what seemed a mixture of curiosity and veiled resentment. On the other hand, Gemma, the middle child, who looked strikingly like her mother, smiled a lot at him and wanted to hear about his experiences in Brazil as soon as the hurling talk lapsed. Afterwards, Ignatius and Padhraig had a long discussion on the state of the economy while Deirdre and the two daughters did the wash up and Cathal insisted on flipping the television channels.

Monday morning, on his weekly visit to the office, he

complimented Deirdre again on the dinner. "Well, fancy you and Padhraig knowing each other!" She was full of pizzazz again. "Funny he never mentioned it when I talked to him about you."

"It's been a long time. And," he might as well say it now lest she expect them to be close friends, "he didn't particularly like me in our last year."

"He mentioned something about that after you left." She stared out the window. "Quite a character, our Padhraig. There are those that he loves and those that he hates, but there aren't too many in between."

"He was always a rather strong personality."

"He's great as long as you treat him with the deference his majesty feels he deserves. But don't get under his skin." This last came out with an unrestrained acerbity.

He should have changed the subject then, but curiosity got the better of him in light of her own subdued behavior at home. "Men can be difficult at times," he probed.

"Indeed! Padhraig's only difficult when you cross him." Her laugh short and brittle. "Then run for your life."

"I'd say he's a good vet." Now he was afraid to hear details of their conjugal troubles."

"He is. And he doesn't quit easily. He'll stick with a sick animal where another would give up." She doodled furiously on a pad that lay on her desk. "I wish he was as patient with his wife." When she looked up her eyes were moist. "Sorry. I shouldn't have said that. Very sorry."

"It's okay," he assured her. If she wanted to complain he'd listen.

"He really does treat us well on the whole." She was doodling again. "As long as we know our place. He'll always let you make your own decisions on the understanding that he can always reverse them."

One morning at the beginning of Lent his God pointed out to Ignatius that he seemed to have developed an attachment to Deirdre McCarthy. *You're seeing a lot of her,* He said. *And I don't think that's good for you.*

But I have to visit her at the fund-raising office, he retorted. It was his duty, his job, and not to be shirked because of an unwanted attachment to his attractive employee, even if that attachment was just as obviously reciprocated. *The Congregation depends on this office for financial survival. And I'm being most careful, aren't I?* In truth, he never did stay long and he stuck to business matters, with only the occasional brief lapse into personal conversation. And yet, for the duration of each visit, the air between them was alive with thrashing atoms of thwarted passion.

You can't be careful enough, his Lord persisted, somewhat huffily. So, brief and business-like Ignatius's calls remained, turning what could have been proximate occasions of sin into remote, just as the moralists advised. As for his Sunday dinners with the McCarthys, which were now regular monthly affairs, they weren't occasions at all, he'd affirm smoothly to his God at each morning-after meditation. Didn't he go to visit Padhraig more than Deirdre? Hadn't the two of them established a solid friendship, despite their ancient contretemps; regardless, too, of their clashing opinions on the future of the euro, not to mention their profound differences on social welfare? Or even their views on the present state of the Church in Ireland, with Padhraig favoring the status quo of eternal truths against the priest who favored change in the interest of survival. And anyway, didn't Deirdre, whose fondness for him she but poorly concealed at the office, don the mask of pleasant indifference in her own home? Though he did occasionally catch her out in a glance of covert adoration when she didn't expect him to be looking. He would devoutly hope her husband hadn't noticed.

But he could not deny that his unfulfilled longing for Deirdre McCarthy did pain him deeply. It wasn't merely the frustration of sexual repression; that could be alleviated for the moment by the self-relief that he had years ago decided was both natural and necessary and, therefore, not sinful. The screams of desire that echoed within him were cries for her physical touch, her embracing arms, the taste of her lips, the softness of her skin and, above all, the undefinable but ecstatic pleasure of her intimate presence. Nevertheless, while he admitted to his Lord that his feelings for her were a source of deepest anguish, he was, he declared, a mature celibate priest who could withstand that pain.

Padhraig McCarthy was early aware of his wife's infatuation with Naeshy Lally – how could he not be? – but he grudgingly tolerated it since the priest himself seemed dedicated to his celibacy. Until Fiona drew his attention to the likelihood that something more serious was going on. "I think they're up to something." Malice in her tone: jealousy of her mother had kept pace with attachment to her father over the years.

"Why do you think that?" They were alone in the house: Deirdre had taken the younger ones to Clyard for the Saturday grocery shopping.

"He's always in her office." Fiona had met him there exactly once, over the Christmas holidays when she stopped in to ask her mother for money. "And Mammy had a package of condoms in her bag last week." This last triumphant news was true: Deirdre had procured them in the forlorn hope of one day seducing her Ignatius.

"Well is that a fact?" Rage engulfed Padraig: the same Naeshy Lally who had once taken his Leinster cap away from him was now threatening to take his wife as well. But this time he was not going to get away with his theft; the mature Padraig McCarthy would thwart him. His revenge – he didn't know yet what it would be but it would be terrible, and satisfying.

When Father Lally came to dinner on the first Sunday in June Padhraig was his usual charming self, talking football and golf and the hope for peace in the North. But all the while he was observing and listening and detecting guilt in both parties and planning retribution. The following Saturday he outlined his revenge plan to Fiona while Deirdre and the other children were gone shopping.

His daughter blanched at his audacious scheme. "Daddy!" She charged upstairs and slammed her door with enough force to send shock waves back down to the kitchen where her father sat stunned by such a violent reaction to a reasonable request.

Fifteen minutes later, having re-thought his strategy, he knocked timidly on her door. "You didn't wait to hear me out," he called in. "It's not nearly as bad as you think it is."

"I don't want to talk about it," She shouted.

"Please!" The word did not come easily to Padhraig McCarthy, but he managed it somehow. And he repeated it many times until finally his daughter emerged reluctantly from her room.

"But I'm only going to listen," she said, with a scowl that would deter a charging bull. "I'm not going to do anything you say."

He presented a revised version of his plan, as though this had been his intention all along. She could do it to herself, he told her, with the help of a gismo that simulated the real thing, if she knew what he meant. There was a shop in Dublin that sold such things. She nodded understanding with barely concealed disgust. "But why can't you just report him to the archbishop for having an affair with your wife?"

"Ah!" Now he was on firmer ground. "The upshot of that would just be your mother looking for a divorce, and then herself and Lally'd ride off into the sunset." Which thought brought on a scowl that outmatched anything his daughter had produced. "I want to nail Lally without giving her any excuse. Do you see what I'm getting at?"

His daughter grudgingly conceded the point, then grimaced with obvious pain. "But wouldn't it be terribly wrong? I mean, it'd be a whopper of a sin for one thing, and if we were ever found out I'm sure they'd put us in jail."

He prided himself on being a moral man, and he had already wrestled successfully with the moral issue involved here. "What we're going to pin on Lally is no worse than what he's already doing and getting away with." He nodded vehemently at that thought. "So his punishment will be just in the sight of God." His own father, he felt, would surely have approved of his scheme. "As for getting caught, there's no danger at all of that. There'll be no publicity and no Gardai involved; just a private word in his Grace's ear and Lally will be permanently out of commission."

"You're sure now? Because I don't want to wind up in jail, you know."

"Arrah, not a fear in the world, pet. Would I suggest it if

there was any risk to you?" And Padhraig McCarthy gave his daughter a reassuring smile, secure now in the knowledge that his plan was going to be effected.

Implementation, he told her, would have to wait till her mother paid one of her weekend visits to her sister in Dublin, a trip she used to make scrupulously once a month until the advent of Lally, but which now occurred less often. In the event, they had to wait till the end of July before she said the magic words, "I think I'll take a run up to see Eavan tomorrow." She left on Saturday after the shopping. Sunday morning Padhraig rang her sister's house and asked his wife if she'd mind picking up a book for him at Fred Hanna's; he needed it urgently. "I'll have to wait over till tomorrow then," she pointed out. "So would you ever call the novitiate and leave a message for Father Ignatius that I won't be in; it's his day to visit the office."

"I will to be sure," he said.

"And maybe you'd stop by the office yourself in the morning and take the stuff to the postoffice for me. Please!" On Mondays, by strongly stated preference of the Clyard postmaster, she delivered the bulk mailing that she had prepared the previous week.

"Why wouldn't I?" But on Monday morning he loaned his car to Fiona so she could do the bulk mailing and stay in the office till the priest arrived. He rang his own office to say he'd be late. His daughter arrived home just before one o'clock. A half hour later he rushed her to the Aherlow Regional hospital, arriving there at the exact moment that Father Lally finished lecturing his five novices on the mystery of the Blessed Trinity.

ACCUSATION

It was a good lecture, if he said so himself; sparkling in both content and delivery. Since it was his first year as Master of Novices he had to prepare his talks from scratch and he wanted each to be not only spiritually uplifting but intellectually stimulating as well. Not that he had to worry about keeping the *attention* of his small audience: his novices at this stage of formation were so attuned to duty and obedience and the will of God that they'd remain alert if he read backwards from a Latin dictionary.

Sean Moylan came to his office afterwards with a question. Sean had become ferociously devout since the second retreat back in February and was inclined towards exaggerated asceticism. Which the Master of Novices had to curb with forceful counseling when Sean decided to forego breakfast and supper during Lent. More recently, he had been developing scruples in his search for intellectual exactitude. So when he said now, "can I ask a question, Father?" – his western accent sharp as a theological conundrum – Ignatius didn't know what to expect.

"Certainly, Sean."

"I hope I'm not being heretical, but isn't it a bit of a cop-out to say on the one hand that there are three persons in one God, and on the other that the only explanation of it is that it's a mystery?" The half-smile reflecting nervousness, but also a shade of triumph; Sean, despite his piety, was hugely proud of his superior intelligence.

This cocky generation of youth! Ignatius wouldn't have dared say the like of that to *his* novice master. But he answered anyway as if he was not surprised. "A good question, indeed, Sean. The answer, unfortunately, is not exactly satisfying to human reason."

"Try me anyway," said Moylan precociously.

"Well, the official church doctrine, which is *de fide*, meaning we must believe it under pain of being branded as heretics, is that all three divine Persons possess the same essence, or substance, or nature, or being." He stopped and smiled. "And now of course you're going to ask what are the definitions of those things? All I –"

"I was just about to, Father." The boy's grin suggested he was enjoying the joust.

"I'm afraid the explanation will have to wait till you do your philosophy degree. You will no doubt regard that answer as another cop-out. Unfortunately, the doctrine of the Trinity, like a great deal of theology, is based on subtle arguments that are based on subtle definitions that are based on subtle distinctions that all require a great deal of what I might call underpinning studies." He smiled at this lad who had only just turned eighteen. "But if you have the patience to wait, you'll eventually know it all. And some day you may even be standing here yourself trying to explain this mystery to an as yet unborn novice."

"I'll take your word for it so, Father." But as he was walking out the door Moylan turned back. "It still sounds to me like we're talking about three Gods." The grin negated the spoken suggestion of heresy.

After supper, the novice Master and his assistant relaxed for a half hour in their small sitting room. "I think it's time to send Kevin Harper away," Ignatius informed Corrigan.

"Indeed," his assistant agreed. "What do you –" At which point the telephone rang in the hall. "I'll get it." Corrigan was out the door in a flash; a nervous young man who always seemed to be in a hurry. He returned with equal abruptness. "Father Kennedy." Rolling his eyes in a give-me-patience expression.

Ignatius got up slowly. Brian Kennedy, the Superior General, was a man who liked to keep on top of things. He'd ring several times a week and want to know every nuance of change in each novice's development. Might as well tell him about Harper.

But Kennedy forewent his usual *how's tricks*? "I had a ring from the archbishop a few minutes ago," he opened crisply. "*Your* AB, not mine." Kennedy lived at the Mother House in Dublin. "He wants to see you and me in his office at ten o'clock tomorrow morning."

"What does he want?" Ignatius had met the Most Reverend Dr. Peter Donnellan, archbishop of Tighmor, only once, when Kennedy had introduced him as the new novice master. The novitiate was in Tighmor archdiocese, though only nominally of it; so a command to appear before His Grace was highly unusual.

"I have no idea." Kennedy's tone was brusque, as if his supper had been interrupted. "I'll see you outside the palace at five minutes to ten. That means I'll have to get up at all hours of the morning." Self-pity rippling across the phone line. "Don't be late," was his parting shot. Ignatius was not renowned for punctuality.

He did, however, arrive at the archiepiscopal residence ten minutes early next morning, to find Kennedy already there. "What can the man want?" he asked as they waited in the episcopal parlor while the housekeeper went in search of his Lordship.

The Superior wrinkled fierce eyebrows at him. "Have your saintly novices been seen smoking in the bushes by any chance?"

The housekeeper returned. "His Grace will see you now. " She led the way.

Archbishop Donnellan, short, tubby, and a noted scripture scholar, was renowned for his affability with the media, a quality not often pronounced among the Irish Hierarchy. Ignatius remembered that he smiled a lot at their previous meeting. But he wasn't smiling this morning in his modest office: his visage was solemn when he greeted them and his handshake for both was perfunctory.

"Have a seat." Waving them to chairs on the far side of his paper-cluttered desk.

"Nice touch of spring in the air this morning," Kennedy tried.

The AB picked up a sheet of paper. "An extremely disturbing accusation has been made to me." He looked at Ignatius. "Against you, Father."

"Good Lord!" Kennedy turned to Ignatius. "You been speeding again, Father?" Twice since returning from Brazil Father Ignatius Lally, CWM, had been issued tickets by the Garda Siochana for driving at excessive speed.

"It's a lot more serious than speeding, I'm afraid." Donnellan's head was down, eyes focused on the piece of paper. "Late yesterday afternoon I had a visit from two very distraught people, Doctor Padhraig McCarthy and his seventeen-year old daughter Fiona. Do you know them, Father?"

"Of course. They're friends. What was the matter?" Something in the archbishop's manner was raising the hairs on Ignatius's nape.

Donnellan continued to stare at the page in silence. Eventually he said, "I don't quite know how to say this." He shook his head, as if to clear it of something. "I don't really want to say it at all." He looked up briefly at Kennedy and then back at the paper. "Doctor McCarthy said that Father Ignatius Lally sexually molested his daughter Fiona yesterday morning in her mother's office in Clyard. And his daughter corroborated the allegation."

"Great God Almighty!" Ignatius heaved his chair away from the desk and shot to his feet, waving his arms as if trying to ward off an onslaught of bees. "That's a terrible lie. I can't believe it! It's incredible! May God forgive the person who told such a lie." His mind was in a state of overwhelmed shock at this unreal charge.

"Sit down, Father." The archbishop seemed to have gathered strength from the release of his verbal bombshell. "There's worse to come."

Ignatius's mind was reeling. He sensed rather than saw that Kennedy had his face buried in his hands. He towered over the archbishop's desk. "But surely you can't believe that –"

His Lordship interrupted, reading from the paper again. "Doctor McCarthy brought medical evidence with him from Aherlow Regional hospital which proves that his daughter had been both vaginally and anally penetrated in the very recent past."

Kennedy moaned. Ignatius said, "good God! I'm terribly sorry to hear that. The poor girl. But anyone who says I had anything to do with it is the greatest goddam liar since Satan himself." He was shouting, in a desperate attempt to escape the awful shame in which the archbishop's words were drowning him.

"Control yourself, Father." Donnellan had regained his poise and his voice was cold and sharp. He read again. "Please answer the following questions: did you go to your fund-raising office in Clyard yesterday morning?"

"I did indeed. I go there every Monday morning. It's part of –"

"And who was in the office when you got there?" The archbishop made a note with a pencil on the piece of paper.

"Fiona McCarthy. I was surprised to find her there, but she explained that –"

"Who did you expect to be there?" Donnellan's pencil was raised.

"Her mother, Deirdre McCarthy, who is the fund-raising manager. But Fiona explained that her mother had gone to Dublin over the weekend and couldn't get back in time, so she came in to take care of the post for her."

"Doctor McCarthy said there are widespread rumors in Clyard that you and Mrs. McCarthy are carrying on an adulterous affair. But since he has no proof he is not pressing any charges in that regard at the moment."

"This is totally ridiculous," Ignatius looked at his Superior. "Brian, for God's sake, will you tell him that I'm not ... Dammit to hell, this is ludicrous." He stood there, looking down from one to the other, wondering when the top of his head was going to come off.

Kennedy dropped his hands from his head and looked up. "Hear him out, Ignatius, and then we can talk about it." Deep pain in the Superior's sad eyes.

Donnellan read from the paper again. "Fiona McCarthy said that you said to her, 'since you're taking your mother's place this morning I'm sure you'll be willing to do everything that your mother normally does for me on Monday mornings.' And Fiona replied, 'I already went to the post office, Father.' And then you said, 'there's one other thing your mother always does for me.' And Fiona said, 'what's that, Father?' And you said, 'she raises her dress and drops her knickers and leans over the desk with her backside facing me.' And Fiona said, 'I couldn't do that, Father, it wouldn't be nice.' But you said, 'arrah go on out of that, don't be prudish, Fiona.' And you stood there and looked at her until she felt that she had to do it, since she was reared to always obey when the priest said to do something. She said she thought you were only interested in looking until you suddenly penetrated her and then it was too late for her to protect herself. She said you were terribly strong and held her against her will until you were finished. And then you asked her if she enjoyed it." Donnellan looked up suddenly at Ignatius, face red and eyes smoldering. "The medical evidence bears out the girl's allegations of sexual molestation."

He swayed on his feet; he was going to wake up in a minute. This wasn't happening of course, though it seemed so awfully real at the moment. And he was paralyzed, as in nightmares when he couldn't move his legs to escape the charging cattle. He heard Donnellan continue. "Doctor McCarthy said his daughter was in severe shock when she arrived home. He took her straight to the hospital, not knowing what was wrong with her or what had happened, since she was totally incoherent. It was the examination at the Regional that showed she had been raped and sodomized."

Ignatius shook himself: shoulders, arms, hips, neck, head. There had to be a way out, a technique for waking up. But all he could see was the top of Donnellan's bald head and all he could hear was the timbre of Donnellan's tenor saying *you may respond now, Father Lally*. And all he could feel was himself stuck to the floor like a big head of cabbage that was buried in wet clay.

"Why don't you sit down," he heard Kennedy say, and for some reason that pulled him out of his stupor.

"You can't," he began. "It doesn't ... This is ... How can I ..." Waving his arms again and again as if to pump up a rational explanation for the surreal scenario painted by His Grace of Tighmor. But it was no use. His legs were suddenly jelly, his body drained of strength. He sat, put his head in his hands and tried to focus his thoughts. The first thing to recognize was that he wasn't dreaming, wasn't imagining, wasn't hallucinating. He really *was* being accused of something monstrous, of a hideous crime that in all his born days he was totally and absolutely incapable of committing. Yet accused of it by people he knew so well. People he was friendly with, whom he thought actually liked him. So how could it be? Then the weakness passed and the adrenaline began to flow. He had fought too many battles in life to cower beneath this outlandish charge. He raised his head, looked first at Kennedy, who was staring at the episcopal desk, then at Donnellan, still focused on his piece of paper. "I don't have any idea why I am accused of this horrible thing, but I can tell you both, as Almighty God is my witness and may He strike me dead this minute if I lie, that I did not do it, that I know nothing about it, and that I'm willing to withstand any investigation that's needed to prove I didn't do it."

"Tell me your side of the story." The archbishop retrieved

a pad from the midst of the clutter and picked up a pen. "What happened yesterday morning?"

He took a deep breath and closed his eyes. "I have delegated to Deirdre McCarthy the primary responsibility for running the fund-raising office. She's an extremely capable woman and I want to devote all my time to my duties in the novitiate. I've explained all this to you in the past, Brian." He glanced at Kennedy, who nodded. "Just to keep abreast of what's going on, and to make any decisions Deirdre needs me to make, I visit the office every Monday morning. Which I did yesterday, as usual. Only Deirdre wasn't there." He paused to swallow saliva. "Her daughter Fiona was."

"I see." Donnellan scribbled in his pad.

"She told me the reason why, which was what she told you. And she told me, too, that she had gone to the post office. So I thanked her and left. I wasn't there more than a couple of minutes in all. I was in a hurry to get back to finish preparing a talk for the novices."

Kennedy removed his glasses and wiped them with his handkerchief. The archbishop scribbled some more. "Did anyone witness your coming and going?"

"They could have indeed. The office is over Regan's shop in Main Street. You go in a door on the side and up the stairs. I don't recall if there were people around or not. Monday morning the town is not too busy of course." He was beginning to feel just a glimmer of hope. Surely the archbishop could not doubt the ringing denial that he, a priest of God, had issued.

Donnellan looked up, straight at him, eyes hostile. "If you didn't do what you have been accused of doing, is there anything you can think of that would lend credence to your denial? Anything at all?"

Ignatius wanted to scoff right into the man's face. *When did you stop beating your wife* he was about to shout, but refrained. Instead he said, quietly, "I didn't do what I've been accused of. And from a forensic standpoint I'm quite sure I'll be exonerated. No doubt there will be semen samples to compare and –"

"Doctor McCarthy found a box of condoms in the office when he returned there last evening. In the drawer of his wife's desk." The archbishop spread his hands wide as in *Pax Vobiscum.* "Need I say more." He scribbled in the pad again.

It was all so diabolical. Or could he possibly have freaked out from the strain of the job and done what he was accused of doing? He felt the sweat all over his body from that thought.

"I'd like you to step outside for a few minutes, Father Lally, while I talk with Father Kennedy." The archbishop got up and held open the door. "You can sit in the parlor at the end of the hall."

Ignatius had no recollection of making his way there. He remembered staring at a large painting of a bishop, resplendent in purple robes and biretta, and with the stance of a man proud of who he was. Ignatius Lally could never stand proud again. His life was ruined. How could he face his novices with this shadow of infamy hanging over him? Talk to them about chastity and self-denial when he himself stood accused of the grossest impurity? Never mind that it wasn't true; the very accusation made him feel unclean. He couldn't even discuss it with his Lord. Instead, he dozed, as one does when overcome by flu or fever.

Then he heard Kennedy say from the door, "come on back in, he wants to talk to you."

Was this how a convict felt entering the court to hear sentence? He sat. Kennedy sat. Donnellan continued to write. Eventually he stared at Ignatius. Again that cold hostility. "This decent Catholic country of ours has been scandalized in recent years with accusations and proofs of clergy misdeeds, most of them dealing with sex. For too long we covered up our scandals, protected the guilty, left the innocent to suffer, with irreparable harm to God's own people and incalculable damage to the good name of religion. But those days are gone, Father Lally. The bishops of Ireland have determined that there will be no more heads thrust in the sand. If the clergy sin we'll admit it, and we have done so already. If the clergy commit crimes they'll pay for them the same as everyone else, and they have done so already. If –"

"I have committed no crime," Ignatius interrupted quietly, almost too softly to be convincing. "I have committed no crime," he repeated, this time in a shout. "And I'll defend myself all the way to the Supreme Court if necessary. They won't get away with it."

"There'll be no court in your case," the archbishop said. "Maybe that's fortunate, maybe it's not. Doctor McCarthy is a fervent Catholic who doesn't wish to cause further scandal to the church, and his daughter is in accord with him in the matter. They have decided not to press criminal charges against you, on condition that you are removed immediately from your post in Clyard. So –"

"Like hell they won't!" He was on his feet again. "If they make those kinds of – of – unspeakable allegations against me then they're going to have to bloody well back them up or bloody well admit they're lying. Even the most elementary principles of justice demand that." He was practically screaming. "You can't just –"

"Ignatius!" Kennedy had his arm around him and was pushing him down. "Please sit and let's talk calmly. All right?" Was this when people had strokes? He slumped back into his chair, breathing hard, the energy drained out of him again.

"I had a priest of this diocese sitting in that very chair six months ago." Donnellan was looking at Kennedy. "Accused of molesting two of his mass-servers. He ranted and raved and denied on the holy bible that he had ever done anything to the boys. Yet a month later he pleaded guilty to the charge in court and went to jail. So you can understand, Father, why I am more persuaded by evidence than histrionics."

"*I'll* stand my ground." Ignatius pulled himself together and spoke quietly but forcefully. "And I *will* go to trial. And I'll prove my innocence if there's even a shred of justice and fairness left in the country. Furthermore, I'll find out why these people have decided to monstrously accuse me of such falsehood. I'll take –"

"Father *Lally*!" Kennedy's tone impossibly sharp on such soft syllables. "You'll take a leave of absence from your post until further notice."

Ignatius turned to him, feeling the tears well up in his eyes. "Brian, at least *you* have to support me in this. Who can I turn to if not my own confreres? This whole accusation is one great big unbelievable lie. And I'll prove it. Please believe me!"

Kennedy glanced at the archbishop, then bowed his head and stared at the floor. "You'll take a leave, Father, while we sort things out."

"I won't do it, Brian. Taking a leave is tantamount to admitting guilt." He slammed his fist on the episcopal desk. "And

I have no guilt to admit to."

Kennedy turned and faced him. "I'm sorry to do this, Ignatius, but you're not giving me much choice. You have a vow of obedience, and I'm commanding you now in the name of that vow to take a leave of absence."

He could argue no further. This was the will of God, as he had explained ad nauseam to his novices these past ten months. If God indeed had a will for him. *What are you up to anyway, Lord?* But he bowed his head, the closest he could go towards acquiescence.

"One more thing." Donnellan's tone was calm and formal and cold. "I am hereby suspending you, *sine die*, from performing any and all clerical functions in this diocese. Is that understood, Father?"

Funny how quickly an act begot a habit. This time he bowed without giving the matter a thought.

DISCOVERY

"I want you to come up to Dublin with me now," Kennedy said the minute they stepped out the episcopal door. "We'll have Noel send on your things."

"I'll do no such thing." Ignatius headed rapidly for his car, forcing the Superior to follow him.

"Now Ignatius, let's not make things any worse than they are already."

He didn't stop till he reached his car. Then he turned. "Listen to me!" At that moment he felt capable of punching Brian Kennedy right in the gob. "Don't push me any further, do you hear me? I'm in a state of total shock. I've been lied about, kicked in the teeth, my life has been ruined, people I thought were friends are out to destroy me, and people I thought I could rely on don't believe me. I'm on my own right now, so I'll take care of myself as best I can." He opened the door, got in and slammed it shut. The Superior stood there with a helpless look on his face. Ignatius rolled down the window. "You might have shown a little more support for me, you know. You know me bloody well enough and bloody long enough to know I'm not capable of doing what those wretched people said."

"We'll go over it all very carefully when we get back to Dublin." There was both embarrassment and retreat in Kennedy's tone.

"I'm not going to Dublin."

"Oh come on! So what are you going to do? You know –"

"Right now, I'm going back to Shankill and I'm going to pack my things. And I'm going to speak to the novices and explain to them that I have a family emergency – my mother is sick anyway – and that I'll be away for a short while. And I'll fill Noel Corrigan in on what he needs to do in my absence. And then I'm going home to Mayo until you and his blasted Grace come to your bloody senses and realize what's been done to me." He backed out of the archbishop's parking space at speed unsafe and roared through the episcopal pillars onto the road leading west north-west to Clyard twenty-two miles away.

The young men's faces showed sympathy for his unwell mother. Noel Corrigan expressed total bewilderment and disbelief when Ignatius told him all; then he expressed his total support and his utmost confidence that the novice Master would be exonerated. Yet Ignatius sensed a vague contentment in his Assistant's sorrow, the comfort that comes to people who not only do not share your disaster but actually profit from it; Corrigan had stated several times that he hoped one day to be Master of Novices himself.

Ignatius packed his clothes, put some books into a satchel, and slipped away while the novices were at prayer. At a quarter to four he parked outside Regan's in Clyard. Deirdre was sitting at her desk, half hidden behind a stack of missionary magazines. And patently startled by his appearance in the doorway. "Jesus God! What are *you* doing here? Hot anger rising from her tone. "I didn't think you'd have the nerve to step foot in the place again." The long blonde hair, usually loose around her shoulders, was pulled back tight and rolled in a bun.

Hands raised in supplication, he stayed by the door. "Deirdre, please, hear me out. At least you!"

"I don't want explanations. My daughter was raped and sodomized." Her voice was cracked and crying. "The medical records show it. And you did it. So get out, quick, before I scream." The look on her face said she was about to. Her poised crouch – half out of the chair with hands on the desk – suggested a hen about to fly off a wall.

"I didn't do it, Deirdre," he shouted. And something in his tone must have gotten through to her, for she slumped back into her seat.

"If you didn't, who did?"

"Well it wasn't me."

"All I know is somebody did. And Fiona said it was *you*. Why would she lie? And the archbishop already suspended you. And your own superior did, too. So what am I to believe?" She wasn't looking at him and her rising pitch indicated she was about to scream.

"They also said that you and I are having an affair." He said it forcefully: the morning stupor had given way to boiling anger.

"Who said that?" Shocked, reflex question.

"Your own husband. He told the archbishop that it was strongly rumored in the community. He said he wasn't going to press charges because he didn't have proof. But he obviously believes it himself."

Her hands clutched her face. "I think I'm going to go mad."

He came forward then and sat in the visitor's chair, a cushioned dining room straight-back that he had loaned her from the novitiate. "Deirdre, you've known me now for the best part of a year. Do you really believe I'm capable of such a horrible crime as raping your daughter?"

The misery in her eyes when she looked up took the anger out of him for the moment. "If you asked me that two days ago I'd have said absolutely no," she whispered. "But somebody did, and she said it was you, and who am I to believe?"

He took a deep breath. "You can believe that Ignatius Lally didn't do it because he didn't. And I intend to prove I didn't, whatever that will take." He spoke quietly, restraining the ferocity within. "If it means I have to prove your daughter is lying, then so be it." He stood. "That's what I came to tell you. And I'll tell you something else, Deirdre McCarthy. I'm more fond of you, God help me, than of anybody else in this entire wretched world. And the last thing I would ever do is to hurt you."

His own tears were welling as he made for the door. When his hand was on the latch she called, "Ignatius!" He stopped and turned and blinked hard. "I do so want to believe you. I just need more time."

"I'm going home now," he said. "You can find me at my mother's."

What are you trying to do to me, Lord, he protested as he drove north-west to Portumna where he'd cross the Shannon.

My ways are mysterious, Jesus replied. *You just have to trust me.*

But is this any way to treat a friend? I'm being destroyed. At least you could tell me why.

It might be related to your overheated friendship with

Deirdre McCarthy. You're not as innocent in my eyes as you'd have yourself believe.

But I didn't do anything wrong, did I? I was so very careful not to step over the bounds.

You have harbored thoughts about her, haven't you? Be honest with me, Ignatius, for once in your life.

That's not fair, Lord. I'm as honest with you as I possibly can be.

Really! Are you going to sit there and tell me that you didn't rejoice deep down inside that you already possessed Deirdre McCarthy in your mind? What I call in my good book adultery in the heart.

He left Deirdre in a state of utter confusion. When he walked into the office she wanted to scream and throw something at him. By the time he left she wanted to believe him, such was the effect of his presence on her. Ten minutes later, still slumped in her chair and her eyes still staring vacantly across the room, she wanted to scream again, this time from the frustration of contradictory truths. Her daughter had been raped, she must believe that. Fiona had accused Father Lally, and why would she lie? But Ignatius? If he had done it, then she knew nothing of character. And he had been so painfully convincing just now. When another ten minutes of staring and sitting yielded no resolution she got up and went home. During the drive she determined to talk with Fiona again, quietly, sympathetically, on her own. The only conversation she had had so far about the rape had been an emotional sobbing session in Padhraig's presence immediately after she arrived home from Dublin last night.

Fiona barely picked at her food through a sullen dinner

whose silence was broken only by Gemma telling Cathal to keep his mouth closed when chewing and Padhraig yelling at Gemma to mind her own business. When her husband left the house as soon as the meal was over Deirdre assigned the two youngest to do the wash up, then led her morose eldest into the parlor and shut the door. "I know it's awfully painful for you," she said gently. "And I'm sure you'd rather put the whole thing out of your mind."

"How can I?" Fiona's grief did not eliminate the hostile tone habitual to her when addressing her mother. "It's there with me all the time. I wish to God you had never anything to do with that awful man. It's all your fault."

She let that pass. "We'll bring the guilty party to justice," she said firmly. "I'll see to that. And though I know it's not easy for you, it'll help me a lot if you tell me exactly what happened in my office yesterday morning."

"I don't want to talk about it, Mammy." Fiona curled up fetally on the sofa.

"I know, pet. But I do need to know the details if I'm to get this man behind bars where he belongs. Please."

Silence for a long time. Deirdre stared out the window. Eventually Fiona said, "he told me to take off my knickers and bend over the desk." She grabbed a cushion and hugged it to her.

"Did he remove his own clothes?"

"How do I know?" her daughter shouted. "He was standing behind me." Then after a pause she added, "he said I wasn't tall enough so he made me kneel up on your visitor's chair instead." She buried her head in the cushion.

Deirdre left her abruptly then and went for a walk, back the road heading west at a furious clip, facing into the low late sun. Fighting it, fighting it, fighting it. She knew now that she had known it from the moment she had arrived home and was given the news. But horrible as it was to believe that her beautiful Ignatius might be guilty of such an atrocious act it was still preferable to *this*; the mind had shut down around it and refused to entertain the thought. But the chair, my God! The kneeling on the chair. How could she deny it further? The only imaginative thing he had ever come up with in their eighteen-year sex life. She stopped abruptly and screamed into the evening air, not caring who heard her or wondered why. To this had her life descended: an incestuous husband, a lying complicitous daughter, and the man she loved accused of their crime.

Ignatius cried three times on the way home: once when he was crossing the Shannon, again when he saw the sign *Welcome to Mayo*, and a third when he came in sight of the townland of Mullagh where he had grown up.

"Musha you're a great stranger, Ignatius." His mother was seventy-six and walked with the help of a cane since she broke her hip last year. But she was spry enough to be out on the driveway when his car pulled up. "I spotted you coming over the road. I was sitting by the window as usual."

"I thought you were supposed to be confined to bed." He gave her the closest he could manage to a hug: Mammy wasn't fond of embracing anyone, not even her own children.

"Arrah sure there's nothing wrong with me. Herself thinks a bit of a cold is cause for viaticum." *Herself* being her daughter-in-law, who came out the front door just then, preceded by three young girls squealing with delight.

"Well, you're heartily welcome, your reverence." Sarah had no reticence at all about full-bodied hugs: she wrapped herself around him and then kissed his lips before stepping back to observe him. "'Tis great to see you, I must say. A most pleasant surprise indeed."

She got an extra squeeze for that. He badly needed the welcome, and he was very fond of his sister-in-law. "And how are my favorite girls?" It was then he realized he hadn't brought them anything: sweets or toys were invariable accompaniments to his visits home.

"Come in, come on inside," his mother said. "You must be hungry after your journey."

He was starved, having scarcely touched his lunch at Shankill. While they fed him at the kitchen table they filled him, too, with local news and tidbits of gossip. And Dan came in from taking care of the cattle and said it was great to see him. It was comforting to end this awful day surrounded by the warmth of family. No one asked why he was home and he gave no reason. Time enough for explanations. When Sarah asked, on his way to bed in the guest room upstairs, if he needed to be called for mass in the morning he said he'd sleep in for a change. He stayed awake a long time into the night, striving unsuccessfully not to brood on the day's calamitous course, and trying to focus on an explanation for what was going to be a prolonged visit home. How could he tell Mammy what had happened? She'd cry for days and then write scathing letters to half the bishops of Ireland. Not a woman to sit back patiently beneath real or imagined oppression. Dan and Sarah would have to know, of course. He'd need their support and patience and understanding. And he'd get it, too: they were bricks, the two of them. The real problem was what to do next. He had been accused but denied the right of defense, convicted without being allowed to face his accusers, put away before given the right of appeal. *I hope you have a good explanation for it all, Lord,* he repeated several times. First streaks of light made shadows on the wall before he fell asleep.

Deirdre felt sick for the remainder of that terrible evening. Her stomach heaved several times as if to send back her dinner but precariously held on to it. She survived several impulses to scream at her husband after he came in and sat across from her in the parlor reading the *Irish Times*. Attempts to read a book failed her. She snapped at Cathal for turning on the telly. When Gemma announced she was going to bed at half nine she got up to retire with her.

"I'll sleep with you tonight if you don't mind," she told her daughter when they reached the top of the stairs. No way was she going to lie in the same bed with him ever again; tomorrow she'd move her stuff into the guest room. In the meantime, Gemma's room had a cot that was used by the girl cousins and friends when they stayed over.

"Oh goodie!" Gemma and she were close. And she was grateful that her daughter didn't ask why. While she was in her own bedroom collecting her clothes Padhraig walked in.

"What are you doing?" he asked.

"I'm sleeping in Gemma's room." She could scarcely get the words out of her mouth with the anger that rose up at the sight of him.

"What do you want to do that for?"

The touch of belligerence in his tone annoyed her even more. "I think you know quite well why," she snapped and slammed shut a drawer.

"I don't know any such thing," he blustered.

"Don't give me that innocent stuff, Padhraig." She grabbed her pillow from the bed.

"All I know is that you've been going round as mad as a clocking hen for the past two years till I don't know any more what's the matter with you."

"Well, figure it out." She gathered up the clothes she had stacked on the bed and headed out the door. The cot was narrow and lumpy, but she wouldn't have slept anyway. Curling and turning and stretching and flipping, she tried to unravel her tangled emotions. Though she put aside brief sharp thoughts of homicide, waves of urges towards bodily injury found a welcome shore inside her. Castration, amputation, declawing, ranked high on her list of attractive alternatives. Leaving this house and not coming back, though she wished for it more than anything else, did not seem a realistic possibility at the moment; children, finances, an alternative residence, all constituted immovable barriers to her freedom from Padhraig McCarthy. For the foreseeable future she'd have to live with him.

What anguished her most and kept her awake was the question of what to do about what he had done. Of his guilt she had no doubt, but for proof she had no evidence. And as long as both he and Fiona continued to lie could their criminal complicity be ever established? Perhaps Ignatius might have some information that, coupled with her new knowledge, would exonerate him of that vicious calumny? Ignatius! Dear God, how she had wronged him, poor man. She ought to have known. How could she even think ...? She had to see him, make amends, give him comfort, plot with him to right this terrible injustice. She'd ring his mother's house in the morning and go to see him as soon as possible.

Lanky, long-faced, perpetually sad-eyed, the Very Reverend Brian Kennedy, Superior General of the Congregation of World Missionaries, drove back to Dublin that afternoon an angry and frustrated man. It was the eleventh time in his five years of office that one of his priests had been accused of sexually molesting a child or adolescent. Seven of them he had known personally and, prior to accusation, would not have believed any of them capable of such indecency. Yet all had admitted guilt in the end. Three had gone to jail, one had died during prosecution, deals with victims and prosecutors had spared others, two had simply disappeared. All had resigned the priesthood except for Harnett who was permanently assigned to a Mother House desk job where he would never again have contact with minors.

So how could Kennedy not believe that Ignatius Lally was guilty as charged? Never mind his protestations of innocence and his fury because his word was doubted: Kennedy had seen those histrionics before, and the first couple of times had initially believed in the innocence of the accused. Never mind, either, the reputation of the priest involved: who could possibly have suspected Michael Harnett, spiritual advisor to dozens of his colleagues, a reputed walking saint, a man some even whispered might one day be canonized? Yet Harnett, in his late fifties, had admitted, after much pious bluster, tears, and denials, that indeed he had a long-standing habit of fondling girls whom he invited to his room for direction when he gave retreats in convent schools.

The question now was, what to do with Lally? All crimes except Harnett's had been committed in other countries and had not generated publicity in Ireland. But the Harnett case four years ago had been a Roman circus for the clergy-baiting media and had done the Congregation no end of harm. Donations to the missions had fallen off to such a degree that the building of a new retirement home had to be postponed indefinitely. One more scandal like that might jeopardize the very future of the Congregation. The only bright spot was Padhraig McCarthy's reluctance to prosecute. Thank God for those few remaining Irish Catholics who were willing to put the good of the church before their personal feelings. But even that ray of hope was now in danger of being extinguished by Lally's obduracy.

Tread lightly, Brian, he cautioned himself as he drove into the Mother House compound. *We'll make no errors in our dealing with this case. Sleep on it for a couple of nights, pray on it for a day or two, and let Ignatius Lally do the same.*

DILEMMA

Padhraig McCarthy, though as nervous of possible consequences as he had once been of his father's wrath, nevertheless spent the day with his head in a euphoric cloud. He had accomplished both objectives by a single act: revenge on Ignatius Lally after all these years, and an end to his wife's infidelity. Which victory was sweeter he scarcely could tell, though he titillated himself endlessly with comparisons and measures as he went about the day's work . Putting Lally in his box, once a fervent schoolboy fantasy, had dissipated through the years because it no longer seemed possible. So it was all the more gratifying now for its sudden unexpected realization. Eye for eye: wrong for wrong; he had suffered for that rugby humiliation day after day, year after year, till it had become embedded in his psyche like a knife in his gut. Now the knife had been pulled and the wound could heal. And God Himself, he was sure, would understand. Hadn't He designed the human heart to rest in peace only when its enemies were punished? As He Himself had punished and promised to continue punishing His own enemies. Hadn’t he once heard the missioners – quoting the bible – saying that God is a jealous God and revenges his enemies. So why not Padraig?

Deirdre, too, had been penalized: her daughter raped – so she thought – and her lover accused of that rape. And she herself left with the guilt of believing that her own unfaithfulness was the cause of both calamities. She'd have her husband's wrath to deal with, too, in the days and months ahead. Though he still loved her as his wife he'd not let her off lightly. The lesson she had learned the hard way must be reinforced: liberation was not woman's lot; obedience was. Hadn't God turned Lot's wife into a pillar of salt just for disobeying her husband? To love, honor and obey was the law of God and man for woman.

His euphoria dimmed when his wife informed him that she was going to sleep in Gemma's room. He had sensed her hostility immediately on his return from Downey's pub, but then she had been so moody recently that he had paid no heed to this current coldness. However, he couldn't ignore her ominous "I think you know quite well why" in answer to his question. Was it possible that she knew! So he, too, stayed awake for hours trying to figure out how to cope with possible disaster. She couldn't really know unless Fiona told her, and his daughter would never do that. At least he didn't think she would. He'd find out in the morning: he was taking her to Dublin as a reward for her cooperation. A day in the city and two hundred punt to spend any way she pleased was the commitment he had to make before she'd agree to do the deed. He had offered a hundred at first but she held out for two. Now he sweated at the thought that she might have reneged and confessed. If she had, nothing in the world could save him. Deirdre would report the matter, he had no doubt about that.

Ignatius woke to Sarah's voice at the door asking if he'd like his breakfast in bed. "What time is it?" he asked.

"Going on twelve." He rolled out, refused food except for a cup of tea, and joined them for dinner at one. Afterwards, when Mammy had gone to her room for her afternoon nap, he invited Sarah to come down the yard with him to where Dan was working and, standing at the entrance to the cattle shed, told them why he was home.

"Christ Almighty!" Dan said.

"You poor man. It must be awful for you." Sarah rubbed a comforting hand up and down his back. "But the truth will have to come out. You'll see."

"I'm going to make it come out," he said savagely. "But in the meantime I need time to think and to pray. If you could put up with me for a while..."

"Arrah why wouldn't we?" Sarah was emphatic. "You stay here as long as you want."

"Our house is yours," Dan added fervently.

"Not a word to Mammy. 'Twould kill her if she found out. I'm going to tell her I have to prepare a series of lectures for the novices and need the quiet of Mullagh to concentrate." He saw the doubt in Dan's eyes. "A white lie, maybe, but to tell her the truth would be a greater sin, I think."

"We'll all be praying a lot for you," Sarah said as they walked back up the yard to the house. "Sure God wouldn't let this happen to you without doing something about it." She put her hand on his shoulder. "Don't you think?"

"I'm sure you're right," he said. But later when he went for a walk out the fields and asked Jesus that same question he didn't get much in the way of a helpful answer. *It's all very well,* he jabbed, *to say that You know best, but it's awfully hard to accept this kind of palpable injustice that strikes at the very foundation of one's sense of right and fairness. Do you know what I mean?* He kicked viciously at a thistle.

Ah, Ignatius! Your life up to now has been free from any real test. You haven't been tried like Job, or crucified like I was.

He climbed a wall, sending several stones tumbling, which he carefully replaced. *But what purpose could You have in subjecting me to this calumny?*

My ways are not your ways. You should know that by now.

I've heard it often enough. "And you have, too, I'll bet," he shouted at the herd of curious bullocks meandering towards him. They shied away at the sound of his voice. *But isn't that kind of statement just a cop-out?*

You're thrashing, Ignatius. Caught like a fish in the net of My ire. Flipping and twisting and trying to get free. But you won't. This is your life from now on. Your word against theirs, and we know already who is being believed. 'Tis the sins of your spiritual brethren, the pedophile clergy, that'll be paid for by you, were you ever so chaste. Which of course you're not anyway.

So is that the way it is going to be?

My ways are mysterious.

He recited his divine office, tonguing every word but no thought penetrating: he might as well have been muttering incantations. After supper Sarah packed him off to the parlor with the newspaper while the women did the wash-up and Dan went to a farmer's meeting. He was trying to do some thinking when Mammy joined him. "So when are you going back?" Lowering herself stiffly into the easy chair opposite.

"I have to prepare a series of lectures," he said. "I thought it would be easier to do them here."

"You're not in trouble, are you?" She was staring into the

fire that Sarah had lit earlier.

He told her the truth, then, with minimum detail but including and refuting the allegation of an affair with Deirdre McCarthy. She responded immediately, almost triumphantly, "I knew you had trouble the minute I saw your car coming back the road." But she was silent after that, with her head on her chest and her eyes shut, for so long that he thought she had fallen asleep. Eventually, without moving, she added, almost dreamily, "but no son of mine would do a thing like that. Least of all you, Ignatius." After another silence she opened her eyes and stared at the fire again. Eventually she looked across at him, blazing anger in the deep dark sockets. "So whose skull must we crack to wake them up to the truth?" The old familiar belligerence in the strong harsh voice.

"I don't know, Mammy. That's what I have to find out. And that's the reason I came home. So I could think."

"The girl and her father," she said after looking into the fire some more. "That could be your problem right there, Ignatius."

"I know. Padhraig McCarthy is using the rape to get back at me. But that doesn't tell us who *did* the rape. And until –"

"But it does! Isn't that what I'm getting at!" Fierce, almost diabolical, malice in Mammy's tone. "Fathers and daughters, the age-old curse of the Irish family. Take your mother's word for it." She wagged a finger that was gnarled from arthritis in his face.

Understanding came slowly, forcing its way into his unwilling consciousness, like dawn dispelling the night. "Oh my great good God Almighty! I never thought of that."

"I'm right, amn't I? Eh?" None more vindictive than Mammy when she had found her villain.

He got up quickly and headed for the door. "I have to go

for a walk now." Over the stile at the end of the yard and up the long hill of the field behind the house. As children they'd race up this hill to see who'd be first to the wall at the top. He was almost racing now, arms swinging, dodging cow plops, breathing hard, trying to keep up with the remains of his sanity. It wasn't possible, something so evil, yet already so obvious. Mammy it was had the nose, unerring and mean, for the source of wickedness. She always had. As kids she'd sort out the culprits and mete out the punishment and never did they know her to be wrong. They hated her for it but could never accuse her of being unjust.

But it made sense, however awful. The veiled hostility of the eldest daughter that he was vaguely aware of but didn't understand; like the time she asked him, "why are you always so happy? Isn't that a bit weird or something?" And the shock of once catching a look of what had seemed like pure hatred on Padhraig's face; at the time he had doubted his own senses. But now ...

So what if Mammy was right? "Oh God, what do I do at all?" He leaned against the wall, puffing and blowing. The hill was steep and he wasn't as fit as he used to be. Denounce them, of course. There must be some tests, some way to prove ... He'd get back his good name, reputation, honor, esteem as a man of God. And they'd go to jail, and serve them right, the bastards, for trying to destroy him. And Deirdre ... Ah, sweet Jesus! What would happen to Deirdre? Her life would be ruined as well, her family wrecked. And all because he was fond of her and she of him, though they never did a thing that even the most puritan of moralists could fault. So it came down to this: one of them must be destroyed, himself or Deirdre. "This is not fair, Jesus!" he shouted into the evening air. "Do you hear me? This is the lousiest thing you have ever done! Who do you expect me to choose?"

Mammy was watching from the back door as he came up the yard. "I'm right, you know," she said. "I know it for sure."

"I have no doubt you are." His legs were lead, and it wasn't from climbing the hill. And his brain was numb, and there was a lump in his belly the size of a turnip.

"So what are you going to do? Eh?" Squinting from the rays of the setting sun. She'd badger him now till the matter was resolved. Which it never would be. Maybe he ought not have told her?

"I'm going to sleep on it." And he went to his room, telling Sarah he was tired as he passed through the kitchen and forcing a cheerful goodnight to the girls. He brushed his teeth and went to bed.

Deirdre was having breakfast when Padhraig came downstairs; Gemma and Cathal had already left for school, Fiona had not yet put in an appearance. She ignored him when he sat across the table from her. Until he said, "what got into you at all last night?"

Her instinct was to yell *what did you do to our daughter, you bastard?* but wariness, born of long experience with Padhraig McCarthy, kept her from leveling that charge. She even regretted her comment last night that might have given away her awareness of what he had done. So she said now, "I don't know what you're talking about," without so much as glancing up from her cereal bowl.

"I'll have a poached egg when you're ready," he said after a short silence. "And a couple of slices of toast." He got up and went to the counter where the coffee maker sat. "You forgot to make the coffee," a touch of petulance in his tone.

"If you want breakfast," she retorted, "make it yourself."

He was quiet then for a long time, his back to her, facing the empty coffee maker. "We're very hostile this morning, aren't we?" he said eventually. "Is this out of chapter four of the women's lib manual?"

"Chapter one." She finished her cereal, put the bowl in the dishwasher, the milk in the refrigerator, dropped an orange into her handbag, and was headed for the door when he stepped in front of her.

"Where do you think you're going?" Deep menace in the dark eyes, hands hanging limply by his sides.

"I'm going to work, of course. Now will you get out of my way; I have a lot of things to do today." Outwardly calm, inwardly taut as a bowstring. Though he had never threatened her with physical violence in all their years of marriage, she had often felt that one day he might strike her. If he ever did, even once, she'd leave him on the spot. Her feeling now was that perhaps this moment had arrived.

He didn't move. "Don't push me too far." In the tone that when addressed to the children elicited immediate obedience. "I know all about you and your bloody priest friend."

And I know all about what you did to Fiona she barely repressed herself from screaming. "You're paranoid, Padhraig," she said instead, very quietly. "Take yourself to a shrink. Now let me pass, I'll be late for work."

He stayed where he was. "I have just one thing to say to you." He took a deep breath. "If you ever leave this house without telling me where you're going I'll go straight to the guards and have them arrest Lally for rape." The expression in his eyes roused fear inside her: this was the face of a man deranged, quite capable of doing what he said, regardless of reason or morality.

"Let me pass," she said again. And this time he did. She was shaking so badly as she drove off that half a mile down the road she pulled over and waited till her body calmed down. As she continued towards the office she decided not to ring Ignatius till she had devised a plan of action that would safeguard them both from the lunacy of her husband.

Fiona was quite amenable to being pampered. Padraig took the day off from work and let her stay home from school again – she hadn't gone the previous day either – and they set out for Dublin. "Are you all right?" he asked her once they were on the road.

"Only middling," she said. "I'm still shook up. Every time I go out I keep thinking people are looking at me and pointing fingers at me and saying things about me."

"You'll get over it."

He could feel her stare and sensed the cold of her silence. "What am I going to say in confession?"

"Arrah, there's no need to say anything at all to the priest. Sure you didn't do anything wrong. If there was wrong in it, and there wasn't, let me tell you, the blame was on me."

When they were passing through Thurles she said, "you promised that that was all there was going to be to it, didn't you? That there wouldn't be anything else going on about the priest."

"I did," he said, "and I meant it."

"I mean, you're not really going to report him to the Guards or anything like that?"

"No, no, not at all. There's not a thing to worry about now.

There won't be any need for anything else. That lad is out of our hair for good. He won't give us any more trouble, I guarantee you that."

"Because I don't think I'd be able to tell lies in front of the Guards. I had enough trouble with Mammy when she was asking me."

"Has your mother being asking you questions?" Now he'd find out; this was the opening he had been looking for.

"She wanted to know what exactly happened; what the priest said and what he did. Stuff like that."

"And you told her just what we agreed on, didn't you?"

"Of course."

"Good girl yourself." That was a great relief; Deirdre might suspect but she couldn't know.

"I threw in a bit about having to kneel on the visitor's chair as well," she added, with a touch of girlish enthusiasm. "Just to make it sound even more real. I saw a scene like that in a movie when we were in London last year."

"Shit!" The word shot out involuntarily.

"What's the matter, Daddy?"

"Nothing. Not a thing. I just remembered that I forgot to call the office before I left." That chair bit! Deirdre, goddam her, without a doubt in the world had made a connection that wasn't there at all! And that's what she had been so upset about. He was morose the rest of the way to Dublin, but as he followed his daughter in and out of shops and boutiques in the vicinity of Grafton Street an idea came to him that revived his spirits. He'd need to pay another visit to the archbishop.

On the way home he told Fiona, "I'm coming up to Dublin again for the hurling match on Sunday. And I have to attend a conference at the Conrad from Monday to Wednesday. So I'd like –"

"You want me to come with you?" she cut in. "Oh, Daddy that's fab!" She bounced up and down in her seat.

"No, pet! Sorry; that's not possible. But I want you to do something very important for me while I'm gone."

"Bollocks! You have all the fun and I have to stay home all the time."

"You're going down to Waterville the week after," he reminded her. His mother had a summer cottage there and the children usually spent two weeks with her, a visit they all looked forward to. "But while I'm gone I want you to keep an eye on your mother for me. I don't want her –"

"I don't want to be in the house with her while you're gone, Daddy." There was extraordinary vehemence in the way she said it, as if she were terrified at the very thought.

"Why not?"

"Please Daddy! Can't you take us to Waterville before you go away? Please."

"What are you afraid of?" Though he had a good idea.

"I don't want Mammy asking me lots of questions while you're gone. You know her, she has a way of finding out things," she added ominously.

She had a point indeed. "We'll see, pet, we'll see. Of course we'll have to ring Grandma first to see if she's ready for you." Anyway, what he had to say to the archbishop this evening would prevent any further contact between Deirdre and Ignatius Lally.

SILENCE

Kennedy rang very early while he was still in bed. Sarah, who was up, fetched him.

"Listen," the Superior's tone was tense, "you need to come here straight away this morning. Something else has come up."

"What's happened this time, Brian? Have I sodomized the Pope?"

"Padhraig McCarthy has just made further conditions for not prosecuting. He wants a signed confession of guilt from you, as well as your written promise never to see his wife or daughter again."

"You can tell ..." He stopped himself. "You know, you and the archbishop are just about as guilty of that horrible crime as I am."

"Please, Ignatius." Kennedy was wheedling now. "If you don't do it you'll be in court and in jail and the church will be sunk deeper in scandal.

"Brian, for God's sake, I can't confess to something I didn't do."

"Let me make a suggestion. Why don't you go on a retreat.

I have arranged for you to do one at the Jesuit house. We can hold McCarthy off till you finish." He paused. "And I'll go further, Ignatius: if at the end of the retreat you can still tell me you're innocent, I'll back you to the hilt. Is that fair?"

The awful sincerity of the Superior was infuriating. "Fuck your blasted retreat, Brian. You're assuming all the time that I'm guilty. Well, I'm not. Do you hear me? I didn't do it. So I won't sign any bloody confession or make any stupid promise. If that lunatic wants to press charges let him. We'll see what comes out in court."

"What harm can a retreat do, Ignatius?"

"A lot. Do you realize what people would say if I went on one now? They'd say I was guilty. It's an admission, dammit, and I'm not going to make it."

"What people are you talking about? Nobody knows a thing about this so far, except the archbishop and the McCarthys and myself. And none of us is telling anybody. We *want* to keep the lid on it. And we will, too, if you'll cooperate."

"Let me spell things out for you, Brian. I did not commit this crime. I will sign no confession that I did. And you won't see me again until I'm exonerated." He put down the phone and went back to bed.

After breakfast he walked up the back hill again, sat on top of the double wall and stared at the mountains to the west. A bright morning at first, till a long dark cloud appeared slowly over the horizon, gradually covering the light blue hills, then spreading east and blocking the sun. Though a shower was imminent he didn't move: there was peace in this inevitability of nature. The first heavy raindrops splashed on his face. Washing away the sins of the world. The rain came down hard then, but he didn't stir; he liked being out in the rain: there was a cleansing feeling about it. Would that it might wash away the awful stigma of McCarthy's allegations.

Brian Kennedy sat in his office, his head between his hands. What on God's earth was he going to do about Lally's obduracy? If it hadn't been for the strength of the evidence and the history of past pedophile denials he might believe in the man's innocence. As it was he was trying to be fair. Last night he had rung Jack Martin, Lally's former Superior in Brazil and now the president of Saint Fursa's, to discreetly inquire into Ignatius's past, hoping for a clean bill of moral health. A terrific fellow, Martin had agreed, one of the very best. Apart from the one incident not a blot on his character during all his years in Brazil. And what incident might that be? Must be all of seventeen or eighteen years ago, Martin guessed. He seemed reluctant to drag it up and Kennedy had to prod to get the story. "It could be terribly important to me and to the Congregation, Jack." Sexual involvement with a woman, scandal to the local community, Lally was very young at the time, was all Martin would say about it.

The Brendan Smyth affair had been a watershed for the Irish hierarchy in the matter of sexual abuse by the clergy. Prior practice had been to deny, cover up, shield the offender, move him elsewhere regardless of the near-certainty that there he'd renew his criminal activities. But the fallout from the horrific case of the Norbertine pedophile had wrought a dramatic change. Admit, apologize, atone, were the three A's of the new episcopal policy. And his Grace of Tighmor had been to the fore in promoting this new approach, so he was not about to tolerate a lackadaisical attitude in dealing with the novice master of Clyard.

"Where is Father Lally?" His Grace had asked on the phone last evening.

"He's at home visiting his mother in Mayo at the moment; she's been unwell for some time. But I've ordered him to come up to Dublin." No point in mentioning that Lally had refused to comply. "And I've set him up for a retreat in the Jesuit house."

"He shouldn't be loose," Donnellan growled. Then, after relaying the aggrieved father's latest demands, he said, "I want the confession and the promise in writing, and I want Lally locked up. Immediately."

"We'll do everything in our power to do just that," Kennedy assured him.

"You know," the archbishop added, "I thought the first evening when McCarthy came here with his daughter that he was simply a good man in a state of shock. But this evening I got an impression of a fellow with a vindictive streak in him. I'm not doubting his version of what happened – the medical evidence is damning and the girl's pointing the finger at Lally is conclusive. But I suspect that McCarthy's motives for keeping quiet about the affair may be personal rather than concern for the church."

"Probably doesn't want any scandal getting out about his wife either," Kennedy suggested.

"Anyway, get those things done straight away," were the archbishop's parting words. So Kennedy rang Lally, endured his recriminations, and now sat in his office wondering what to do next. It was time to share the burden with the General Council and seek their advice.

"I've got something to show you, Ignatius." Mammy always called him Ignatius except when there was company; then it was *Father* Ignatius. "Come and take a look." Her face had that neutral expression she always wore when she wanted to surprise you with either calamity or diversion. "It's in my room."

Her bedroom, across the hall from the kitchen, had been the children's playroom before she broke her hip. And a big bright room it was, with large windows facing back and side. When Dan and Sarah designed their new dwelling next to the drab stone-and-slate abode where generations of Lallys had grown up, they made it everything the old house was not. Where the old was dull gray stone, the new was bright cream stucco. In place of dark interiors they had lots of light. And rooms small and few gave way to spacious and many: on the first floor, kitchen and scullery, dining room and parlor, playroom and bathroom; upstairs, two more bathrooms and four bedrooms, including a permanent guest room that was Ignatius's when he came to visit.

Ignatius stared in disbelief. “Where in God's name did you find this?" On the floor next to her bed was a battered black steamer trunk that he recognized instantly; it had sat in the tiny room he shared with his brother John; under the window, it use to be the only sizeable object in the room other than the bed. They kept their clothes in it and sat on it and stood on it and jumped off it.

"I kept it with me all these years. It was your father's, you know." Jim Lally had emigrated to America before the war and returned home when threatened with conscription into the United States army. "Lift it up on the bed now and open it."

He plopped it on the duvet, undid straps and clasps and raised the lid. "His books! I was wondering not long ago whatever happened to them." Dad had loved his books. A man with no formal education beyond the National School, but a great reader.

When he'd have the odd pound to spare after swearing off the drink, he'd go to Galway on the bus and come back with a few carefully chosen volumes: Frank O'Connor and Liam O'Flaherty and Maria Edgeworth and Walter Macken and Mary Lavin and the plays of Sean O'Casey and once a book of W.B.Yeats's poems. He didn't like Joyce at all, he said, after reading *Dubliners*.

"When he got sick he made me put them all in his trunk. 'Ignatius is the only one who'll ever want them,' he said. And he told me to keep them for you till you came back from Brazil. So they're yours now."

He dragged the trunk up the stairs to his room and browsed through it. A brown-paper-covered schoolbook, called *Fíon na Filiochta* – wine of poetry – his own from Saint Fursa's, caught his eye. He skimmed the pages, read stanzas here and there, some of which he could still recite from memory. *Tighe Molaga*! Even as a callow youth that poem had struck a chord: meditation amid monastic ruins, lamentation on what used to be: *do bhi aimsear ann a raibh / an teach so go soilbh subhach.* – was a time when joy and gladness reigned within this house. Ancient monasteries of Ireland, pillaged and destroyed by the conqueror; abodes of peace and prayer and industry and learning, that were no more.

Maybe he *should* have gone on that retreat. But not to the Jesuits as Kennedy had suggested; they were too organized for his needs. To a monastery maybe. He thought of the Franciscan monastery ruins on the river banks near Drumnamwika, destroyed by Cromwell. Perhaps he'd find in those ruins the answers and peace he sought. He went there after dinner. The absence of people, the sprightly sounds of water racing over rocks, all provided the soothing solitude he needed. He sat on a rock and meditated on his predicament. *Why, Lord? Why have you done this to me?* It was then that the sudden silence inside him spoke only of God's absence. Something was happening to him. Right now, this minute, deep inside him, amid these peaceful ruins, a terrifying separation of mind from faith was taking place, creating between them a yawning fissure of nothingness; like an earthquake opening a cleft in the ground.

My God! My God! Why hast thou forsaken me? He felt that the God in whose presence he lived, Who was always there for him, had suddenly vanished. Completely, without trace, as if He had never been. How he knew this he didn't know, but he was absolutely certain of it, as if the very absence of God were a being that had made itself known to him. Was he going mad? He clutched his head to keep it from exploding. *Where are you, God? Where have you gone? You can't leave me alone like this just because I asked you a question.* But his God was silent. And Ignatius Lally felt the emptiness of a universe suddenly bereft of anyone in charge. Despair surrounded and enveloped him, like that black cloud covering the mountain.

The seven members of the General Council met with Brian Kennedy to be briefed on the latest catastrophe to strike their Congregation. They sat around the oval table in the conference room, eight middle-age men in somber clerical garb, and listened to the tale of human perfidy with downcast eyes and solemn expressions. When Kennedy finished, two of the Councilors, Fathers Barry and Farragher, said they refused to believe in the possibility of Lally's guilt.

Barry was particularly outspoken. "I've known Ignatius since the novitiate. We went through the scholasticate together. We served in Brazil together. He could never do a thing like that, I absolutely guarantee you."

"He was involved with a woman in Brazil," Kennedy pointed out.

"Terezinha!" Barry, overweight and with mischievous eyes, snorted in derision. "God, Brian, even you'd have fallen for that lassie if you were there. Every single CWM that ever visited Ignatius's parish and met her fell in love with her. Including myself, I might add. There was something about her ... But anyway, there's no argument that because a young lad fell victim to Terezinha's charms he's capable of committing rape."

"After Michael Harnett anything is possible," Father Mullen retorted grimly. Mullen was the Bursar and a hard-liner in matters of discipline. "So, regardless of our personal beliefs we have to act on the assumption that there may be guilt here, and take whatever steps we think are necessary to ensure that there's no chance of it happening again, and that there's no damage accruing to the Congregation because of it. Any more scandals and we're all up the creek."

"Would you be willing to punish an innocent man to achieve those ends?" Farragher asked, with just a touch of acerbity. A quiet man, Brendan, with a soft voice amd a very acute mind; a scripture scholar, he was the acknowledged intellectual of the group.

"It's not our business to punish," Kennedy noted. "That's not what we're trying to decide here. What we have to do is protect the Congregation – and the Church – from any harmful effects that could occur as a result of the accusation made against Father Lally, regardless of whether the accusation is true or false."

"And what about the victim?" Farragher asked quietly. "If there is one. Are we not concerned about her protection?" Nobody said anything.

"What about Ignatius Lally?" Sean Barry's tone was belligerent. "Doesn't he need protection, too? How would any of you like it if you were accused of something like this? If you were wouldn't you expect support from the Congregation to which you have devoted your life?"

Kennedy drummed his fingers on the table. Trust Barry to throw in a red herring; a fierce man for the underdog, even if the underdog were an axe-murderer. Father Donohue, the canonist, came to the rescue in his precise measured tones. "Sometimes it *is* expedient that one man die for the people, Sean. I don't want to be hard-hearted, but it seems to me that this is a case where the common good must come before the individual good. Better to risk an unjust accusation against Ignatius Lally than to put the Church and the Congregation in jeopardy."

"Easy for you to say, Matt, you're not the one in the hot seat."

"At this stage," Kennedy said in summary, "*we're* not accusing Father Lally of anything. However it has been alleged that he raped a teenage girl. There is medical evidence that she was indeed raped. And the girl's father is threatening to prosecute Father Lally for the deed unless we take a certain action. So the question before us is, do we take that action or do we presume Father Lally to be innocent and let justice take its course, with all the consequences of adverse publicity and possible conviction that that course will entail?"

"We can't take that risk." Mullen, red-faced, thumped his fist on the table. "We could wind up being totally destroyed." The rest were silent.

"Let us pause then for a few minutes," Kennedy said, "to

pray and think of possible solutions." All heads bowed immediately. Pot-lids clanged in the nearby kitchen. A twitter of birds came through the open window. A passing motorcyclist revved his engine, then screeched his brakes.

Eventually Matt Donohue raised his head. "Suppose you were to assign Father Lally to a post at the Mother House." He paused for a moment. "And guarantee to this fellow McCarthy that we'd keep him here permanently. Perhaps he might then be willing to compromise on the confession-signing condition."

"I could use an assistant," Mullen put in quickly.

Kennedy saw several heads nod. Barry and Farragher remained frigidly silent. "We can try it," he said, "unless someone has a better idea?"

"It's a terrible thing to do to an innocent man," Barry objected.

"Even if he's innocent what we're doing is protecting him from the consequences of a criminal prosecution," Mullen said sourly. No one else said anything. Donohue's proposal was carried on a vote of six to two.

"One more thing," Kennedy added, "he won't be allowed to say mass. His Grace of Tighmor has suspended him *sine die* from all clerical functions in his diocese. And although canonically he could say mass in the Dublin diocese I think it would be politically prudent to maintain the suspension here, at least for the time being."

A man laughed loudly in the street outside as the meeting was breaking up.

REVENGE

Despair did not vanish with the night. Sarah said, "what are you doing up so early?" when he surfaced before she had even roused the children out of bed for school.

"I woke at four and couldn't go back to sleep." He had lain awake for hours, watching the gray shadows on the wall turn slowly to bright morning, wondering who, if not God, made the sun to rise. For that Being to Whom he always gave his day's first greeting was still conspicuously absent. He made porridge in the microwave and peeled an orange, and had just finished eating when the girls came down, sleepy-eyed and grumpy.

"Will you look at them," their mother said. "You'd think the weight of the world was on their shoulders."

He escaped before he could be involved in conversation, and was at the end of the yard staring over the wall at some grazing sheep when six-year old Cara came running up. "There's somebody on the telephone wants to talk to you, Uncle Ignatius," she said breathlessly. "Mammy told me to come and get you quick."

He dragged himself back to the house. As he feared, it was Kennedy. "Good morning, Father Lally." The Superior's tone heavy with formal politeness.

"What is it this time, Brian?"

"Listen. We want to be sure we do the right thing by you. We owe you that, and we will. So this is what I've done. I've held a special meeting of the Council and placed the facts before them and –"

"What facts, Brian?" He couldn't keep the savagery from his voice. "The same ones the AB used? You give them the guilty verdict first and then you ask them to determine the sentence. Aren't you leaving something out?"

Kennedy's silence was as calm as his speech. Eventually, he said, "If you'll be patient for just a moment, Ignatius, I'll try to explain. First of all, nobody has condemned you. We are trying to do the best we can about a most frightful accusation that is backed up by very strong evidence. And the only way we can do that is by a due process of examining all the alternatives and their consequences, and then deciding on the best course of action. So I have laid all the information before the Council of the Congregation and asked their advice and recommendations. And after much reflection and prayer we have agreed on what should be done."

The measured tone, the meagerly spooned information, bespoke a decision unpalatable to the victim. "Spit it out," he said brusquely.

"You have only two real options, Father. One, you accept the accusations – whether you believe they're true or not – and do nothing about them. In that case there will be no publicity and no criminal charges. We'll find you a post at the Mother House that won't involve your dealing with the faithful. In time you may even be permitted to say mass again." The Superior paused. Ignatius was too stunned to respond. Kennedy continued. "I most strongly urge you, Father, for your own good, and the good of our Congregation, and indeed the good of the whole Church, to accept this solution." He paused again.

"You said there was another option," Ignatius managed.

Kennedy's heavy breathing was audible across the line. "That alternative, I'm afraid, is not one either of us would want to contemplate."

"In other words, you've given me the *good* news, Brian!"

"That's about it," Kennedy said bleakly. "If you don't take that option, the McCarthys will prosecute and you will be arrested and tried for rape."

"I don't believe this is happening," Ignatius whispered. "I'm your Novice Master, for Christ's sake. I give good example to my novices, I lead an exemplary monastic life. I have done nothing since I came back from Brazil that cannot bear the scrutiny of God and man. How can I be in this appalling predicament?"

"I'd like you to take some time, Father, and think about this, carefully and prayerfully." Kennedy all *plámás* now. "Take a couple of days if necessary. Then ring me when you have decided. Okay?" Ignatius said nothing. "We're counting on you to make the right choice," the Superior added.

"Goodbye." Ignatius hung up.

"Is everything all right?" Sarah asked when he returned to the kitchen.

"No," he said. "But I'll tell you about it later." He shambled back down the yard to resume his contemplation of grazing sheep. After a while he opened the iron gate leading out of the yard, wandered through long grasses, climbed over walls, stepped through gaps, scrambled beneath electric fences, meandered in the midst of curious bullocks and frisky calves, avoided their plops, and threw stones into the pond that was their watering hole. All the while his conscious mind refused to dwell on what Kennedy had said. The sun was shining, a fresh breeze was blowing and, although his God was still silent, the world at this moment was in harmony with his body. The future was in abeyance.

Eventually his solitude was disturbed by the arrival of Dan on the tractor, pulling a trailer. "I'm going to sell a few of those lads at the mart today." His brother herded several calves up the ramp into the trailer. "How are things?" he asked as he climbed back on the tractor. "Sarah said you had a phone call this morning."

"I'll tell you about it again," was all he would say. But the anaesthesia was wearing off and he returned to the house.

Mammy was watching from the back door. "I thought you had got lost, Ignatius." Her way of asking what was going on.

"Just went for a walk, Mammy." He needed to get away from here. Into total solitude. Ah for the wilds of Brazil! He escaped to his room, sat on the bed, picked up his breviary, put it down again: how could he pray if there was no one to pray to? He stretched out and slept.

Mammy's cane tapping on his door woke him. "Are you all right, Ignatius?"

"I'm fine, thanks. Just taking a nap."

"The dinner is ready."

He splashed water on his face in the bathroom and brushed his hair. Just Mammy, Sarah, and himself for the meal, Dan having left for the cattle mart. Not much was said while they ate. Even Mammy, the ever loquacious, didn't get beyond a few comments on the weather and the questionable wisdom of her youngest son selling calves at this time of year. Sarah looked quizzically at him several times and seemed about to ask something, but each time drew back. He waited till Mammy went for her nap before saying anything.

"Things are going from bad to worse." He told Sarah about Kennedy's options.

"Oh Ignatius, you poor thing!" She dropped the clothes she was about to put in the washing machine and put her arms around him in a tight sympathetic hug. "Have you decided what you'll do?

"Not yet. You've been wonderful, Sarah. You and Dan."

She tossed clothes into the machine. "Isn't that what friends are for?"

"Mammy, too, has been a brick. I didn't know how *she* was going to react."

"She's been good all round, mind you, lately. She seems to be mellowing a bit with the years." Sarah smiled.

"So I hope you won't misunderstand me," he said then, "when I say that I need to be alone for a while."

"The place is yours. You know that. We won't bother you. I'll keep the girls –"

"I was thinking actually of getting away altogether for a bit. It's nothing to do with anyone being in my way. I just need solitude right now."

Sarah poured detergent and dropped the lid. "All right. You know yourself what's best for you. Did you have some particular place in mind?"

"I was wondering about the house you rent in Louisburgh every summer. Do you think it might be available?"

She rang the owner. Because of a cancellation it was vacant at the moment and he could have it for the next ten days. "I'll head off in the morning, then." he said. Later in the afternoon he got Dan on his own down the yard. "I came away with very little money," he told him. "And I have no way of getting any at the moment."

A quiet man, Dan, and much teased as a youngster for his devotion to his elder brother. Now he pulled a wad of notes from his pants pocket and handed them to Ignatius. "I got seven hundred today for a calf."

"That's much too much," Ignatius protested. "I just need a couple of hundred. And I'll get it back –"

"Take it." Dan's tone said don't argue. "And I don't want to see it again."

That night, when the girls had gone to bed and the adults were watching television, Ignatius rang the novitiate. Corrigan answered. "How are things, Noel?"

The assistant Master coughed. "Hello Ignatius." Even a novice would have detected the forced quality of his cordiality.

"I just called to see if all is well with our boys." He tried to sound casual.

"Listen, I might as well tell you up front." Corrigan coughed again. "I've been told to report any calls you might make here."

"Indeed! Are they afraid I might attack the novices next?"

"There's no one as sorry as I am, Ignatius, that ..."

He left after breakfast, to the tears of his mother and wild waving from the children, and with a large bag of groceries from Sarah, and a map and detailed directions from his brother. "If anyone is looking for me you don't know where I went," were his last instructions to them before driving off.

Since it was Sunday, he had told them he'd catch mass on the way. But he couldn't face his old parish church without being able to stand at the altar himself. Besides, he was too angry with his God to take part in the holy sacrifice this day. He drove almost recklessly through Drumnamwika, as if to escape some invisible pursuer. Later, the narrow winding coast road to Louisburgh took a level of driving concentration that for the moment befogged the despair from his thoughts. On impulse at Murrisk he pulled into the car park at the foot of Croagh Patrick. The day was fine. The great holy mountain stood clear, inviting, against the blue sky. He got out and headed for the path to the ascent. He'd go as far as the statue of Saint Patrick, about a hundred feet up. A few people passed him on their way down. From the monument he surveyed the grandeur of Clew Bay below, with its myriad islets, and the great hump back of Clare Island just visible away to the left. *Where are you, God? Is all this beauty the work of your hands or merely the result of chance? Are you alive, Patrick, up there in heaven somewhere, looking down with care on your spiritual descendants? Or are you, too, no more than a far distant memory, mingled dust in the ancient soil of Ireland?*

But silence was the only reply. He was tempted to continue climbing all the way to the top. Perhaps up there his God would talk to him, like He did to Patrick and Moses. Maybe God *did* reside on mountain tops, as the Greeks believed. The physical exertion, too, might mitigate the tensions within, even banish the demons of doubt. A burst of enthusiasm for the effort roused him briefly from his torpor. He was dressed for the effort, in casual shirt and jeans and well-cushioned sneakers; and he was reasonably fit, having regularly engaged in manual labor with his novices and played basketball almost daily with them. Then he remembered that he had no provisions for what would be an exhausting four-hour trek. Without water, at least, he'd be dehydrated by the time he reached the top. Reluctantly he returned to his car. Tomorrow, for sure, he'd make the climb, and clamor at the gates of heaven.

Dan's directions were accurate, and the key to the house, located on the cliff overlooking the strand, was under the doormat. A modern two-bedroom cottage with bathroom and shower, a suitably-equipped kitchen, including a dining alcove, and a furnished sitting room with television and telephone. He could hide here in comfort for the next ten days while he sorted out his future. He unpacked his clothes, put the groceries away, plopped into an armchair and fell asleep.

He was awakened by a loud ringing sound. Ignoring the phone, he went for a walk down the road till he found an entrance to the strand. The sandy path opened out onto a glorious white beach. He sat on a dune, removed shoes and socks, and rolled up the legs of his jeans. The sand was cool to his feet and, though the sky was clear, a stiff breeze blew in off the Atlantic. He walked down to where the tide was lapping and let his feet get wet. The water was cold. He trudged ankle deep in the frothy waves and a couple of times was surprised by exuberant swells that came all the way to his knees, soaking the ends of his jeans. Kennedy was lapping at his heels, too, wasn't he? Only a matter of time before he overwhelmed him with a demand in the name of obedience. *Return to the Mother House to begin your sentence.* What then? Other than his assignment to Brazil almost twenty years ago he had never until last week received a command in the name of obedience. That wasn't how the religious system worked: you were asked to do things and you did them, without formal injunctions. The habit of obedience was instilled into novices from the very first day, and it had never occurred to him before not to carry out the request of a religious superior. But this particular request, or command, or whatever Kennedy would choose to call it, was different. To obey would be to subject himself to a life sentence of hell on earth. Too well he knew what that job in the Mother House would consist of. Another Tom Reidy, that's what he'd be! Tom had been a member of his ordination year who was never ordained. The night before Holy Orders the highly-strung Reidy woke screaming and demented and had to be hurried away to the Saint John of God psychiatric institute for deranged clerics. But, though he was never after ordained a priest, neither was he released from the obligation to lifelong celibacy attached to his sub-diaconate ordination. So he was assigned to the Mother House with the amorphous title of assistant to the Bursar, and there ever since he eked out an existence performing menial jobs.

Ignatius kicked viciously at an incoming wave. He could not, would not, become another Tom Reidy. Yet the alternative was to reject his vow. Ten days to make up his mind. But if ten, why not twenty? While he couldn't be found he couldn't be commanded. How long could he stall? A month? A year? Forever? What if he vanished? There was precedent for that: a few years ago the Bishop of Galway disappeared to save the church embarrassment after a scandal. So why not the Novice Master of Clyard? But was he prepared to do it? Leave confreres and family and – and Deirdre McCarthy, God help him. But he'd lose all of them anyway when he went to the Mother House. *When* he went? Ah, the finality of that statement. *Father Ignatius Lally, CWM, laid to rest at the Mother House in Dundrum, Dublin, on August 18, 1999. Requiescat in Pace, the poor unfortunate bugger. We'll say no more now. A weakness of the flesh, you see. Especially for young females. Ah sure it was a terrible business altogether. Nice little girl raped down the country. In Tipperary it was. And he Master of Novice, no less. Not to be talked about, God help us. Mind you, the Congregation took swift and certain action. No nonsense at all there, unlike some previous cases of pederasty. Brian Kennedy deserves a lot of credit for that. Locked him up in the Mother House straight off and threw away the key. Fortunately for everyone the miserable fellow died a few years later. I suppose he couldn't live with himself. Or maybe it was he couldn't live without access to the children.*

A huge wave reared towards him. He moved backward, till it dissipated, swirling, spent, about his ankles. He would *not* allow himself to be victimized. He couldn't. They had no right. "Do you hear me, God?" he shouted into the wind. But his God, if He heard, paid him no heed.

He was hungry. Six o'clock already. He had neglected dinner again. He returned to the cottage, delved into Sarah's bag of groceries, and fried a pork chop and a sliced potato, and heated a can of beans. Not much of a cook, but he could survive. He had just finished cleaning up when the door bell rang. Who in God's name? Ah, the landlady of course – Sarah had said she'd drop by to see that everything was okay. But it was Deirdre McCarthy on the doorstep. He stood gaping at her.

"Hello!" Her tone, if he could have focused on it, he'd have classified as bright.

"What ...?" He was stunned. "How did you manage to get here?"

"Do I have to answer now, or do I get to come in first?" She smiled, as if their relationship were perfectly normal.

"Come in, come in." At this moment all he could register was the fact of her presence.

She preceded him into the living room. "Very nice indeed." She sat in one of the armchairs and crossed her legs.

"What ..." he began again, towering over her before

dropping onto the sofa. "How did you find me? Nobody is supposed to know where I am."

She smiled sweetly, though with a touch of sadness. "It took me four hours, but what's important is that I'm here. I had to find you, Ignatius." The old intimate Deirdre of the fund-raising office and Sunday family dinners.

"Why?" This past week had made him suspicious of everything and everyone.

"Oh God, Ignatius!" Her brightness vanished, like a candle flame snuffed after mass, and tears appeared. "My whole world has been turned inside out." She tried to smile and wiped her eyes with long slender fingers. "What you said to me in the office the other day is true. Only it's worse. Much worse."

He wanted to say, *I know*. "Tell me about it."

The fists clenched, she drew deep breaths. "I can't bring myself to say it. Padhraig ..." She stopped. "My own husband and daughter ..."

"I know," he told her then. "You don't have to say any more."

She looked at him, the sorrows of the Virgin in her face. "I'm so ashamed. My own flesh and blood. And then to accuse you, my dearest friend ..." She frowned suddenly. "How did *you* find out?"

"Mammy. My mother. When I told her what happened she put her finger on it straight away. Mothers always know!" A fierce anger at Padhraig McCarthy swept over him. If he could get his hands on the fucker at this moment he'd surely kill him.

"Mothers always know," she repeated softly. "So why didn't I?" She covered her face with her hands.

"If you don't mind my asking, how did *you* find out?"

"I questioned Fiona ... I know my daughter." Anger in *her* voice now. "She can't fool me with her lies."

"Did she admit it?"

Deirdre shook her head. "Not her. She's as stubborn as her father. Torquemada himself wouldn't force her to recant. But she will. By God she will. Padhraig, too. I've decided to call the Gardai and have an investigation." She was shouting now.

Yes, get them both. Lock them up and throw away the key. Then there'd be hope for him. But of course there wasn't. Greek tragedy at its most dramatic. The wife, to save her lover, must destroy her family. Was he her lover? At least a serious friend. The stuff of theatre certainly. But real life did not demand or expect or countenance such sacrifice. "You can't *do* that," he said.

"I certainly can. I'm not going to allow you to be destroyed because –"

"You can't," he interrupted.

"Why not?" almost belligerently. "I have to do it."

"It would destroy your entire family."

She laughed, a harsh high-pitched cackle. "You're a funny man, Ignatius. Don't you realize my family is already destroyed?"

"But a *public* scandal is a different matter. And you probably couldn't prove your case. Besides, my reputation would be gone anyway." He didn't quite know what was driving his argument but he knew he was right.

"Why do you say that?" She uncrossed her legs and leaned towards him.

"That you couldn't prove your case? Because I don't –"

"Why do you say your reputation would be gone?"

"You know what happens the moment an investigation like this begins? The media hounds smell blood. A priest accused of rape. No smoke without fire. They'd be checking into every detail of my life from the day I was born."

"So! You've led a blameless life, I'd imagine. I mean – well haven't you?" Her wide-eyed look demanding assent.

"Not quite, I'm afraid." He told her about Terezinha, reliving in the narrating a hint of the eroticism he used to feel with his Brazilian *namorada*. She listened wordlessly till he finished, then slipped across from chair to sofa and draped an arm around him.

"You dear man! It must have been awful for you." She squeezed his shoulder. "If I had been her I would never have let you go."

"It was my own fault. I shouldn't have got involved." Weak protest to her closeness stirring his blood even as her hair tickled his nose.

She drew back and looked at him. "what am *I* going to do? They've ruined my life, too, with their carry on." The tears were there again, rimming her eyes like pools overflowing. "How can I ever go back to living with them?"

He opened his arms and held her close. She clutched him tighter. He pulled her towards him. She moved to his lap. He wiped a tear from her cheek with his finger. She kissed his lips. He responded with a savagery that surprised even him. Her tongue slid into his mouth. He lay sideways on the sofa. She sprawled on top of him. His hands slid down to her backside. She moaned with pleasure.

"I want to make love to you," she breathed in his ear. She pulled his shirt from under his pants and ran fingers up his diaphragm and chest. Then she rose and pulled him up after her. “Which way the bedroom?”

He pointed. Without letting go his hand she led him down the short hall. His empty suitcase was atop the bed. He removed it with his free hand. She pulled down the duvet. "Let me undress you," she said.

A fierce amalgam of emotions coursed through him. Not the righteous sadness of the offended good, nor the implacable fury of the impotent, rather the vengeful spleen of the unfairly accused. Lust and anger, directed at McCarthy, and the Almighty, and Jack Martin who had separated him from Terezinha Gomez. He savored his revenge as Deirdre slowly and sensuously stripped and fondled and licked and nibbled and bit and sucked his flesh, which during all those pitiful years had borne their deprivation. The satisfaction of retaliation fueled the fires of his passion. When she removed his shorts he stood erect, exuberant, triumphant. "Now I'll undress you," he proclaimed.

"Be quick," she gasped. "I can't wait much longer." He unbuttoned and unzipped and unclasped and unhooked till she was as naked as he.

"Are we safe?" The thought had been burgeoning in the back of his mind.

She pushed him down on the bed and leaped astride. "Nothing to worry about, my dear." And the swift envelopment of bodies, the vigorous interaction of loins, the mingling of lips and tongues, the sliding and sweating, the panting and purring that crescendoed to screams and shouts, left neither space nor time nor contemplative peace in which to pursue either reasoned analysis or moral decisions about the deed in which he was irredeemably involved.

When vigor gave way to languor and they lay quietly side by side under cover of the duvet he was conscious only of profound satisfaction at what they had done. "That was fantastic," he murmured, not once but three times.

"For a man who is supposed to have no practice you were quite extraordinary." Smiling slyly, one hand massaging his inner thigh. "Are you quite sure you haven't ..."

Just flattering him, of course. "With you for teacher I'd soon be an expert." Would there be a next time? Now that pleasure had been achieved and passion spent and revenge obtained, sanity and sense and ethical issues wanted to push their way to the fore. *But not yet, Lord,* he admonished his absent God. "Unless I'm just a one-night stand?"

She rolled on top of him again. "If I have any say in the matter, Ignatius Lally, you're going to be getting a lot of practice." Passion shone through her smile and, though his body was spent for the nonce, he desperately wanted to respond. But he didn't reply, for the forces of good that had ruled his life from the age of reason – with the exception of that one mad interlude in Brazil – were now massing within to deliver him back to his prison of virtue. She must have seen the distress in his eyes for she cupped his face in her hands and kissed him lightly, tenderly, as a mother would her unhappy child. "What's the matter?" Pushing up with her arms till her face was removed from his and her small breasts dropped like perfectly inverted cones.

"Reality. I have a vow and you have a husband, and we both have an angry God looking down with disfavor."

She collapsed beside him. "Bother!" She nibbled his ear. "Well, the husband at this stage I don't give a fig for." She kissed his nose. "And God, I'm afraid, hasn't meant very much to me for quite a long time." She looked at him then and her eyes were wide with what he could swear was mischief. "So that leaves only *your* vow to be taken care of."

He heaved himself up onto his elbow. "Are you telling me Father Norton engaged a non-believer for his missionary work?"

"It wasn't my fault, honest to God. He asked me if I went to mass every Sunday. I said I did – I do, too." She posed an innocent pout. "And that was all he asked."

"But you don't believe in God?"

"I don't know, to tell you the truth." Then she, too, raised up on her elbow. "I'm prepared to believe whatever you want me to, as long as I can keep you for myself."

Longing for her swept through him. They made love again. Afterwards he put to her the question he had been holding in abeyance. "Now will you tell me how on God's earth you were able to find me here?"

"Your mother. I told her I was your friend and that I had good news for you. So she gave me your number, but said she didn't have your address. I've a friend in Eircom and she was able to find the address for me."

"I can hardly keep awake. Stay the night and we'll sort things out tomorrow." And that was all he remembered till he woke to the morning light.

VISION

He awoke alone in the bed, and not only because Deirdre was clattering plates and pots in the kitchen: his God was also still absent. He tried prayer: *I know I have sinned, Lord, but please let me repent.* It was like trying to make a phone call without a dial tone. *You didn't leave because I sinned,* he challenged. *You were already gone.* No response. *In fact, I sinned because you had left me,* he goaded. Silence still, but not the peaceful quietude of a summer evening by the lake; rather the soundless noise of nothingness. *I want to do your will, Lord, but I need to know it first,* he pleaded, but his inner voice dissipated like chatter in the wind. *If you had given me the slightest support, you know, I wouldn't have done what I did last night.* The echo of those words carried a ring of mockery. *So what do you expect me to do now, if you won't even acknowledge your existence to me?*

"Good morning, dear." Deirdre in the doorway, smiling brightly.

"Good morning to you." Blonde hair tousled and hanging sensuously loose. Gaily flowered robe reaching scarcely to her knees, the v-shaped opening extended to her sternum. "Where did you find the robe? I didn't –"

The smile expanded to beatific. "You didn't think I'd drive all the way from Tipperary without an overnight bag? I was hoping you'd let me stay." She glided to the bed. "Would you like your breakfast now, Father? Or," she undid the belt and let the robe drop to the floor, "would you rather have me for your first course?"

He was powerless to resist her voluptuous nudity. This time their lovemaking was a little less fierce though even more tender, and then they lay side by side, bodies touching, holding hands and saying nothing. Until Deirdre, sniffing, leaped from the bed and ran naked through the doorway, shouting "Oh my God, I forgot the rashers." They made do with boiled eggs, and *caiscin* that Sarah had sent, as well as oranges and instant coffee. Then, still dressed only in robes, they went outside and surveyed the morning. "Not a bad day for a swim," Deirdre suggested.

"An even better day for the Reek," he countered. "Would you be up to it?"

"Is it me? I've climbed Galtymore, and that's higher." She linked her arm in his and leaned her head on his shoulder. "I have a backpack and a pair of walking shoes in the boot. I do a bit of hiking sometimes on weekends so I always keep them there."

They packed a lunch, after sharing a shower and dressing each other with much touching and kissing and laughing, like a pair of adolescents, and then drove the few miles down to Murrisk in Deirdre's car. They bought pilgrim staffs from a teen-age boy at the end of the car park and walked up the short road to the beginning of the trail. From St. Patrick's statue they could see the ragged path traced out by the feet of myriad pilgrims over more than a thousand years; it meandered upwards for a long distance, then turned to the right across a hump-backed ridge and disappeared around the back of the rocky cone that was Croagh Patrick. A wispy fleece of cloud lay over the ridge and partly covered the top of the cone.

"How long will it take? Deirdre asked.

"I got to the top once in two hours," he told her. "But I was young then and the bones weren't creaking like they are now."

"I don't think it was the bones that were making all that noise last night," she said with a smile. "Or this morning either."

The terrain was rough and stony, requiring attention to every step. Parts were quite steep, others appeared almost level, though the effort required to move forward indicated that even the apparently flat was really an upward slope. After about half an hour they halted by a flat outcrop of rock. Deirdre pulled the water bottle from the pack on Ignatius's back. They drank deeply, then sat on the rock in silence, drawing breath and admiring the view of Clew Bay far below.

An old man clambering down at a steady pace stopped by them. "Are ye coming or going?" he asked, almost belligerently.

"We're on our way up," Ignatius said. "We have a good way to go yet, I'd say."

"And ye're tired already?" Disgust in the old fellow's tone. "Musha God help us." He removed his cap and wiped his forehead with it, then placed it carefully back on his head. "When I was yere age I used to run up."

"It's this younger generation," Ignatius admitted indulgently. "We don't have the stamina of the old people."

"A hundred and nine," the old codger said.

"My goodness!" Deirdre sounded awestruck. "You certainly don't look that old."

He waved a gnarled hand. "I'm not. That's how many times

I have climbed this blessed mountain."

"You're a real mountain goat," Ignatius said.

"I am indeed, faith. 'Tis no trouble to me at all to climb it, and I with eighty-seven years last month. But I'll tell ye something." He stepped a bit closer and leaned on his staff. "I wasn't always this hardy. As a ladeen I got the TB. 'Twas a terrible scourge to the country in them days. They sent me off to the sanatorium to die, that's what they did; there was no cure for it then but to kick the bucket. But I got down on my knees every day and I prayed to Saint Patrick – I always had great devotion to him, being born within sight of his holy mountain. And I promised him that if he cured me I'd climb his reek twice a year in his honor for the rest of my life. And he cured me, too. And I've kept my promise, so I have."

"Isn't that wonderful," Deirdre said.

"So my advice to ye now, when ye get to the top, get down on your bended knees and pray to Saint Patrick. He's our man up there, you see." Pointing skyward with his staff. "They tell us everyone has to have someone to speak up for them, even with the Man Above. And Saint Patrick is *our* man in heaven. They say, too, that no Irishman that has faith in him will ever go to hell, and I believe that myself. Sure you can't trust the priests any more, with all the terrible things some of them are going on with. And even the bishops, God help us, aren't much better." He lifted his staff and planted it firmly, then leaned heavily on it. "The pope, I suppose is all right, but he's a foreigner. You can only really trust your own."

"I'd say you're right there," Ignatius said, with more feeling than the humoring of an old man required.

"Good day to ye now." The eighty-seven year old raised his cap briefly to Deirdre and returned to the trail. After a few yards he turned back and shouted up at them, "let ye not delay there now or ye'll catch yere death of cold."

"I wish I had his faith," Deirdre said after they had resumed climbing, she leading.

"Why did you stop believing in God?"

"I don't know." She allowed him to catch up. "Let me carry the pack for a while." He gave it to her without demur: her slender body was as vigorous on the mountain as it had been in bed.

A little later he asked, "did something dramatic happen to shake your faith?"

She stepped sideways off the trail to get around a protruding rock. "Not really. I just began to think that God was an anachronism in today's world. I mean with all we know about the origin of the universe and how we ourselves came to be, and then look at the stories of religion and how everything we don't understand is explained by the mysteriousness of God, it all began to look a bit foolish to me." She turned and smiled at him. "Sorry, but that's how I feel." Then she moved on ahead, as if to end the discussion.

The argument was old, he ought to have taken it in his stride. Yet he was acutely disturbed, and mulled his disquiet as they trekked across the ridge. It seemed his discomfort stemmed from his caring for her and his concern for the welfare of her soul. *But if that were the case you wouldn't have engaged her in sin*, said his conscience.

"My God!" Deirdre exclaimed, when they came in sight of the path to the top of the cone. "We have to climb up *that*?" A wide swath of loose rocks rose steeply to the peak.

"This is the real challenge." He felt a little bit smug.

"I need a drink." She dropped the pack off her back. "And

a breather. And I'm going to put on my sweater; it's cold up here."

"If you don't feel up to it we don't have to go all the way," he said, patronizingly.

"Well, if that old man could do it a hundred and nine times, then I can certainly do it at least once." She got to her feet. "You take the pack again for a while," and she started off without waiting for him. It was a long slow climb as they picked their way carefully through the unsteady rocks, sometimes close to each other, often well apart, seeking safe footing on the treacherous slope. Twice they stopped for breath and a drink and to look back down. Away in the distance they spotted several groups of people slowly wending their way upwards. After each stop Deirdre was first to move on, and when finally they sighted the little chapel at the summit she broke into a run of sorts and touched its white wall while he was still many yards away. "I won," she shouted exultantly.

The wind was strong and chilly. They sat at the base of the chapel wall after they discovered the door was locked. "I'm starved," he said. "Since they won't let us in to pray we might as well eat."

"Mammy will feed you right now." She took sandwiches from the backpack and unwrapped them. Afterwards they walked around the narrow summit and marveled at the views of mountains and lakes, the town of Westport, awesome Clew Bay, and Achill Island far off to the north west.

"Mullagh is down there somewhere." He pointed at the haze away to the south east. "I can see this top from my bedroom window on a clear day. And I can pick out that rocky path we just climbed.".

"I have to visit the ladies' room," she said. "Which is down there beside that rock."

Are You here, Lord? he demanded as he gazed north towards the bay and the islands. *I came all the way up here just to talk to You. Give me at least some indication of Your presence and Your Will for me.* He paused and waited, but experienced no manifestation of Divine Presence. *Ah please do, Lord; even a minimal sign that You know what I'm going through, or that You still care for me.* But all he heard was the whisper of the strong west wind, and Deirdre saying from behind, "the men's room is down there, too, if you need it."

"I'm all right for now," he said. But he wasn't, of course; the depression, which her presence since last evening had alleviated, had returned with all of its dull dead weight.

They went back to the shelter of the chapel wall to rest before beginning the descent. "Have you decided what you're going to do?" She rested her head on his shoulder.

"Not yet. The choices are bleak." He told her about Kennedy's phone call and the options he had given. "Damned on earth if I take the one and damned in hell if I take the other," he concluded.

"Tell *them* to go to hell." She wrapped her arms about her knees. "I can't believe that the God of love we're taught to believe in would want you to throw away your life just because someone lied about you."

"So you do believe in God!" he said mischievously.

She bent over till her forehead touched her knees. He held his peace. Eventually she raised her head and stared across the mountain top. "What bothers me most about God is that I don't know who He is. I can relate to the God of love – Jesus I suppose – who cares about us, but I just can't accept the God of laws and hell and damnation and all those terrible things." Then she waved her arms. "And why would a good God want to treat us like this? Both our lives destroyed by those we loved; and then we're forbidden to love each other." She looked suddenly at him. "Would you love me if you were allowed?"

He returned her gaze, looking steadily into her eyes. "I love you whether I'm allowed or not, my dear. God help me, I have no control over that."

She took his hand and kissed it and then held it against her cheek. "I needed to hear you say that, Ignatius. I've loved you from the first minute I set eyes on you. Do you know that?"

They snuggled then and kissed. Eventually he drew back and looked at her. "So you don't think the God of love has any objections to what you and I are doing?"

"Well, He told us to love one another, didn't He? God knows I've heard you bloody priests spout that often enough." She looked archly at him. "So when did He ever say we're forbidden to love each other?"

He had to laugh. "The Church could use a theologian like you."

"The Church is all bollixed up." She jumped to her feet. "Do you hear me, Saint Patrick?" She cupped her hands and shouted into the wind. "This bloody Church you founded here is a big fecking bollocks. Come back and do something about it. Can you hear me up there?"

He got up and stood beside her. "You're going to give scandal to the faithful," he said into her ear. A man and woman had reached the summit and were heading towards them.

"Let's go." She swung the pack onto her back. The cone trail was even more dangerous on the descent, but with the help of staffs and careful footwork they got down safely. Less than two hours after they left the top they reached the car park, tired but not exhausted. As Deirdre drove onto the road Ignatius spotted a pub.

"I've a thirst no money could buy," he said. "Are you ready for a pint?" At four o'clock there was quite a crowd of thirsty patrons, most of them standing around the bar. They found an empty table but had to wait a while to place their orders.

"It'll take a few minutes now to draw the pints," the lad who served them said. But the black creamy white-headed drink was worth the delay.

"Haven't had one of these for years." Deirdre's upper lip was mustachioed with foam. "I'd almost forgotten how good it tastes."

"One of the great pleasures in life." He took another deep pull. "Though it's only recently I've learned to savor it myself."

"You're learning to savor a lot of new pleasures these days, aren't you?" Her smile was lecherous.

"Which is something we'll need to discuss." He felt himself redden as he added, "unfortunately."

She lowered her glass, her forehead creased. "Can't it wait till tomorrow. Today has been so good, why spoil it?" But after they returned to the cottage and showered and changed and ate a dinner that Deirdre cooked from Sarah's groceries, he felt obligated to raise the matter again.

"I've only got a few days to surrender myself to the Mother House. After that I've a feeling the Guards will be out looking for me. Unless, of course," he looked hopefully at her, "you think your husband is bluffing."

She shook her head and the tears came to her eyes. "I wouldn't count on it. I've never, in all my life, met a man so stubborn, or thick-headed, or contrary, or downright vicious when you cross him. Once he thinks you've done him wrong he's your enemy for life. I've seen him let cattle die on a farmer who had told him lies earlier on, rather than go and help him like a decent Christian. That man could have sued him, but I was told by his neighbor that he was afraid of what Padhraig might do to him afterwards if he did. That's the kind of man my husband is, God help me."

"In that case, it seems to me I have three options." He paused to reflect. "Three, that's it: I can go to the Mother House and serve a life sentence there; or I can defy them and take my chances with the legal system; or, I can go on the run." He smiled bleakly at her. "Not one of them looks terribly appealing."

They were facing each other from opposite ends of the sofa. She stretched out her hand and took his. "I wish to God there was something I could do. But I can't think of anything, other than to kill him. Which I'd consider doing if I thought it would do us any good. He's furious at me, of course. You were right when you said he believed I was having an affair with you." She laughed, but there was no humor in it. "Isn't it funny, though? His own daft behavior made his belief come true." She raised his hand and pressed it to her cheek. "And that's the only part of this whole woeful mess I'm not sorry about."

So like Terezinha in her single-minded passion. Was that how all women loved? He had so little real experience of them. "I don't regret it either," he avowed. "Unfortunately, as a priest and a Christian, I must ask myself now what does God want of me?"

He saw her quick, impatient, intake of breath and prepared for a blast. But she deflated slowly, let go of his hand, tucked her knees up close to her face, and rested her chin on them. "God gave you common sense, didn't he? So I think you should use it to make a sensible decision." She sucked her knee. "Never mind that old resignation to God's will stuff. Put your intelligence to work to figure out what's best for you, and that'll be what God wants."

He nodded agreement. "If I go to the Mother House I'm admitting my guilt and taking their medicine and I'll never get out of there alive."

"Good man, Sherlock." She sucked her knees again. "Continue."

"I'd probably lose my case in court. Nowadays everyone seems willing to believe the worst of priests. Isn't that strange? Ten years ago it would be almost impossible to convict a man of the cloth, no matter what he did. But now ..."

"So go on the run." She shot to her feet. "I'll join you."

"Elvira Madigan!" He had to smile at her enthusiasm. "But you know what happened to that pair."

She sat. "I have to go home tomorrow, anyway. If he had even an inkling that I was here with you your goose would be properly cooked."

"So where does he think you are?" A question he had been meaning to ask since she came.

"He thinks I'm at home. He's up in Dublin himself at a conference, or whatever it is that vets do when they get together. And the children are down in Waterville with their grandmother."

"I have one other option." The thought had come to him half way up the mountain, but he had squashed it with a mental heel as unworthy of consideration. "I could ask to be laicized."

"Oh Ignatius! You don't want to do that?" There was sadness, yet incongruously a trace of hope, in the way she said it, head down, not daring to look at him.

"No," he told her with conviction. "I don't. I'm a priest and

I want to stay a priest." He touched her chin with his finger and when she glanced up at him he added, "even though I love you, God help me."

"I vote you do what makes you happy." She opened his palm, stroked it lightly with her fingers, then bent over and kissed it.

They sat in silence, fingers interlocking. He was fading away, mind detaching from body, like pure intellect unencumbered by earthly needs, or even, impossibly, earthly desires. *Wandering through a long narrow field with Sarah, his sister-in-law. Sparse grass, strewn boulders, rocks, gravel, deep crisscrossing tractor-wheel ruts that made walking difficult, the whole field hemmed in by thick hedges of blackthorns. "There appears to be no way out," said Sarah, "no matter how far ahead you look. "Those thorns will destroy us if we try to get through."*

"What does it matter?" he retorted. "There's nowhere to go."

The rain came down from a lowering sky, at first lightly, then in sheets that drenched. "We have nowhere to shelter," Sarah complained. "We're getting awfully wet."

"What does it matter?" he retorted again. "We're not wearing any clothes."

"Is it all right to be naked?" Covering bare breasts with her dripping hands.

"How should I know? I'm naked, too."

"But you're the priest. It's your job to know those things?"

"I don't know anything any more." Wondering that he felt no shame. "Though I used to know everything. I suppose it's all right since we have no choice. And we never will again, now that God has died."

"Is He really dead?" she asked. "It's so terrible to be left all alone."

"We have each other," he reassured her. "And our nakedness. But that's all we have, now and forever in saecula saeculorum."

"I don't think I can live without Him," she wailed. "How can we go on with no one in charge?"

"I'm afraid, too," he said. "He had no right to leave us like this."

"You must find Him, Ignatius," she said. "That's your job. Seek and you shall find. Isn't that what He said?"

"First, I must knock on these hedges and see if they'll open – knock and it shall be open to you. I can't do anything till I get out of here." He hurled himself in vain at the menacing thorns.

"Are you all right, Ignatius?" Deirdre was leaning over him, rubbing his face with both hands.

He sat up. "I'm so sorry. I must have dozed off." Then he remembered the scene, with its frightening clarity of detail. "I had this weird dream."

"You scared the life out of me." There was concern in her eyes.

He took her hands in his. "I must have been tired from the climb."

"It wasn't just sleep. You were curled up in a ball and pale as a ghost. I was sure you had stopped breathing." Her lower lip quivered. "I thought you had died."

"This dream." It was still there, clamoring to be told. "I ..." So clear, yet he could not describe it. He waved his arms as if to crank-start his brain, started half a dozen sentences, but could find no words to match the experience.

"Are you all right now?" She felt his forehead with the back of her hand, like a mother testing her child for fever.

"I'm fine. I wish I could explain ..."

"You're going to bed now, this minute." She stood and took his hands and helped him to his feet. "You'll feel better in the morning."

Standing, he felt an awful lassitude, as if all his strength had drained into the sofa. He made no objection as she led him away to bed.

DECISION

Moonlight beaming through parted curtains relieved the blackness. It took a while to recall where he was. And the touch of his leg against her flesh to confirm he had not imagined it all. Silence so dense as to be eerie: only the faint rhythmic puff of her breathing disturbed the total stillness.

Then the chaos of his world came crashing in, like a wall knocked over by a panicking sheep. *Dear God, let it be but a nightmare from which I am now awake*. But the God he addressed was silent. And the feel of her silken flank was no illusion. And his recollections of Kennedy and Donnellan were too vivid to be the stuff of dreams. He was trapped, hooked, imprisoned, as he had been in that strange awful dream – which came back vividly to him now. Life as he had known it had been destroyed. Never again would he be Master of Novices, or missionary priest, or man of the cloth with earned respect. He must face a future stark and fearsome, from which escape might be through death alone.

And the dream! What was it? Self-delusion? Wish-fulfillment? Subconscious analysis of options? A direct communication from God Himself? *What did you mean by it,*

Lord? Are You saying You have abandoned Ignatius Lally, leaving him alone and naked, locked in a misery of no escape? Was it your way of showing me there is a hell and I am in it? But that would make You mean-spirited, wouldn't it? Capricious, irrational, antithesis of all that You claim to be – the God who loves sinners. Or you might have just sent me into the soul's dark night, like John of the Cross? But You'd hardly do that in my present sinful state, now would you?

His God made no response.

Or maybe! He sat up in the bed at the very thought. *Did You mean to show me how lost I am in the overgrown meadows of casuistry? Were You goading me to seek You in the wasteland of truth? Filching my comforting idols, as a concerned mother would steal her adolescent's security blanket? But why make so poor a thing as me your trailblazing seeker of the third-millennial? Your Church, it's true, is an overfed charlatan – there, I've admitted what I've long believed but could never acknowledge – puffed with the pride of possessions, paralyzed by the fear of sex, glued to a theological past of its own making, while the rest of the world moves on. Would a truer image of You raise her up again to light the way for mankind? But still, why me, Lord?*

The silence of emptiness answered his plea.

Perhaps it was merely my subconscious speaking, after all?" He slumped back beneath the covers. *Telling me there is no God? That I have been addressing a non-existing Thou? Worshiping a fabrication of the historical human mind? Is there only a world and no creator? A chance confluence of molecular mutations pridefully claiming a divine originator? Have peoples and nations fought wars, killed millions, persecuted and tortured, created schisms and enmities, all from mistaken belief in Your*

Being?

Only the sound of his sleeping love responded.

What ráiméis, Ignatius! What heresy! What bile of desperation! Save me, Lord, I perish. Denying You to protect myself. Belief is easy when it makes no demands. But when faith is plunged into the fire of pain and white-hot hammered on the anvil of truth its mettle is fairly tested. And mine has been found pathetically wanting, has it not? I'm pious and brave while my Lord holds my hand, but a cowardly lion when left on my own. A saver of souls while my ship is afloat, but an abandoning rat when the waters pour in.

Deirdre stirred, turned, her arm slid over his middle, down his thigh, fingers wrapped his genitals. She uttered a contented sigh. Her hair was in his face. She draped a leg over his. The hand covered him gently, yielding to his rising tension. He turned and kissed her cheek softly. She purred. "Are you awake?" he whispered.

"No." Sensuous murmur. "I'm dreaming about a big man with jet black hair who's making love to me." She nibbled his ear.

He got an arm underneath and tipped her over till she lay atop. The rest she did herself: the long hair brushed his face, the breasts dipped down and up to tickle his chest, the haunches caressed his inner thighs. The pleasure turned fierce, blotting out for now all else but this union of flesh. When it was over and she let her body drape loosely over his, he stroked her backside and held her hands and kissed her lips and wondered why God chose not to confine his gifts to only this. Then he remembered no more till his eyelids opened to bright morning light. She was leaning on her elbow looking down at him.

"Good morning again, love." The tenderness in her eyes

would have tempted the pope himself.

He sat up. "I need to do some serious thinking." He pushed back the duvet, slid out of bed and headed for the door.

She was instantly accommodating. "I'll get us some breakfast." By the time he had showered and shaved she had scrambled eggs and toast at the ready. "It's so terribly stressful for you, isn't it?" She poured him tea.

"We must make some decisions today." He was regretting, as the words came out, their almost censorious tone.

"I have already made mine." The bleakness in her voice startled him.

"Everything inside me screams I must not go to the Mother House." Afraid to ask what she had decided. If she said she'd stay, which a part of him desperately wanted, he would have to say no, at least for now. He nibbled at his eggs.

"I'm going home today," she put in, urgently, as if afraid he was about to suggest an alternative.

Relief and worry and frustration made an unpalatable salad. He made several attempts to say something useful, or at least meaningful, before grabbing that most pathetic of epithets, "ah shit!" And biting deeply into his toast.

"Ignatius!" She laughed, almost hysterically. "That's the first dirty word I've ever heard out of your mouth."

"I used to be good at it, but it's a luxury not permitted Masters of Novices." He took a forkful of egg. "What's going to happen when you go home?" A novel sensation this, to be intimately worried about the safety and happiness of another; the kind of feeling that priestly detachment always kept at arm's length.

"It's what would happen if I *don't* go home that worries me most." Spoken in the unhurried tone she'd used in her fund-raising report. "I can't allow him to come after you, and that's what he'll do if I don't toe the line."

He had to agree with her logic, though it ran counter to his instinctive male reflex that wanted to place her within his protective strength. "I wish we could stay together," he said weakly.

Again the tender look that made a fool of reason. "Thank you, dear. I needed to hear that. And I do really hope that some day we can." Her hand reached out and ran lightly over his arm. "But it's not practical at the moment, is it?"

They finished eating in silence, then washed and dried the dishes and put them away. She said she must get ready. He sat in a chair, trying to think, but no constructive ideas came. Her going home might protect him from McCarthy, but what would save him from his vow of obedience? And if he did circumvent it and not go to the Mother House, where *would* he go? Sarah and Dan would put him up indefinitely, but he couldn't live out his life with them. He was still circulating those notions in his mind, uselessly and for the umpteenth time, when she returned.

"I'm off then." Forcibly bright, her overnight bag hanging by a strap from her shoulder. In her summer frock and straw hat she looked fetching.

"Are you sure you'll be all right?" Though it was himself he most feared for.

She handed him a piece of paper. "This is my sister Eavan's phone number. Ring her if you want to leave me a message." To his enquiring look she added, "I was told to report if you rang me at the office." Then she laughed. "But they didn't say anything about my ringing you." She dropped the bag, wrapped herself around him all too briefly, kissed him quickly, and was gone. He heard her car start, the crunch of gravel, the acceleration, the fading motor hum, and he was alone.

He walked to the strand. The tide was out. The stiff wind pushed hard at gulls seeking breakfast in the sand. It seemed to blow strength into his torpid mind. He wouldn't stay here without her. Nor would he go back to Mullagh. Dublin maybe. What better place to vanish till he sorted things out? He knew people there. But priests, mostly. He could hardly stay with them. Then it came to him. Dominick! Dom McElligott! The very man! The closest to a buddy in novitiate and scholasticate when *particular friendships* were not permitted. And a very real buddy in Brazil until Dom decided to leave the priesthood. Must be ten years ago now. Burnt out and disillusioned were his words to describe why he was pulling out. But they had kept in touch by letters, all through Dom's laicization, law school, and marriage. And last year they had met again when Ignatius was in Dublin to receive his new assignment.

"Of course you're most welcome to stay with us! Dominick will be thrilled." No doubting the enthusiasm of Aoife. "I'll ring him now and let him know you're on your way."

He was out of the cottage within the hour, leaving the key under the door mat with a note of thanks and giving Dom’s address where the bill should be sent. The first splash of rain hit his windshield as he drove through Louisburgh. Croagh Patrick was blanketed in cloud. Westport was thronged with tourist umbrellas as he inched through the car-crowded streets. He stopped at a pub outside Castlebar for a sandwich and a pot of tea. Afterwards, he drove as fast as conditions permitted, sometimes faster, to escape his self-pitying thoughts. But they crowded him anyway. Forty-seven years of age and here he was, without home or belongings, except for a few clothes. And a car that belonged to the novitiate which would soon reclaim it. Cut off from the source of his livelihood, cast adrift from his spiritual home, the knot that bound him to God loosening. Never before had he felt so bereft, not even in those first days alone in his Brazilian parish when he scarcely knew the language and was surrounded by strangers. At least then he knew life would get better: his Portuguese would improve and strangers would become friends. Now, he had nothing to hope for.

The towns slipped by in the rain that was steady now. He crossed the Shannon at the Athlone bypass and then it seemed but a short time till he was pushing through Horseleap, Tyrrellspass, and on to the dual carriageway that landed him in Dublin just after four o'clock. Getting from the carriageway to Dominick's suburban home was another matter: Dublin traffic had grown far beyond the capacity of its streets, and he had to stop-and-go the maddening commuter trail for more than an hour, from Islandbridge to Mount Merrion.

"'Tis great to see you, Ignatius!" Dominick, short and squat and bald as an egg, kept his deep wide grin long after he shut the door and led the way to the bright-lit parlor.

"Thank you for having me," Ignatius told Aoife, a slender woman, inches taller than her husband, with prematurely gray hair and a sad expression that belied the mordant wit of her published poetry.

"You're more than welcome." The briefest of smiles replaced by a look of concern. "Did you have any trouble getting through the city?"

"Have a seat man, and take the weight off your feet," Dominick cut in. "Sure Dublin is gone mad, between traffic and money, and everyone fighting for status. 'Tisn't the city you and I knew twenty-five years ago."

"Traffic was a bit slow, mind you." Seated, he looked discreetly around: the room had the trappings of affluence, with leather-upholstered chairs, deep-polished hardwood tables, crystal lamps, modern paintings, oriental rug, expensive-looking ornaments.

"We'll have dinner shortly," Aoife said. "Maybe a glass of wine while you're waiting?" Her wifely glance a command to her husband.

"Yes, of course; I'll go get a bottle." Dominick shot to his feet and headed out the door.

"I haven't seen him so excited in years," Aoife whispered. "He came home early so he'd be here when you arrived, and he's been singing since he came in."

"That must have been hell for you." He chuckled; his friend's tone-deafness had been a seminary joke.

"So tell us, what's going on with you at all?" Dominick asked after they had dinner in the dining room and returned to the sitting room for drinks. "Playing hooky from the novitiate for a few days?"

Ignatius felt himself redden. "It's a little more complex than that, I'm afraid."

Aoife seemed to sense his discomfort and made to get up. "I have things I need to do in the kitchen."

"Not at all, no, please don't go." He'd need all the support he could get, and Aoife impressed him with her air of sympathy. He told his story, omitting only his more recent involvement with Deirdre. When he finished they sat in a deep silence that was like the aftermath of prayer.

"Christ Almighty!" Dom eventually erupted. "What kind of

bloody people are they at all?"

"I don't think too highly of Father Kennedy or the archbishop either," Aoife added sourly.

"It's them I'm talking about." Dominick was almost shouting. "That arsehole, McCarthy, is obviously a head case. But good God in heaven, your own people! Surely they know you better than that, Ignatius?"

"It appears the bad press about deviant priests has put the wind up them."

"I'll tell you this much though, I never did have much time for Kennedy." Dominick's expression was a cartoonist's vision of apoplexy: bulging eyes, reddened cheeks, eyebrows reaching for the hairline he didn't have. "Never trusted the bugger."

Aoife's sad eyes were on Ignatius. "Have you any thoughts as to what you might do?"

"I'm baffled," he admitted. "It seems that I'm damned if I do something, and damned if I don't."

Dominick passed a palm across his dome. "Let's look at it from a legal perspective." The barrister's cool tone replacing the yelp of insulted friend. "If I understand the situation correctly, the only evidence against you is the accusation of this creepy hoor of a girl. Right?"

"There's medical evidence that she was sexually molested – raped and sodomized – though no sign of semen, they said, so the rapist must have used a condom. As I told you, we think we know who did it, but I don't know if we can prove anything."

Dominick leaned forward. "You might be able to sue the bastards for slander. They have defamed you to a third party, haven't they? To the archbishop of Tighmor himself, no less." He rubbed his hands as if in glee, then joined them in prayer while raising his eyes heavenward. "Oh God, if you let me get that bloody bishop on the witness stand I'll be good for the rest of my life." He slapped the top of his head in rebuke. "Stop it, Dom, let's get serious. Slander can be a bit tricky in the courts, but I'd say you might have a chance. You'd have to prove actual material loss, you see, but you can certainly prove that – you were sacked from your job as Master of novices, right?"

"Yes. But –"

"There's something else in the slander law." Dom's eyes glazed over, like a man delving deep into the bowels of memory. "You can sue even if there's no material loss, providing the slander imputes that you committed a criminal offence that's punishable with imprisonment." He glanced at Ignatius. "They certainly imputed that, the buggers." He grinned. "And in this case buggers is the right appellation."

Aoife poked a finger into her husband's shoulder. "Would filing a slander suit prevent them from pressing criminal charges, do you think? I mean, what if they come back and allege he really did it? Which case gets tried first?"

Dominick sat back. "If they pressed charges the DPP – Director of Public Prosecution – *could* indict you. However, if you pre-empt them with a strong case the DPP might decide to hold off till after the civil suit. On the other hand –"

He had let them talk on only because it was difficult to stop his friend when he got going. "Time out," he interrupted now, waving both arms. "There isn't going to be any slander suit."

A film of neutrality descended instantly over both spouses. "Ah," Dominick said, and folded his arms. Aoife said nothing, just dropped her gaze to the carpet.

"I appreciate your ideas very much. And in other

circumstances I would certainly take your advice. But *Deirdre* McCarthy is my friend and ..."

"Ah," Dominick repeated. "Yes indeed. I understand. As your lawyer I'd certainly be duty bound to dig up every bit of dirt on her family that –"

"Exactly."

"But Ignatius!" Surprise, even a trace of annoyance in Aoife's tone. "Isn't your own reputation more important than protecting the feelings of a friend?" Still looking at the floor. "Even a *good* friend?"

How to answer that? "Good question indeed." Should he explain that he'd rather die than bring disgrace on his Deirdre? Oh dear God, *his* Deirdre! "But I can't destroy an innocent person's life," feeling the inadequacy of his words to express the indescribable.

His response produced a silence that, while perhaps not exactly disapproving, seemed to contain a definite element of concern for his sanity. "I suppose," Dominick said, but with no concession in his tone. "On the other hand, Ignatius, remember that it's not her that's on trial."

"And keep in mind, too, that you have an awful lot at stake here," Aoife added urgently.

He covered his face with his hands. They respected his silence. Eventually he said, looking between them at what appeared to be a Chagall print on the wall over the sofa, "Deirdre is more than a friend."

They nodded in unison – as if they had been awaiting this confession all along – with the kind of approval they might give a child for swallowing an unpalatable medicine. "Understand."

"However, there was nothing illicit going on between us at

the time the accusation was made."

"Of course not," Aoife affirmed.

"But that's no longer true." Might as well tell them all.

"Aren't we all human?" Aoife looking at him with the sympathy of a doting mother.

"It's nothing to be embarrassed about," Dominick added. He grabbed the brandy from the coffee table. "Another spot?"

"We'll support you in whatever you decide to do," Aoife said.

"Anyway, now you know everything." Except, of course, the dream. That he would keep to himself. He lay awake far into the night in the stylish guest room, ruminating on what he had experienced during that brief nap in the Louisburgh cottage.

In the morning at breakfast, after Dom had left, Aoife said, apropos of nothing, "I should let you know that Dominick and I no longer practice our religion." She smiled. "I'm telling you now so it won't come as a surprise to you later."

"No surprise," he told her. "Several other confreres who left have told me the same thing."

"I'd like to think we're still spiritual people. It's just that we don't practice a formal religion any more." No apology in her tone.

"So long as your conscience is comfortable." Which was more than he could say for his own at this moment.

"Lately, I've been delving into some of W.B. Yeats's ideas on spirituality." She brushed crumbs from the tablecloth into her palm and shook them onto her plate. "I'm very fond of his poetry."

"Wasn't he into theosophy or the occult or something of that sort." Though he knew little about William Butler's religious beliefs. "The Universal Brotherhood of Humanity and that kind of thing?" Careful not to sound disapproving.

"Well yes, he did study the occult, though not for its own sake. He did it, he said – and I think these were his own words – to enrich his art and thereby benefit humankind. He said he wanted to give the purest substance of his soul to fill the emptiness of other souls." When she looked up the sad eyes were glowing. "That's an idea that has inspired my own poor efforts at poetry."

"I see." He didn't really.

"Yeats thought each one of us had his or her own personal daimon that –"

"Well, we certainly all have our demons." He had a feeling she was warming to her subject and he wasn't sure he wanted to hear it in his present confused state.

"Oh no! Not a demon. The *daimon*. He looked on it as a sort of occult self that survived our various reincarnations. He thought it was capable of both good and evil, and that it had a lot of influence on our destiny."

"Very interesting indeed."

"It's fascinating. The daimon emanated, he thought, from what the theosophists called the *Anima Mundi*, which turned out to be a lot like Jung's notion of the collective unconscious. What's most interesting about that is that Yeats never studied Jung."

"Well, well! You know, I'm not too familiar with any of that stuff myself." No point in pretending he knew what she was blathering about. "Did Yeats believe in God, do you think?"

"Oh yes." Her thin eyebrows raised at the question. "He certainly believed in God. Now whether it was the same God that we Catholics were taught to believe in is not too clear." She took the cozy off the tea pot. "Would you care for a little more?"

He held out cup and saucer. "Thanks a lot." He needed to get away.

"I have a very different concept of God myself now from what I grew up with." Aoife poured for herself after filling his cup. "No, not a female God – the feminist position is just as absurd as that of the patriarch. I think of God now as the life force of the universe. We're just bits of a body of which God is the soul."

"Used to be known as pantheism, I think."

"And he – she, it – communicates with us somewhat in the way our brains communicate with the different parts of our bodies. Only we have to make an effort to listen: we don't just respond automatically, like a knee jerk. So that's the importance of exercises like yoga and meditation to help us listen to our inner selves which are always in close touch with God."

"Fascinating." It wasn't. He stood abruptly and pushed back his chair, "I think I'll take a run into the city." He took the bus on her advice: parking in town was so terribly difficult, she said. She gave him a house key in case she was out when he returned. He meandered down crowded Grafton Street, feeling positively old amid the horde of chic young shoppers. How did this fashionable set, so recently affluent and materialistic, view the faith of their fathers? Many of them were apparently abandoning the practice of their religion.

He turned into Johnson Court and, on impulse, into the Carmelite Church. Cool and quiet and a world apart from the noisy bustle of the city. He sat in a pew and tried to pray, but no thoughts of piety came. People – older mostly – drifted in, genuflected to the tabernacle, knelt in pews, rattled rosaries, did the stations, lit candles at the various shrines. For the first time in his life he wondered, with an irritation he didn't understand, what lighted candles had to do with the human relation to God. What *was* the human relation to God anyway in this new chaotic world? The elders offering traditional homage to ancient saints, the young obsessed with the here and now, the middle-aged turning away from the faith handed down, yet feeling the need of a spiritual anchor. Like Aoife. *And where do you fall yourself, Ignatius?* A week ago this would have been a meaningless question. But, today ... *Dear Lord, let the faith I have lived for, and renounced all else to serve, be true.* His God made no reply.

He left in a hurry when Deirdre came into his mind, feeling a desperate need to talk with her. Back on Grafton Street he bought a phone card and walked briskly up to the Westbury to find a quiet booth. "Would you ask her to ring me about four this afternoon," he told Eavan, and gave her the McElligott's number. After a plate of pasta at a nearby restaurant he spent an hour browsing books in Fred Hanna's before catching a bus back to Mount Merrion. He was home by three. Aoife was out. He fretted by the phone for the next hour, wishing she'd ring now and that Aoife would stay away. At exactly four she did ring.

"It's good to hear you again."

"I thought I'd never hear from you." her voice sounded strained.

"You're having difficulties, aren't you?"

"Yes." Bleakly, followed by silence.

"Padhraig, I suppose?"

"Of course." More silence. Then, "he's being a real stinker; verbal abuse spewing out of him at all times when we're in the house together. And that's the way it's going to stay, he says, till he gets my infidelity out of his system. The imagined one, of course, not the real thing. If he only knew ..." Her laugh was brittle. "Anyway, he threatens that if I dare to walk out on him even one time, he'll expose you. He's just waiting for the chance, he says."

"Shit," he said.

"That's twice!" He could imagine her forcing a smile. "It's getting to be a habit with you, Ignatius." She chuckled. "How are you doing anyway?"

He told her about Dominick and Aoife, and then to his own surprise – for he didn't know his mind was finally made up – he added, "I'm not going to the Mother House."

"You're not?" He could feel the lift in her voice. "I'm so glad."

"I just can't do it."

"So what *are* you going to do, if I may enquire?"

"I haven't decided yet. But I'm going to call Kennedy now and tell him."

"I love you," she said, with a brevity and absoluteness that left him without words. "Hello?" she called into his silence. "Are you still there?"

"And I love you." He wondered for a moment if he was levitating. Then, through the glass panel of the front door he saw Aoife coming up the path. I have to go now," he said. "Call me at this time tomorrow again."

He rang Kennedy while Aoife was preparing supper. "How are you, Father?" The Superior's tone was coolly formal.

"Not a good question, Brian. How would you feel if you were suddenly told you were a pariah?"

That brought a moment's silence. Then Kennedy said, slowly, as if choosing his words with the greatest care, "there are consequences to particular types of conduct."

"One more time, Brian: I had nothing to do with the horrible act I've been charged with." He spoke calmly though he felt like screaming.

"The evidence is –"

"Fuck the evidence, Brian. You ought to know me better than to believe I'm capable of anything like that."

"Maybe in the wrong circumstances we're all capable –"

"I called to tell you something important," he interrupted. "I'm not coming in to the Mother House."

"Ignatius!" Kennedy's sigh, with its timbre and temper, was audible across the line. Followed by a pause. "You know the consequences?" With just a hint of scold.

"Don't bother to threaten, Brian. It won't do any good to you or to me."

"But you know you're under obedience to –"

"My first obligation right now is to protect myself from those who are trying to destroy me. Including you and Donnellan, as well as that lunatic McCarthy. And I intend to protect myself, Brian, both body and soul. So you go ahead now and scream obedience till you're blue in the face; it's not going to get you anywhere."

"In that case, Ignatius, I suppose we have nothing more to talk about."

"Not until you and the AB come to your senses, we don't."

"I wish you well then, Ignatius," Kennedy said peevishly. "Though I fear for your future."

He rang his mother. Ever since his return to Ireland she expected and received a weekly phone call from him. "I'm fine, Mammy," he assured her. "I decided to come to Dublin. Yes, that's where I am now. I'll probably stay here, at least for the time being." No, the matter was not yet resolved, but he was working on it. He left her his phone number and promised to ring soon again.

"I gather Aoife told you we don't go to mass any more." Dominick was shouting to be heard over the din in Muldoon's pub. Nine o'clock and the place was full of bodies and smoke and voices vying to be heard.

"She mentioned it." Aoife had declined when Dominick suggested they all go out for a drink. "But you don't have to worry that I'm going to lecture you." He grinned at his friend and took another sip of Guinness.

"It wouldn't do you a bit of good anyway." Dominick leaned forward to let a young woman squeeze past behind him. "But since you're a broad-minded chap I'll tell you where I'm at."

"I don't think I've ever been called a chap before." Dinner and wine and now the Guinness had produced a euphoria he had not felt since Donnellan's charge.

"Here's a theological problem that I've been grappling with for a long time." Dom screwed up his face till his glasses did a little dance on his nose. "In fact since before I left." He sipped his whiskey. "The problem is this: we learned in philosophy that all our information comes to us through our senses, right? I know that Aoife has different ideas – about the immanence of God and yoga and that sort of thing – but the evidence seems to indicate that whatever we know comes ultimately from what we perceive with our senses." He tapped his finger on the low table for emphasis. "So we know only the physical universe and whatever we can deduce or derive from it through our senses. However, God, by definition, can't be defined by any part of the universe, and therefore is totally unknowable through the senses, right? So the God we claim to know can't be really God. In fact all we have are some set of concrete images or ideas that we think relate to God, but that are derived from the physical universe. And if we worship those images or ideas aren't we then worshiping false gods?"

Ignatius could only stare at him. "Until this past week I haven't had a discussion on the nature of God since the seminary. Now the subject is popping up all over the place." He finished his Guinness before telling Dom about the dream.

"First year theology was a lot simpler than this," Dom said. "We knew all the answers then. Now I feel like I'm drifting somewhere in the universe." He waved his arms. "But do you know the good thing about it? I'm not worried. If you have no control over your destiny what's the use of fretting about it?"

"So you've given up on religion?"

"Almost, but not quite." He finished his whiskey and waved at a waiter. "I'm friends with a small group of former priests and nuns. We meet now and again for a drink and a chat and a discussion on what we think religion is really about."

"Maybe I could meet them sometime," Ignatius suggested.

Dom got the waiter's attention. "Another Jameson, please. Have one, Ignatius?"

"No, thanks; I've reached my limit this side of drunkenness."

"I'd say you're not ready for this crowd then. Either inebriationally or theologically. A couple of those people are off the wall. And they'd drink you under the table." But after Ignatius said again that he'd like to meet them, Dom agreed to take him to their next gathering.

MEANING

Brian Kennedy brooded all through supper on Ignatius Lally's latest defiance, taking almost no part in the community conversation, which this evening focused on Mullen's pessimistic views of the Euro's future. Afterwards, he went for a solitary walk through the quiet streets that surrounded the Mother House, testing and rejecting as he went a series of scenarios that might protect the Congregation. Frustrated, he was returning with the intention of going to the oratory to pray when he was collared at the front door by Barry. "Tighmor is looking for you, Brian. You can pick up in your office."

Donnellan was brusque. "What have you done about Lally?"

The question Kennedy had been dreading since Ignatius said no. "We had a meeting of the General Council," he heard himself say. "And we concluded that the best solution is to place him in an administrative post here in the Mother House, with little or no access to the outside world." God forgive him for the half-truth. "He refuses to sign anything," he added.

"I didn't expect he would." Donnellan didn't sound put out.

"But make sure you keep a close eye on him," he added sternly. "As long as he stays locked up he'll keep out of trouble. I'll inform McCarthy then. I think I'll be able to persuade him to forego the confession bit. A terribly unreasonable request in the first place anyway."

Kennedy found Mullen and Barry in front of the telly. "We need to talk, Dermot," he told Mullen, his most trusted confidant, and led the way out the back door to the courtyard. "Here's what's happening." As they strolled around the flower beds he briefed the Bursar on Lally's obstinacy, and on his conversation with Donnellan.

"We're sitting on a powder keg, aren't we?" Mullen bent to tie his shoe-lace which had been flapping for some time. "All that's needed," he looked up at Kennedy from his kneeling position, "is for McCarthy or the AB to find out that Lally's still at large." He straightened. "We have to find some way to coax or coerce the bloody fellow to come in."

"He won't budge." Kennedy shook his head vigorously. "You know, Dermot, he's behaving terribly like an innocent man." In spite of his past experience of pedophile denials, Ignatius Lally's awful sincerity was getting to him.

"So was Michael Harnett," Mullen snapped. Then his grim visage lightened a shade. "I just remembered something: I had a ring from Noel Corrigan this morning; he was wondering if we were going to get back our car that Lally drove off in. Now there might be some way to convert that to leverage." He pursed his lips and whistled softly. "Let me look into it."

Padhraig McCarthy was relaxing after the trip home from Dublin, with half an eye on the television program his wife was watching, when the phone rang. He went slowly out to the hall: probably Fiona calling from her grandmother's.

"This is archbishop Donnellan," the voice at the other end announced. "I've got an update on your concern." Low-pitched, precisely articulated, as if the matter were most distasteful to the speaker.

"Thank you for calling, your Grace," Padhraig said, with the right amount of respectful fervor, "I hope that –"

"Father Lally has accepted a post at the Mother House of his Congregation in Dublin. He will be kept in close confinement there and will not bother you or your family in the future."

"Great. That's good. Did he sign the confession?" A stroke of genius this idea of his for a written admission of guilt; it would protect himself from being accused in the event that his daughter ever reneged on her promise.

"He didn't and he won't." Donnellan's tone was peremptory. "You'll have to be satisfied that he's locked up."

Padhraig breathed deeply. He wanted to scream *I want that fucking signed confession or I'm going to the Guards*, but he held back: calmer reflection had already raised the specter of being caught out should he allow the case to be investigated. Better to accept whatever he could get; at least Lally was going to be out of harm's way. "All right so. Providing he never bothers us again I'm willing to put up with it." Then he added piously, "with the help of God it's all over now and we can put it behind us." But he was still brooding on his enemy when he went to his solitary bed that night. One thing was for sure, Deirdre would make no more trips to Dublin to visit her bloody sister.

Veronica stepped onto the coffee table in her velvet

platform pumps and hoisted her flowered frock till her lacy underpants showed. "I ask you!" She whirled and bunched the skirt further up to her navel. "Are those good legs or not?"

"I'd need to get a feel of them before I could tell." Turlough reached a hand towards the lady's gams.

"You do and you'll get your balls kicked in." Veronica raised a threatening toe.

"A well-fed arse, I'd say." Dominick raised his glass in salute. "No stinting in the making of them buns."

"Arrah you're more than just legs, Veronica." Rosemarie swept her long red hair back off her forehead. "Why don't you drop your knickers and show these starving celibates what a woman is really made of."

Veronica leaped off the table and shouted, to no one in particular. "I went down to the Gaiety today to audition for a musical, and do you know what the bastard said?"

"That your boobs drooped," Turlough guessed. "They always do when the legs are good."

"He said they were too chubby. Now, any *amadhan* can see there's not an ounce of fat on those legs. And no bloody cellulite, either."

"I warned you they were off the wall," Dominick whispered to Ignatius.

"Nice flat you got here, Veronica." Monica's quiet tone said let's change the subject and become a bit civilized.

"It's not a flat, it's a town house," Veronica corrected sharply.

"When did you get it?" JJ tapped a wall with his knuckles. "The last time we met at your place you were holed up in a dingy dump in Rathgar."

"The brother finally came through. He's been promising it to me ever since I left. Almost three years, would you believe?"

"He must be loaded to afford a place like this at today's prices," JJ said. "Even my dump is worth money in this market."

"Ours," Rosemarie corrected, giving JJ the elbow.

"He's making a packet," Veronica told them. "Selling education software on the Internet. Mostly to American companies."

"Meeting to order." Dominick shouted about the din.

"Silence in the court," Rosemarie yelled.

"The cat is pissing," Turlough added.

"Is everyone's drink topped up?" Veronica asked.

"I could use a little more sherry." Monica raised her glass in supplication.

"Before we start," Dominick continued, "I'd like to introduce a very special friend, Ignatius Lally. *Father* Lally to you lot: he's still a priest in good standing. Or almost, anyway."

"I thought we didn't allow good standing priests in here," Rosemarie objected.

"Good sitting nuns maybe," Turlough allowed. "With well-padded arses."

"What if he tries to convert us?" Veronica raised horrified hands. "I refuse to go back to poverty, chastity and obedience; especially chastity."

"What did you mean, Dominick, by almost?" Monica sipped her refill.

"Perceptive question indeed." Dominick straightened the glasses on his nose. "To which I shall give an audacious answer. But only on condition of your totally indulgent silence."

"We'll be mute as mutton," JJ promised.

"Shall I tell them everything?" Dominick whispered loudly, applying an elbow to Ignatius's ribs.

"Might as well." He'd have to get used to people knowing the wretched story.

The silence held while Dominick told. And for several seconds after he finished. Then cacophony broke out. "We said definitely no pedophiles," Rosemarie shouted, passion reddening her cheeks. "We voted on that."

"The bloody pendulum has swung too far," Turlough yelled. "Now it's the men who're being victimized. Some women are real hoors," he added gratuitously.

"Incestuous bastards are the lowest forms of life." Veronica raised her skirt to scratch her knee. "McCarthy should be strung up by the gonads."

"Did you do it or did you not?" Monica asked earnestly when the noise temporarily subsided.

"Of course he didn't," Dominick retorted. "Listen!" Hands uplifted beseeching silence. "Listen! I've known Ignatius Lally for thirty years. I've never known a more dedicated priest. He –"

"They're the fucking worst kind," Turlough cut in viciously. "The dedicated ones. They'd cut your balls off to save your soul, so they would."

"Ignatius Lally has done nothing wrong," Dominick yelled. "If I had the least suspicion about him I wouldn't bring him here, I guarantee you that."

"He wouldn't be the first pedophile to proclaim his innocence," Rosemarie said with scorn. She lit a cigarette and pulled hard.

"Nothing personal." JJ stared at Ignatius. "It's just that we're terribly particular about who we admit to this extraordinary group.

As you can tell from our conversation we're frightfully elite altogether."

"Fornication is fine," Veronica explained. "Even adultery is acceptable to some." She wrinkled her nose at Turlough. "Sodomy is okay, too, though gonorrhea is not. But we definitely draw the line at molesting the under-aged or the under-privileged."

"Never mind them at all," Monica said. "They're just trying to shock you."

"I'd like to propose a motion that we accept Father Ignatius Lally as an honorary member of our society." Dominick intoned formally.

"Are you still a virgin, Father?" Veronica jumped up excitedly. "If you are you can count on my full cooperation. I've always wanted to make it with a virgin. Around here, of course," she waved her arms dramatically, "they're as scarce as hens' teeth."

"The bye-laws don't make any provision for honorary members," Rosemarie objected.

"That's because we don't have any bye-laws," Turlough retorted.

"Seconded." JJ raised his hand.

"Thirded," Veronica added. "On condition that I get first dibs. *Droits de signorina*."

"Are you still a signorina?" Turlough asked.

"Order!" Dominick shouted. "Motion passed. What else is on the agenda?" He looked at Rosemarie.

Monica put up her hand. "I'm still suffering from the guilts. No matter how hard I try."

A general bleating emanated from the group, as though a flock of invisible sheep were present. "Listen, Monica, as long as you believe in God your agony is going to continue," Turlough retorted. "The only cure is atheism."

"Rubbish!" Veronica leaned back in her chair and kicked her heels in the air. "Sex is the answer. I believe in God and sex, and I don't have the guilts. So there! When was the last time you did it, Monica?"

"You know very well." Monica finished her drink and shook her head in self-pity. "Anyway, who'd make love to an old hag like me, even if I wanted it?"

"Turlough!" Several voices sang in unison.

"As long as you have a skirt to take off, Turlough will do it," JJ added.

"It's still on my conscience that it was wrong of me to leave the convent." Monica staring into her empty glass.

"You have the wrong notion of God entirely, Monica," Rosemarie said. "I keep telling you that."

"Why do you say that?" Ignatius turned to Rosemarie. The God question again.

"She's back into Calvinism and pre-Vatican II Catholicism, for God's sake." Rosemarie blew smoke towards the ceiling. "Am I glad I didn't grow up in such an environment. Hell yawning before your feet at every step. What kind of a God is that anyway? Do you believe in hell, Father?"

"Oooh! Checking the good priest's orthodoxy, are we?" JJ wagged an admonishing finger at Rosemarie. "No fair, my dearest, no fair. We might have a John Paul mole in our midst ready to turn the poor man in."

"Turlough!" Veronica yelled. "It has to be. I suspected him all along. No one could really be quite as depraved as he says he is. Turlough the mole! I bet you're still a virgin, too." She poked her toe at Turlough's shoe. "Pity there's no male hymen to check."

"I take it *you* don't believe in hell," Ignatius said aside to Rosemarie. "I'm a bit ambivalent myself. When I think of people like Hitler I desperately want there to be one."

JJ was listening. "Why would God want to engage in petty vengeance anyway?" His tone loud and dead serious. "To accuse Him of that is to turn him into a miserable power maniac – like Hitler for example. If He's the God of love who invites us to the sweet hereafter, surely He's not going to embroil Himself in our juvenile squabbling after what we call justice. He –"

"End of sermon, JJ," Turlough cut in. "Go back to the Jesuits if you want to preach. Some of us don't believe in God, you know."

Others joined in and they argued God over several rounds of drinks and through the tea and cake that Veronica produced. When Dominick asked on the way home what he thought of them Ignatius said, "mind-boggling."

"They're a wild crowd all right."

"I was referring to their ideas rather than their behavior."

"We do manage a bit of serious discussion in between times, don't we?" Dominick puffed at the compliment.

"They're all hung up on the notion of *who* God is, I noticed."

"Ah sure it's the fundamental question, isn't it? When you know who God is – that is, *if* He is – you're home free. But until then you're lost in the wilderness."

When he got into bed Dom's last comment came back to him. *That's what you're telling me, isn't it, Lord? That's what the dream was all about. A whole world of Christians out there who don't know who You are or even if You are. And You want me to hurl myself out of the thorny confines of our barren theology and tell them?*

He anticipated silence, and he got it.

FUGITIVE

"The McElligotts are awfully nice and they're willing to put me up indefinitely," he told Deirdre when she phoned next afternoon. "But I really have to start thinking about finding a flat for myself."

"I wish I could help you. Dammit, I wish I could join you," she exploded.

"I wish you could, too." Shocked at his own vehemence. He had stayed in his room long after rising, pacing the floor, seeking to justify before his absent God his fearsome craving for her. Spewing out the arguments he had once made for Terezinha, reinforced by the pain of *her* loss, a pain that was augmented, he told his God, by the example of Dominick and friends who had made the – to him terrifying – leap from celibate priesthood to human love. But of course he got no answer from on high.

Who are you anyway, God? he cried after Deirdre reluctantly hung up. A bellow of pain that reverberated through the empty house a half dozen times that summer afternoon before he spotted Aoife's car turning in the driveway. *I've got to find out*, kept echoing through his tortured mind for the rest of the evening.

"You look a bit under the weather," Aoife remarked at dinner. "Are you feeling all right?"

"He's still in shock from that crowd last night." Dominick grinned. "Hell of a crew, aren't they?"

"They seemed more than a bit confused," he let slip unwisely.

Dom's grin disappeared. "Don't you even think of trying to convert us, Father Lally." He tapped the butt of his knife against the table. "Hell hath no fury like an ex-nun suborned. Not to mind an ex-priest. Anyway, they'd spot you coming a mile away, and chew you up and spit you out."

"Not to worry. I'm just as confused myself these days." He sipped his brandy. "Maybe more so. I'd like to have a chat with JJ sometime; he might be able to help me."

"Brilliant lad, our JJ. PhD. and all that. Studied at the Gregorian, Harvard, the works."

"So why did he leave the Js, if I may ask?"

"Actually, nobody is quite sure; he doesn't talk about it. Apparently he taught at a University in the States for a while. One time he let slip something about being restricted in what he could teach. But I don't know if that was the reason."

"I gather he's a writer." Several jibes about famous authors had been directed at JJ during last night's session.

"Oh indeed. Psychology of religion and that kind of stuff. His books have sold in England and America, too. In fact he has made enough money on them to be able to write full-time now. And he puts out a Journal of very avant-garde theology a couple of times a year."

"And he and Rosemarie have some kind of ....?"

"They've been living together for some time now. First

romance for the group. Though whether it'll last is hard to say. She wants to be a priest and she's heard of a bishop in the States who's ordaining women, so she's thinking of going over there. JJ on the other hand, while he's at theological odds with the institutional church, would like to remain within the fold. So we'll see how the romance works out."

Ignatius went early to his room, though not to bed, sitting instead at the elegant escritoire doodling on sheets of writing paper he found in a drawer. Former priests and nuns seeking God in post-religious life. Disdainful of dogma. Impervious to platitudes. But, withal, if God was to be found in their concept of truth they'd accept him. *And what is truth, dear Pontius Pilate? The truth is that the Lord is not in the wind and the Lord is not in the earthquake and the Lord is not in the fire. But after the fire a still small voice... which Ignatius Lally thinks he might once more hear: that somewhere, somehow, he may find his Lord again, and restore to Him those lost sheep of the fold.* But right now he was lost himself in a silent fog of despair.

He was getting his breakfast when the phone rang. Aoife, who worked three days a week at the National Library, had just left. He debated until the sixth ring before deciding to pick it up. "What's the matter?" Deirdre sounded as if she'd been crying.

"Padhraig." He detected a sniffle. "He's turned Cathal against me now, with his lies."

"What happened?" He never could quite like her youngest.

"I told him to pick his clothes off the floor so I could do his laundry, and when I turned my back I heard him mutter 'slut'. So I yelled at him, 'what did you say? And he said, 'I know what *you* are. And I said, what am I? And he said, 'Daddy says you're a slut.'" She sniffled again.

"I'm sorry," Ignatius said. "It's a fierce situation for you to be in."

"If it weren't for what he might do to you, I'd pack up and leave this minute."

"I think the time has come for you to take care of yourself, regardless of me. What would you do about the children?"

Silence for a bit. Then she said in a strained voice, "the only one left to me now is Gemma. She's always been great; and she's been extra attentive lately. I suspect that he tried to poison her too, but she wouldn't buy it." He heard a muffled sob.

"Take her with you," he said, "and come on up to Dublin. There are plenty of jobs here."

"Oh! I forgot to tell you." Forcing cheerfulness into her tone. "I had a visit yesterday from Father Corrigan."

"Indeed. And how is dear old Noel?"

"He said he was just passing through and thought he'd drop in to see how things were going. Very friendly altogether. Which immediately put me on the alert because he has gone out of his way in the past to ignore me, as if my very existence were a threat to his chastity."

"Which I don't doubt it is; look what it did to me?"

"Anyway, he eventually got around to telling me why he came. The novitiate is moving to Dublin in September and they're going to move the fund-raising office up there, too. So I have a choice of moving with it or quitting."

"See! There's your opportunity. Grab it." Sheer bravado: he was terrified of being dragged to jail.

"You know I can't, Ignatius. I'd never forgive myself if it cost you ... Oh, and when he was going out the door he turned around and said, 'if you hear from Father Lally tell him to get the car back as soon as possible.'"

"Well, he can wait another couple of weeks for it," Ignatius retorted savagely.

After lunch he rang JJ. "Certainly, come on over. The ex-Jesuit seemed pleased. "I've enough Paddy for an all-day chinwag." He gave directions to his flat near Christ Church. Ignatius took the Honda rather than the bus, a metaphorical nose-thumb at Noel Corrigan, he acknowledged as he turned into Foster's Avenue. On the Stillorgan Road he noticed the police car behind him. He checked his speedometer: under the speed limit, nothing to worry about. But the car was still tailing him as he turned into Leeson street and it stayed with him all the way across St Stephen's Green. Then, as he was passing Saint Patrick's Cathedral, its flashers lit up. Shit! Then, just as he was about to pull in to the curb Corrigan's request registered for the warning it probably was. He stayed in lane. The lights continued to flash and the police car moved closer. The traffic light at the High Street intersection turned red as he approached. From the middle lane, without stopping, he made a left turn just ahead of a lorry that barreled across from the Dame Street end. The lorry's horn blared, brakes screeched. At the Cornmarket he swung left again, into Francis Street. The Gardai were no longer behind him. But half-way down the street the flashing lights were in view at the far end. He did another quick left and found himself in an alley with nowhere to go: two concrete phallic pillars blocked the exit. He turned off the engine, unbuckled, got out, and ran. Through lanes and down steps and then he was back on Patrick Street. He slowed to a brisk walk. They must have checked the Honda's license plate, but they wouldn't recognize him on foot. He headed briskly for Christ Church. In a few minutes he was knocking on the door of JJ's second floor flat.

"Another triumph for the computer," JJ pronounced, sitting behind an ancient-looking desk in his livingroom. "They drive around doing spot checks, and they picked on you by chance."

"I felt like a gangster in a movie." He sat across from JJ, still unnerved by the escapade.

"You didn't leave anything personal in the car, I hope?" JJ, tall and lean, with thick graying hair, had a long crooked nose that wiggled as he spoke.

"Oh shit!" The piece of paper on which he had scribbled Aoife's instructions to their house was still in the glove compartment. "So now they know where I'm staying."

"Car theft is a felony," JJ noted. "They'll arrest you on sight." He was silent for a bit. "But I don't think Rosemarie will mind you sleeping here on the sofa until such time as we find you safe accommodations." From somewhere in the desk he pulled out a bottle of Paddy and two glasses, and poured.

"I think I may be having a crisis of faith." Ignatius tried to make it casual, but his tone betrayed anxiety.

"You are, huh?" JJ examined his drink. "Not terribly surprising, of course, after what you've been through." His nose twitched. "And you feel like talking about it, I suppose?"

"I'm not quite sure where to start." The anxiety still coming through.

JJ handed him a glass. "Start with this." He himself sipped, savored, nodded approval. "I should tell you straight off, in case it didn't come across on Monday night, that my theological views are rather unorthodox. However, I do know a bit about the psychology of belief that might be of some help."

"I always took my faith for granted," Ignatius said. "It never occurred to me that it would ever falter. But now I don't know if I even believe in God."

JJ inspected him as if he were a frog to be dissected. "What has just happened to you is what has challenged your faith in God. It's probably the first time in your life that you've been forced to examine your most fundamental beliefs. And so you've panicked."

He hated JJ at that moment for his dogmatic tone and supercilious stare. "I don't feel so much that I have lost faith in God as that God has lost faith in me. He just vanished from my life."

"In other words, your faith up to this has been pampered by gooey feelings and goosy sensations, and now they're gone."

"I'd hope there was more to it than mere sensual feelings." *Fight back, Ignatius; you're a theologian for chrissake, not a simple rustic to be talked down to.*

"Maybe yes, maybe no. Do you remember the first time you believed in God?"

"I think I've always believed. But I do remember the first time I actually talked to Him. I was just seven years old."

"So you were socialized into believing in God because everybody you knew believed in Him – parents, teachers, peers. And you were taught to talk to Him the way a child talks to her invisible friend. God was your invisible friend, wasn't He?" A tinge of sardonic smile raised the corners of JJ's mouth.

"That doesn't necessarily mean that what I believe in isn't true."

"It might be true. But if you were like most Catholics, including most priests, you spent your religious life trying to understand what you already believed, instead of trying to determine what was worthy of belief; *fides quaerens intellectum* instead of *intellectus quaerans fidem."* JJ paused to sniff his whiskey. "Faith should be based on reason, Ignatius, not on imagination or wishful thinking, or ancient myths, as so much of it in fact is. Take, for instance, all the nonsense written and pontificated about regarding the Virgin Mary: does it have any reasonable historical basis? Or the papal sex claptrap about every act of love being open to the possibility of new life: does that have any basis in reason or biology, or even a shred of biblical backing? I could go on and on, but it probably wouldn't help you in your present state." He let his tongue run along his upper lip. "I think what you need to do is examine what it is that you believe, and determine the basis of your belief: these might give your faith some kind of foundation."

Why are you angry at him, Ignatius? Because you have for long in your heart subscribed to what he has just said but were afraid to admit it? "I hear you, and I don't disagree. But at the moment I'm totally confused about my own beliefs. Do you believe in God yourself?"

The ex-Jesuit threw back his head and laughed like a man enjoying a huge joke. "Ah yes, the big bugaboo itself! The question we all have to face sooner or later if we ever in our lives do a bit of serious thinking. But there's no simple answer to the question, let me tell you straight away. Who or what do we mean when we say God? That's the question." He pushed back his chair and hoisted shod feet onto the desk so that Ignatius was staring at well-worn soles. "Yes, I believe in God, Ignatius, but in a God of my own definition, a God who is plausible to *my* intellect based on the knowledge *I* possess. And that's the notion of belief I try to define in my Journal. More Paddy?" He held up the bottle.

Ignatius held out an eager glass. "It sounds terribly arrogant when you put it that way, doesn't it? As if you were the creator yourself and you were defining the deity." He slugged the whiskey in a way he had never done before. It scorched his throat.

"Maybe. But it's arrogant only to minds accustomed to obeisance before the deity." JJ stared unrepentantly at him before returning to contemplation of his drink. "In my thinking if there is a God, and I happen to believe there is, he has made no serious attempt to let us know who he is or what our relationship with him should be; we have to seek him out individually for ourselves. And that's a highly intellectual exercise, since the clues are vague and the false trails are endless."

The whiskey was going to his head, making his crisis of faith recede somewhat for the moment. "Tell me more about your Journal."

The shoes came off the desk. The glass was put down. JJ swivelled to a shelf behind him and lifted off a thin publication with a bright yellow cover.

WHY DO YOU BELIEVE?

the bold headlines across the center asked. "That's the latest issue; it caused a bit of a flap: the AB threatened me with excommunication, but I thumbed my nose at him. So I'm expecting to be drummed out of the corps one of these days."

"Who reads it? I mean, I hardly expect the clergy or the hierarchy to look to –"

"It's a small readership: a few hundred; some clergy, mind you, and even one bishop, who shall be nameless; a fair number of university types, as you might expect; and a sprinkling of what I call lay intellectuals – there's actually a growing number of those fellows around the country these days."

"And how – "

The front door opened and Rosemarie came in. Not at all, she didn't mind him staying with them till he found a place of his own. "It makes you sort of one of us, being on the run." She added this with a certain amount of satisfaction. Tall, statuesque, with a glorious crown of long red hair, she was an attractive woman even if the proportions of her facial features denied her the privilege of classical beauty.

While she prepared dinner, Ignatius rang the McElligotts. "That explains it," Aoife said when he told her about the episode with the police. "There were a couple of fellows sitting in a car across the road when I arrived home. Hold on a minute till I see if they're gone." She returned a bit out of breath. "I had to look out the upstairs window because of the bushes. They're still there."

"I better stay put so," he said.

"I'll pack your suitcase and when Dominick comes home I'll have him drop it off to you."

"Aren't they likely to follow him?"

"I think you can leave it to Dominick to work that out." She chortled. "He always did want to be a sleuth."

After dinner, while they were still at table drinking coffee, Rosemarie said, "One of my authors is a woman in the Garda hierarchy. She's a good friend, so I can trust her to find out why they're after you."

"Rosemarie is an editor with a feminist publisher," JJ explained. "And if you're not a feminist watch out: you might end up with your throat slit on the altar of one of their goddesses."

"You bloody males with your sexist fantasies and sacrificial virgins to hoist your cocks." Rosemarie made a face at her companion. "We women, when we're free from your domination, have a much more down to earth view of divinity."

"You talked about male bias in the definition of God the other night," Ignatius recalled. "I'd like to hear more about that."

She swept her hair over her shoulders, pushed back her chair and crossed her legs beneath the long green dress. "I was a ferociously devout nun in my young days and I wanted in the worst way to become a priest." She laughed without humor. "I still do, and one of these days I shall." She glanced slyly across at JJ. "Anyway, one day I picked up the autobiography of Saint Teresa of Avila. Now there's a woman for you! If she'd been a man they'd have made her Pope. It was the way she was treated by the system that brought home to me that *I* was being discriminated against, and would always be discriminated against in the Catholic Church, just because I didn't have a penis."

"And you look a hell of a lot better without one, I can tell you." JJ stuck out his tongue at her.

"I came to the conclusion that Rome rule was penis rule and so I left the convent and the Roman Church and became an Anglican."

"But what do you think of –" Ignatius was interrupted by a knock at the door.

"Garda, Special Branch," Dominick called loudly from outside. "I'm here to arrest a notorious car thief," he said when Rosemarie let him in, carrying Ignatius's suitcase.

"I hope they didn't follow you." Terror of being arrested assailed Ignatius again.

Dominick dropped the suitcase at his feet and drew himself up to his full five feet six. "Are you insinuating, sir, that Gumshoe McElligott couldn't give the slip to a couple of flatfoots?" He swung around to JJ and chortled. "Jaypers! You should have seen me."

"Were they actually following you?" JJ asked.

"Oh yes." Dominick spotted the bottle of Paddy on the

sideboard. "And if yous bowsies'd give a fellow something to wet the whistle with I'll tell yous all about it."

"*Give the woman in the bed more porter*!" JJ sang. He got up and poured a glass.

"That's better." Dominick sipped appreciatively, pulled up a chair next to Rosemarie and put an arm around her. "Hiya, shweetheart! Is your man here treating you dacent? 'Cause if he isn't I'm waitin' in the wings. You know that, me luv. Any time o' day or night."

"Tell us," JJ commanded.

"It's like this." Dominick waved his arms as if to clear a space. "The G-men are waiting across the road, see. So I marches out the front door lugging this huge suitcase and puts it in the boot of me car. Then I gets in and drives away, acting as if I were totally unaware of their snooping presence. But of course in the mirror I can see they're following me. So we proceed all the way out to Butterfield Avenue, where Justin Kelleher, one of my partners, lives. I pulls up in front of his house, gets out, takes the suitcase out of the boot and carries it in. Justin's missus lets me in the door, I stays a few minutes, comes out *sans* suitcase, and takes off again. And guess what?"

"You're brilliant." Rosemarie patted his cheek affectionately. "They didn't follow you?"

"You got it, shweetheart. Last I saw of them rozzers when I was driving off they were out of their jalopy and heading for Justin's front door."

"Do we have to beat out of you how you got Ignatius's suitcase here, or were you going to tell us?" JJ demanded.

"Nothing like a good straight man, I always say." Dominick beamed and bowed, and winked at Ignatius. "I was just coming to that part, as a matter of fact. I –"

"You had put it in the huge suitcase before you left your house, and then you left it behind in the boot when you took the huge one out," Rosemarie cut in.

"Ah sure I always knew you had brains as well as beauty." Dominick stroked her hair affectionately. "As I've told you many a time, when you get tired of this eejit here ..."

"I need a safe house," Ignatius pleaded. "Any ideas?"

"Just have a bit of patience me lad, will you?" Dominick gazed at Rosemarie. "These bloody RC clergy are so demanding, aren't they?" He turned and faced Ignatius. "I'm here to tell you, Father Lally, that the Mount Merrion sleuth has not been sitting down on the job. I rang our gang from the office after Aoife informed me of your outlaw status. Veronica has a spare room at her Dublin 4 address and she's willing to put you up. You can't do better than that."

"Jeez!" JJ exploded. "We better find you a bloody chastity belt first."

"Never mind him," Rosemarie said. "Veronica just likes to talk about sex, sort of like a schoolgirl. And she likes to shock us with her fantasies sometimes. But it's my belief she's still a virgin."

Ignatius noticed JJ and Dominick exchange rolling-eye glances, but neither said anything. "I'll drop you off there on my way home," Dominick said. And he did.

AUTHORITY

Veronica's town house was tiny. "It's all of four meters wide and eight long," she informed him with a laugh as she showed him around. "Two floors of course." On his previous visit with Dominick he had seen only her sitting room, which occupied most of the ground floor. Now he got to see her minuscule kitchen just inside the front door, separated from the narrow hallway by cafe doors. And the two bedrooms upstairs, with the bathroom in between. "This boudoir is yours." She waved a dramatic hand at the little front room. But it had a bed and a chest of drawers, and the house promised shelter against the law that sought to apprehend him.

"I'm most profoundly grateful to you," he told her solemnly.

"Arrah not at all. We have to protect the innocent, don't we?" But the strain of generosity showed in her voice. "Would you like a cup of tea or anything?" Which offer was definitely forced. They were standing in front of the bathroom door.

"I'm right as rain now. I was well fed by Rosemarie and JJ."

"Well in that case I'll take myself off, if you don't mind. I have to be at work early. As you can see, I was on my way to bed when I got the phone call." She spread her arms as if inviting him to inspect the flowered robe that hung from the tips of her shoulders and descended less than half way between hips and knees.

"Of course. I'll do the same myself."

She made for the bathroom; he closed the bedroom door and sat wearily on the bed. He removed his shoes, unpacked his things into a drawer, hung his one spare trousers on the back of the door, found his bag of toiletries and went out to the bathroom. Veronica was just coming out, naked and carrying her robe.

“Sorry,” she said, but made no attempt to cover up. “I like to go naked around the house.” She stepped close and kissed him on the lips. “Goodnight,” she said, then sauntered to her bedroom. He hurried into the bathroom, quivering from both the kiss and her nakedness.

He didn't sleep well: the mattress was hard, the pillow was lumpy, there was no top sheet, the duvet was too warm. When he woke the sun was shining on the wall. Ten to nine by his watch. *Are you here, Lord, by any chance?* Feeling the belligerence in his interior voice. But though the silence remained deep, in the cheerful sunlight of this room it seemed to him just a little less desolate than on previous mornings. He bathed in the tiny shower stall, shaved, and went downstairs in search of breakfast. A note was taped to the left cafe door.

> *Father I left orange bread and tea bags on the counter and there's butter and jam in the fridge. Hope you can manage with that. Sorry for the meager provisions. I left you a key to the front door hanging from the inside knob. Be sure to lock it from the outside when you go out. I'll be home at six and cook us dinner.*

He thought of Deirdre as he peeled the orange, and decided to ring and tell her where he was and why. But not from here, lest *they* trace the call. Was he getting paranoid? And he'd better gloss over Veronica, saying merely he was staying with a friend of Dominick's.

Afterwards he walked up Serpentine Avenue, onto Merrion Road, past the RDS, and over the Dodder. A balmy day; a walk to the city center instead of taking the bus would do him good. Meditation time, of which he'd had too little lately. No prayers either, or mass, or divine office. Plenty of material here for examination of conscience, but anger at his God blocked out all feelings of guilt. *Are you listening to me, Lord? I want to talk to You.* But though the traffic was ceaseless and pedestrians plentiful, his God was nowhere in sight. He walked by rows of three-story brick houses with steep stone steps leading up to brightly painted doors raised high above basement windows and separated from the footpath by iron rails and flowered gardens. Built, he guessed, in the late eighteenth and early nineteenth century, well before this endless stream of horseless carriages began to flow. A different age: less frenetic, more in tune with nature. And with God? Hardly indeed. The age of Enlightenment that challenged the need for Him, who He was, even His very existence: Voltaire and Scleiermacher and Hegel and Feuerbach, leading up to Nietzsche and the death of God. His seminary theology classes had only briefly touched on those heretical thinkers, and then only to demonstrate their errors against the infallible teaching of Popes and Councils - *de fide definita*, and the slightly less certain doctrines of Fathers and Doctors - either *fidei proxima, certa,* or *sententia communis.* But you had to wonder now at such casual dismissal: wasn't it possible that those so-called heretics *had* legitimate ideas about God? What was the Church afraid of anyway? What harm was there in exploring ideas? Wasn't that what arrogant JJ was doing? And perhaps he only seemed arrogant because he was challenging accepted truths? You can never have too many angles on the truth, was what he had learned in Brazil, though he kept many of his wilder ideas to himself. Was he lapsing into heresy? So much had happened in recent years to challenge his faith in the Church: from financial dishonesty to protected pederasty and episcopal sex. And then that most egregious act of dogmatic pigheadedness, that JJ, too, had pinpointed: denial by celibate men of the sexually actives' right to contraceptives. That in particular he had mulled a lot in Brazil, tormented by the spectacle of overburdened parents and hungry children; and through it he had lost his faith in infallibility. Although he had suppressed those feelings of rebellion when he took over as Novice Master – a position that demanded total orthodoxy – now his heterodox ideas were rearing their heads again. But could one really challenge the church's teaching, as JJ was doing, and still be a Christian? Conversely, as a Brazilian priest once said to him, could one be a true follower of Christ and *not* challenge it?

He crossed Haddington Road, then the canal bridge, and headed up Mount Street. He was probably a heretic by orthodox standards, but did it really matter? Wasn't pursuit of the truth the paramount consideration? Surely God wouldn't fault him on that? To thine own self be true, even when it meant asking whether Christ was really God? A question that had been bothering him when he was called home to Clyard and that he had put in abeyance since. If He *was* divine, then He was the solution to the problem of God: the Man whose doctrine boiled down to *love one another*? A doctrine which surely all could accept as coming from

God. But the Church, over the ages, had confounded that simple teaching with an intolerable legalistic and authoritarian mess, so that He who once said *call no man master* they now called Christ the King. JJ was right: understanding must precede belief. Church doctrine was now as confusing as this chaotic traffic. He needed to sort out his own conflicting ideas and restore order to the anarchy of his mind. Sort out what it was he believed about what. He'd try writing down his thoughts as soon as he got home. Home? He had no home any more.

He came through the north end of Merrion Square into Nassau Street and was passing the railed walls of Trinity College, heading for Fred Hanna's book shop, when the urge came on him to continue his enquiry into JJ's *Journal* that Rosemarie had interrupted yesterday. He strode around the front of Trinity, up Dame Street at a fast clip, past Christ Church, and up the stairs to the ex-Jesuit's flat.

"I'm glad you came." JJ sat himself in an armchair in the small parlor. "I still have a little Paddy left."

"Would you mind if I made some phone calls first while I'm still sober?"

"Use the extension in the bedroom," JJ said kindly. "You'll have a bit of privacy there."

"Father Lally!" Kennedy answered the phone himself. He seemed surprised.

"What are you up to, Brian?"

"I beg your pardon, Father?" Formally, as if for the record.

"Siccing the Gardai on me like that. What kind of religious are you anyway?"

That produced a pause at the other end. "You must realize, Father, that you are in unlawful possession of a car belonging to the Congregation." Again, Kennedy spoke stiffly, as if speaking into a microphone or tape recorder.

"Was," Ignatius retorted. "I'm sure you have retrieved it by now."

"When you come in to do your retreat we're prepared to drop the charges," Kennedy said.

Ignatius hung up and rang Dominick at his office. "Is this legal?" he demanded.

"If they genuinely believe you stole their car, of course it is. On the other hand if, as you think is the case, they're just using the Gardai for their own devious ends, they could be up on charges of harassing you, or even of criminal mischief or something of that sort."

"So what should I do?"

His friend was silent so long that Ignatius had to ask him if he was still on the line. Eventually Dom said, "you can tell him that you have consulted your lawyer and that unless the charges are withdrawn immediately you will file a charge of harassment against him."

"Thanks, Dom."

"And when he does drop the charge you'll come back and stay with us again. Unless of course Veronica seduces you first," Dominick added slyly.

"I've been thinking that maybe I should be looking for a place of my own. I can't be sponging on my friends forever."

"Eventually, I suppose. But we'll have to find you a source of income first. What we need is a rich widow with an appetite for renegade priests." Dominick chuckled.

He rang Kennedy again and had to wait several minutes while the receptionist located the General. He passed along

Dominick's message and hung up without waiting for a response. Then he debated safety before ringing Deirdre, and decided to risk the call anyway.

"I was terribly worried about you." He could almost taste the concern in her voice. "I had a premonition that something bad had happened."

He told her about his escapade; she listened in silence. "So are you coming to Dublin?" he asked.

"I've thought about it, Ignatius, thought about it a lot. But I can't risk your safety. What I did instead was turn the tables on Padhraig: I told him last night that if he makes the slightest accusation against you I'm walking out. And that I'll tell the world he's had incestuous relations with our daughter. And I'll do it, too."

Ignatius felt the breath had been knocked out of him. "You said *that*?"

"Why not? No more Mrs. Nice Wife." The breathless fury of a woman he didn't know in her tone. "And it's got him off my back for the time being. He never said a word, just stalked off to his room, and I haven't seen hide nor hair of him since."

"You're a brave woman, but I wish you were here." For mostly selfish reasons, he had to admit.

"I do, too." The fervor of that wish brought him close to tears. "But by staying here I'm keeping you safe."

He told JJ about Kennedy, and about Dominick's threat. "Let's give the bastards until tomorrow," JJ suggested, "and then Rosemarie will find out if they actually did withdraw the charge. By the way, she's leaving me next week."

"Who's leaving?" His mind still on Kennedy.

"Rosemarie. She's hooked up with a group of women in America who are studying for the priesthood. Apparently they found a bishop who's willing to ordain them."

"I'm sorry to hear that." What would he do if Deirdre walked out on *him*? "I mean, I'm sorry she's leaving you."

"It's not the end of the relationship. I hope," JJ added wistfully. "Anyway, are you ready for that Paddy now? I've been thinking about your crisis of faith," he said as he poured. "Might make an interesting article for the next issue of the Journal. That's if you're interested, of course."

"What would it entail?" Ignatius sipped greedily. Was he getting too fond of the drink?

"Whatever you want to make of it yourself." JJ waved an expansive arm. "How are your writing skills?"

"Reasonably good, I'd say. I always did want to do some serious scribbling."

"I could use an assistant," JJ said casually. "The pay wouldn't be very good, but it might tide you over till you find something better."

He was about to be excommunicated, JJ had said yesterday. Did Ignatius Lally want to share that fate? "What kind of topics do you have in mind for future issues?"

JJ smiled modestly. "I have a whole bucket of ideas."

Ignatius settled into his armchair. "Let's hear some of them."

JJ condescended one of his rare smiles. "I'm writing a piece for the next issue that I call *The Fallacy of Loyola*."

"Provocative title."

"Ignatius – Loyola, not Lally – viewed God as a remote Father, because that was the experience he had of his earthly father. Stiff and stern and demanding complete obedience. That perspective colored – in fact it dominated – his entire Weltanschauung." The glaze in JJ's eyes suggested he was embarking on a lecture, so Ignatius cut in facetiously:

"Fortunately, we didn't have any Weltanschauung in Mayo in the old days."

JJ glared at him. "In the thinking of Ignatius, all mankind had a duty to behave towards God as a dutiful son should behave towards his authoritarian father. Hence his concept of blind obedience, you see."

"Some of us are still struggling with that notion," Ignatius acknowledged.

"On the other hand, Ignatius was a power maniac himself. He always had to be in charge, and he was happy to take over the role of Superior who stood in the place of God for his subordinates, who of course owed *him* the same blind obedience they owed to God himself. That attitude permeates the Spiritual Exercises." JJ poured more Paddy for himself, then offered the bottle to Ignatius.

"'Twould be hard to argue with that." Ignatius topped his drink.

"The thesis in my essay is that the Exercises, based as they are on notions of medieval chivalry and monarchy and belief in the devil, are actually harmful in the light of our present-day knowledge of human nature." JJ ran vigorous fingers through his hair, as if to stimulate his brain. "They produce attitudes in the exercitant of humility and self-abnegation and obedience, and even fanaticism, that are not only useless in today's world but that are positively detrimental to a person's mental and social development."

"You're really taking on the Establishment, aren't you?" Could this be how history was made? Was this crooked-nose man sitting across from him, sipping whiskey, going to topple one of the great pillars of Christian spirituality? "Almost every Catholic religious in the world, male and female, has done – or is doing, or will do – the Exercises in one form or another."

"Unfortunately. I'm still trying to undo their effects on my own life. You did them yourself of course?"

"Indeed."

"My argument is that Ignatius anthropomorphized the notion of God in the worst possible way. Christ the King! Who needs a bloody king, much less pledge him blind obedience? Do you see what I mean? It's my belief that this concept of blind obedience that was crystallized by Loyola and propagated by the Holy Roman Catholic Church ever since for its own peculiar reasons has been one of mankind's most terrible curses of the past four hundred years. Look at the dictators it has helped to prop up in this century alone: "Hitler, Stalin, Mussolini, Franco, Salazar."

"Do I get the impression that you left the Js because you didn't like being ordered around?" He was grappling with the poisonous thought that obedience, that bedrock of religious life, might not be the work of God after all.

JJ sat up straight in his chair. "The whole thing is a bit like the three card trick, you see." He waved his hands in the manner of the trickster rearranging his cards. "You keep your eye on the card that says *obedience to the will of God*: how can you argue with that if you believe that God is the Creator and Sovereign Lord? But look what happens next: the cards are turned over and obedience has been switched to this goddam twit who claims to be your Superior and tells you that he speaks with the voice and authority of God. And you're prevented from trying to find out how this magic occurred because if you question it you're being disobedient, not to mention lacking in faith."

Ignatius felt the sweat on his neck and under his arms. The

argument resonated, but there had to be giant holes in it: fifteen hundred years of monasticism couldn't be entirely wrong. "You're throwing out the entire foundation of religious life," he said brusquely.

JJ was smiling with his eyes. "That one got to you, didn't it?" The slightest curl of cruelty in his mouth.

"So you're totally against obedience of any kind?" He had a feeling the ex–Jesuit was needling him. "But wouldn't that produce complete anarchy."

"I'm not an anarchist." JJ frowned. "Obedience has its place in the world. Obviously you can't have a civilized society without laws. My point about Ignatius – and indeed about the whole monastic tradition – is that they built their power structures on the deceit that the Superior represents God, and that by obeying the Superior you are obeying God Himself. And conversely, that when you disobey your Superior you are spitting in the eye of the Almighty. They'd have us believe in effect that it is God, not themselves, who is the tyrant of monastic minutiae."

"But you have to have some kind of authority in the monastery." He had been a Superior himself for the past eight years.

"Democratic authority, yes; the kind that can be taken away for misuse; subjects having the right to criticize. But not the Ignatian absolute. Do you know what that kind of authority does?" JJ leaned forward and glared at him. "It destroys your critical faculty, that's what it does. You're conditioned to accept everything that's bloody well thrown at you, to believe everything told you by any kind of authority figure, and to do whatever you're told to do by fucking Superiors. And that attitude spills over into the rest of your unfortunate life." He sat back and breathed hard for a bit. "I only realized this a few years ago," he continued, calmly now. "I was asked to review a film for a newspaper and I discovered that I had been watching movies all my life without ever subjecting them to any serious critical analysis. So in my view the church has a lot to answer –"

Time to get him back on track. "I thought your Journal was focusing on the *nature* of God, not on the shortcomings of the church."

JJ relaxed, joined solemn fingertips. "My Journal is concerned with what we believe, and how our beliefs, and others' beliefs, affect our lives. You'd be wasting your time trying to discover the nature of God, Ignatius; the philosophers and theologians and every other pseudo-intellectual Tom, Dick, and Harry have been poking at that for thousands of years without coming up with anything of consequence. What *would* be useful would be to explore what we really believe about God."

He fought briefly, then squelched, his inclination to be stubborn and reject JJs argument. "It's a starting point," he agreed reluctantly. "Which needs to be explored as a preliminary. But the search for God is the most sublime endeavor we can engage in."

JJ scrutinized the carpet, as if he had discovered a hole in it. "The harm that's been done to mankind by the power maniacs, religious and irreligious alike – all of them hiding behind the name of God, mind you – is incalculable. From the divine mission of popes to the divine rights of kings to the power of the People." His eyes, when he looked up and past Ignatius, seemed focused on infinity. "To me, the only difference between the first two types and the third one is that popes and kings abuse power directly in the name of God, while the People do it indirectly: the People being just another fictional name for the deity. The People, you see, is almost as elusive a concept as God."

Ignatius shook his head vigorously. "All that may be true, but it's just telling us about power and its abuse, not about God."

JJ's face took on the slightly pained look of a good man abused. "You need to let me finish my train of thought," he said, so mildly that Ignatius felt guilty for interrupting. He finished his whiskey to cover his embarrassment. "For Ignatius the soldier," JJ continued, "power meant subjecting everyone to the service of his king. When he converted, God became a divine version of the earthly king. Hence his rule of absolute obedience, especially to the pope, the visible representative of the omnipotent ..."

Going back out to Ballsbridge on the bus Ignatius tried to engage his Lord once more. *I'm going to remain a priest, Lord, whether you want me or not. And I'm going to find out who people think You are. And then I'm going to find out who You really are. That's how I'm going to serve You from now on.* And though his God remained silent, he didn't mind too much this time; he was beginning to accept the situation.

JUSTIFICATION

"It was a bad idea to begin with anyway," Brian Kennedy growled, his fixed-sad visage even more glum than usual.

"Arrah sure 'twas worth the try," Dermot Mullen retorted, standing in the doorway of the Superior's office. "And personally, I'd be inclined to stick with it and call his bluff."

"We can't afford even the possibility of any more lawsuits against the Congregation, Dermot. You of all people should know that." Kennedy's grimace looked almost like a precedent to tears.

"I'll ring Mangan right away then and have him drop the charge." But Mullen leaned against the doorjamb to indicate he wasn't about to do it this very minute. "So what are you going to do now?" Just a hint of the sly in both tone and expression.

"I don't have a single idea at the moment." Kennedy rubbed long-fingered hands over his gaunt face. "We're caught between the devil and the deep blue sea, aren't we?. He won't come in willingly, that's obvious. And we can't bring him in against his will. On the other hand if we leave him out there and he molests someone else there'll be hell to pay."

"We could expel him from the Congregation for

disobedience to his vow." Mullen straightened quickly at that thought. "You know, it mightn't be a half-bad idea, Brian, come to think of it."

Kennedy stared at him, then shook his head. "We can't do that. If we were absolutely certain he did what those people claim he did we could do it all right. But I'm not convinced yet." He saw Mullen's eyebrows go up. " Yes, I know that on the face of it the evidence is strong. And I'm well aware of the way pederasts have lied in the past. But I was there looking at him when Donnellan made the charge and Ignatius Lally behaved exactly the way I'd have done myself if I'd been the one accused." He took in Mullen's supercilious glare. "I tell you, Dermot, he's either innocent or he's the most extraordinary actor I've ever come across."

"But he did break his vow, regardless. And that's enough reason to expel him. Which would get us out of our present jam, wouldn't it?" Mullen banged knuckles together to emphasize his point.

Kennedy glowered at him. "If you were in his shoes and you were falsely accused of the same crime, how would you behave? I think I'd do exactly what Ignatius Lally is doing right now."

"And if you were guilty you'd do the same thing, too," Mullen retorted sourly.

"So we don't know whether he's innocent or guilty at this stage. But expelling him would be the same as pronouncing him guilty. And that we can't do till we have proof positive."

"Your decision." Mullen turned and walked away.

"Don't forget to ring Mangan," Kennedy shouted after him. Then he joined his hands and sat perfectly still, staring at the phone on the desk. Eventually he picked up the receiver and dialled.

"I'll see if he's available," the voice at the other end said."

Kennedy tapped his fingers on the desk while he waited, as if he were playing the piano. "We have a problem, your Grace," he said when the line came alive again. He explained the situation.

"Didn't I understood you to say the last time we talked that you already had him locked up?" Donnellan's peevish tone projecting his deep annoyance.

"Actually we were in the *process* of doing just that at the time I spoke to you," Kennedy said carefully. "But unfortunately, Father Lally chose not to cooperate with us."

Donnellan condemned him with a long silence. "So what are you going to do now?" he asked eventually, the level tone carrying dire threats of unfathomable consequences.

"We'll keep trying to get him in. That's all we can do at the present."

"And what if he molests another young girl in the meantime? We're back to Brendan Smyth again, aren't we? Knowing the man is dangerous and doing nothing about it. That's not acceptable, Father."

"If you have any ideas ...?" Kennedy said stiffly. He was running out of patience.

"You think he's in Dublin?"

"We're pretty sure of that. We even knew where he was staying, only he skipped before the Gardai could get him."

"I suppose I should ring Whelan then; if the man is in the diocese of Dublin his Grace of Dublin ought to know about it. He's the one who's going to have to deal with him." A touch of malice in Donnellan's tone.

"A good idea, your Grace." But the prospect of dealing with Michael Anthony, Archbishop of Dublin, didn't help Brian Kennedy sleep any better that night.

Ignatius woke to the sound of swishing water. He imagined Veronica naked, showering on the far side of the wall on which the morning sun was shining. Stop! Pray! He needed to pray. Drop his anger with the Almighty and beseech Him to stay *His* anger with Ignatius. *Wilt Thou forever be angry with me, Lord? Your ire I could put up with, if only You'd speak. But if You won't talk to me then I'll talk to You. I'll take that job with JJ and write for his Journal. And maybe by so doing return souls to your allegiance. Even if not perhaps to the fold of the institutional Church. I'm beginning to wonder anyway if You care any longer about that bureaucracy. Do You, Lord?* Maybe a surprise question would elicit an answer.

It didn't, of course. The shower shut off, the bathroom door squeaked, Veronica's bedroom door opened and then it shut. He thought of Deirdre. *Why is sex wrong, Lord, when it's responsible?* Something was happening to his conscience. He was the Novice Master, for God's sake: spiritual nurturer of delicate souls, orthodox teacher of priests-to-be, pillar of rectitude in a dissolute world, model of holiness to those in his charge. *Yet I keep company with women, my friends are heretics, my lover is married, I'm hiding from the law, and I'm disobedient to my vows. My life is a shambles, Lord. Wilt Thou not save me from my iniquities?*

Somewhere the phone crake-craked. Then his door opened and Veronica was by his bed. Clad in the very short robe of his first night here. "A Mrs. McCarthy would like to talk to you." Leaning over and speaking loudly, as if he'd not hear her otherwise. "She says to hurry, she only has a minute. The phone is in my bedroom." She stood aside to let him pass. What could he do but throw back the sheet and race naked out the door.

"Deirdre!" Sitting naked on Veronica's bed, every nerve in his body on edge. "Where are you? Is everything all right?"

"Yes, but I'm using a phone card and it's about to run out. I'll explain everything later, including how I found you now. I'm coming up this morning on the train, getting in at half eleven. I'll take a taxi to where you're staying. I have the address. See you about –." The line went dead.

"Is everything all right?" Veronica solicitous on the door side of the bed, dressed in underwear now and struggling into tights.

"Yes. A friend is coming up for the day." Flushing at the prospect of having to walk past her.

"She's Fiona's mother, isn't she?" Standing to straighten her sheer black hose.

"Yes." He got off the bed and headed quickly for the door.

"Ignatius!" The soft gentle call of an intimate friend.

"Yes?" He replied without turning, his hand on the knob.

"You have a very nice backside. I hope you don't mind my telling you." Her tone of respectful admiration could scarcely be faulted.

"Thanks." He fled to his room. Later, after she had left for work and he had just finished breakfast - rashers and a fried egg, and fresh bread smeared with marmalade - the phone rang again, this time somewhere in the parlor. He had to search to find it under a cushion at one end of the sofa.

"Good morning, Father Lally."

"Brian?" Oh God! Kennedy. How did he –"

"It's Turlough, Ignatius. Sorry if I woke you up."

"No, not at all." Relief coursing through him as the sound of throat-clearing scratched at his ear.

"I was wondering if you had a few minutes to talk."

"Certainly. Of course." He didn't particularly like Turlough, but Ignatius Lally was still a priest, with consequent obligations to lost sheep, etcetera.

There was an awkward silence then, so just to keep the conversation going he asked, "what seminary did you go to?"

"Clonliffe. I was a priest in the Dublin diocese for ten years." Just the faintest whiff of pride in the way that came out.

"Good college." He paused but there was nothing more forthcoming from the other end. "You rang me for a particular reason, I'd say?" The lost sheep trying to find his way home, perhaps?

"Well, I didn't want you to have the impression that I'm a complete bowsy altogether. I have this thing for Veronica, as you no doubt divined, but I wasn't very gentlemanly about it the other night, was I?"

"She's a very attractive woman; it's understandable that you might lose your head over her."

"She ..." Turlough stopped. "No ..." He paused again. "Let me be honest about it, the problem is me, you see. I'm obsessed with sex. Always have been. I don't know why I ever went to Clonliffe. And I don't know why they didn't throw me out the very first day. All I thought of from the time I was twelve years of age was girls, girls, girls. And all I learned about them in school was that they were sin, sin, sin. So I think I went to the seminary to escape from myself. Cold turkey on the prick, if you know what I mean."

"You weren't the only one with that problem, I can tell you."

"The difference is that most lads settle down after they're

ordained and make up their minds that women are out of bounds. But I didn't. That was the trouble."

"Some fall and rise again." What would he do himself when Deirdre came today?

"I've concluded that I'm a sort of Saint Augustine in reverse. After ten years of battling the flesh – falling and rising, as you say – I quit the priesthood. I met this girl, this woman I couldn't live without. So I didn't even wait for a dispensation: they told me it would take years at best, and might never happen at all since John Paul was taking such a hard line on priests who wanted to leave. We got married in a registry office in London and I thought my troubles with sex were finally over. Hah!" This last an explosion of exasperated contempt.

"I gather it didn't work out?" JJ had told him that Turlough was divorced.

"She left me after six months. My own bloody fault of course. Giving the glad eye to every good-looking bird I came across." His tone brightened. "At least I got a job out of it. From her father. As a car salesman. I'm so damn bloody good at selling cars that he kept me on even after she walked out on me."

"That was something, anyway." Where was this conversation leading?

"Actually I didn't ring to tell you all this stuff about myself. I just wanted to apologize for my behavior the last night."

"That's very nice of you," Ignatius felt himself warming a bit to this man he had previously considered annoying.

He showered and shaved and all the while Deirdre was on his mind. After dressing he took his breviary and ploughed through Matins and most of Lauds before the despair of spiritual dryness overwhelmed him. *How long, Lord? How long must this desert go on? And what am I to do when she comes? My whole being quivers at the thought of her. I'll want to kiss her and touch her and make love to her. But I may not, Lord. I know. Isn't that right?* He might as well be addressing the floor. *And I won't, either, Lord, if you don't want me to. Though I do recall, before you closed down on me – it was back in Brazil, actually – that You had gone a bit tepid on sins of the flesh. You really had! Remember that time when I was Superior and I had to drive from Marilia to Brasilia to see some of the brethren, and Maureen and Siobhan, the two Irish Sisters, came along for the ride because they had never seen the Capital. On that thousand mile journey through hard-packed dirt roads and clouds of brown dust, through desolate scrub and lush green forest and green open graze-land we all let our hair down and told bawdy stories and laughed till we ached and teased and slapped and touched each other in the friendliest way. And when we stopped for the night at a pensão used by lorry drivers and only one room was available we all bunked together and made not too much effort at modesty though we did nothing terribly bad except we shouldn't have all showered at the one time in that makeshift bathroom on the plea that we had to get going as quickly as possible. I thought then You'd flail me for gross misbehavior but You only said 'watch it.' Not even confessional matter, you allowed. And for years, too, You let me see those scabrous films in the art houses of São Paulo without so much as a twitch of annoyance.*

So where do I get off now? How much can I do without causing You offence? Was Louisburgh mortal? I know by Your rules it had to be: adultery, You said, thou shalt not commit. But You were so gentle with adulterers Yourself, as though You understood and almost condoned it. Did You love Mary

Magdalene? Is it possible You even made love to her, as some have alleged? And would You understand if I made love to Deirdre today?

But he had to make his own decision now: his God was away, with no forwarding address, no telephone number, no e-mail id., and no date for return. Had He abandoned the entire human race, or just himself? Who could he ask? They'd think he was daft. For who but himself had a friendship with God like the one he had enjoyed since age seven? Would he be jealous if he discovered that God, this minute, was on the friendliest of terms with any number of people he knew?

He owed Mammy a ring: it had been a week since he talked to her and she'd be fretting. She wasn't just fretting, she was hopping mad. "Garda Finnegan from Drumnamwika was here yesterday asking about you. I said what do you want him for and he said that a car had been stolen from the novitiate in Clyard and there was a suspicion that you were the thief. I –"

"I can explain that –"

"I gave that Garda a good piece of my mind, let me tell you. 'Who in God's name do you think you are?' I said. 'To come into my house and accuse my son, a holy priest of God, of stealing a car?' I said. 'A car,' I said, 'that belongs to him as Novice Master of the novitiate of the Congregation of World Missionaries in Clyard, County Tipperary. Have you nothing better to do,' I said,'than to go around falsely accusing God's anointed when,' I said, 'the country is going to the dogs with crime of every conceivable wickedness?' I tell you," Mammy ended triumphantly, "I sent that lad packing with his tail between his legs."

He explained to her why the Garda had come to visit, leaving out the bit about the car chase and the fact that he was now hiding out. "But it's all been resolved now," he assured her confidently.

"Isn't it a terrible world we live in, God help us," Mammy concluded dolefully, "when even the priests themselves are not safe from the law."

For the next hour or so he tried to read a book he had found on a chair – a collection of short stories by Irish women. But much of the time he was checking his watch and calculating where she'd be. When the bell rang at eleven minutes past twelve he charged for the door like a horse out of the starting box. A momentary vision of a bright blue suit, then she was through the doorway and wrapped around him. "Oh God, it's good to see you," she gasped eventually. Head thrown back to get a look, arms still holding him tightly.

"I was afraid I'd never see you again." Haunted all week by fear of a Terezinha tragedy. She enveloped him again, lips pressing hard, tongue probing deep, groin gyrating fiercely as if consummation were achievable in despite of clothes. Then without relaxing she freed a hand and began to unbutton his shirt. "Now," she breathed, suddenly shorter as her shoes came off. "I can't wait another minute."

Better let the thinking wait till after. He took her hand and led her up the stairs to his tiny room.

They had a late lunch in a pub up on Merrion Road. "Now let me have it all," he said after their pints arrived and they waited for sandwiches.

"I thought I just did." Her smile so lascivious that he reddened to his roots. Their love-making had been so savagely intense that he was in a lather of sweat when they finally collapsed. "Sorry," she added. "I'm a most wicked woman, aren't I?"

"You're a wonder to behold," he said fervently.

"Padhraig went off to a vet's meeting in Cork and he won't be back until late tonight. So I thought I'd avail of the opportunity. The children are still with their grandmother in Waterville and I rang Father Corrigan to say I wouldn't be in. So I've covered my tracks."

"I'm so glad you came," he said.

"Several times!" Then she put her hand on his neck and rubbed it gently. "Sorry. I'm as high as a kite all day. But sure it's all your fault."

"How is he behaving?"

"Staying out of my way." She sipped her Guinness. "When we're together, which is just for meals mostly, he has nothing to say. But I have no illusions about him. The man is like an otter: once he gets you in his jaws he never lets go."

Afterwards they walked up along the Dodder to Herbert Park and sat on a bench. He told her about JJ and his offer of a job with the Journal. "It's been such a nightmare few weeks for you." She held his hand and stroked his palm with her fingers.

"Except for you." He put an arm around her, heedless of passing strollers. "You're the one solitary beam of light in my darkness."

"I'll always be here for you." Then she looked at her watch. "But now I must get back." They found her a taxi and when she was gone the well of his emotions overflowed. *Out of the depths I have cried to You, O Lord. I was yours, all yours, in soul and body, dedicated to training your future priests, faithful to my vows, firm in chastity despite fierce temptations, constant in prayer, a model to my charges. So why did you do this to me? The cruelest of calumnies, destruction of my character, loss of my livelihood, scorn of my confreres. And, most perverse of all, you removed Yourself from me. The rest I might have withstood if You had stood by me. But You, too, Lord? Can You blame me for cleaving to Deirdre? We all need someone to love us. I once had You, but when You went, to whom should I turn? Even now, if you come back I swear that I'll leave her and return to You.*

If that's what You really want, of course. Though I have to tell You that I do love her, Lord, and I have to wonder why I should not, even were You to take me back in Your favor. Surely You have nothing to fear from human love. All that nonsense about You being a jealous God I don't believe any more. Jealousy is an anal-retentive state of mind; how could the Lover Who gave His life for us all indulge in such petty meanness? Jealousy has to do with love as cancer has to do with life – it's an aberration that destroys what is beautiful and good.

You said love one another; this is My commandment. So if You're not a jealous God, what purpose could You have for barring Your priests from love of woman? Perhaps You have no reason, Lord. Perhaps You don't so wish to keep us. Perhaps we're just paying for the bad conscience of Augustine, whose ancient response to guilt has been lacquered and glossed till it shines like virtue. But must I go to my grave frustrated and sad because a man long ago was ashamed of his lust?

Feck it, Lord – excuse the French – I can no longer accept that that's what you want from me. And I won't. I, Ignatius Lally, hereby solemnly state that I firmly believe – against all arid decrees of dried-up divines and all sterile proscriptions of ancient misogynists – that You, my only Lord and God, do indeed want me to extend my love to all human persons, and do not wish me to exclude either emotion or passion from the purview of my caring.

Therefore, in the absence of a specific indication from You to the contrary, I will offer my love to Deirdre McCarthy.

Yes, I know, Lord: technically we're talking adultery in this particular case. But really! Isn't she stuck in a loveless union, in a relationship with a man who has shown that he hates her? So how can I not conclude that their marriage no longer exists? Because how could You demand a union of hate in defiance of your command to love?

I'm done, Lord. Resolved. I'll think no more on the subject. If You don't agree, it's up to You to let me know.

His God remained silent.

VIOLATION

The first three weeks of September went by like a dull headache that stifles pleasure but does not incapacitate. He returned to living with Dominick and Aoife after Kennedy had called Dominick and said they had dropped the car-theft charge against Father Ignatius. Veronica expressed regret at his leaving: "I'll miss you," she said emotionally. "I got used to having you around." The McElligotts were delighted to have him back, they said, but he assured them that he'd find his own place as soon as he had saved enough money from his job with JJ to rent a flat. More than anything he needed space and solitude to rethink his life.

JJ found a tiny desk for him and placed it next to his own in his small office. He also bought a secondhand computer for his use. The *Journal* had to be out before the end of September, he said, if they were to have any chance of selling a decent number of copies.

"Do you have any idea how many different magazines and periodicals and reviews and the like this blessed country is currently churning out?"

"Not a clue," Ignatius admitted. "Fifty or sixty, maybe. I'd imagine that most of the stuff you see in the shops comes from

England and America."

"Two hundred and seventy-five at last count," JJ announced the figures slowly, with a kind of morose satisfaction. "From this country! And the number is growing. There are over twenty religious publications alone, would you believe?"

"So what chance do we have?" He was feeling very down, still learning to use the computer, missing Deirdre something fierce, and wondering daily if he wasn't going into a state of clinical depression.

"There's a fair amount of interest in serious religious publications, mind you," JJ said. "*The Furrow* and *Doctrine and Life*, for example, have been around forever. And of course the Js put out *Studies* four times a year. But there's nothing out there of the sort that we're going to put on the stands."

They worked long hours each day to get it ready. Ignatius typed and edited and scrambled to learn about formatting and design and size and margins and illustrations and the cover and all that went into getting the *Journal* into the format the reader would see. Though his heart wasn't in the work he stuck to it doggedly, reminding himself that the money JJ was paying him was his ticket to independence. And when copies of the finished product were delivered from the printer he felt a touch of pride in having helped to produce this elegant publication. He even felt cheered that JJ had placed his name below his own on the inside page, with the title of *Assistant Editor*.

But all the while, lowering at him through his waking hours, was fear for his future. Did Ignatius Lally have a future? Any hope at all of continuing in his life's calling? Despite the continued absence of his God he was a priest and wanted to remain a priest. But what chance did he have of removing this Damoclean sword that Padhraig McCarthy held over his head? And even if by some miracle it were taken away, what then? God help him, he loved Deirdre McCarthy and could no longer envision his life without her.

He heard from her a couple of times a week. The fund-raising office had been transferred to Dublin at the beginning of September and she had reluctantly decided to quit. "He'd crucify you if I left and went to Dublin," she told him in her last phone call from the office. She daren't ring him from home, she said, because Padhraig would know when he got the phone bill. So she bought phone cards now and rang from Clyard whenever it was safe. He was getting nastier by the day, she said. Sometimes she wondered if he were really sane, with his muttering to himself when the children weren't around, and his obsession about knowing where she was at all times.

"Neither you nor I can go on like this indefinitely," he told her the last time she rang. "We'll have to do some serious thinking and make some long-term plans. Just know that I'm committed to you," he added, "no matter what happens."

Padhraig McCarthy, as the weeks went by, felt less and less secure that his nemesis was locked up, despite the archbishop's assurance. Or, if indeed he *had* been locked up, that he remained so. He experienced a brief mitigation of anguish when his wife quit her job: Lally on the loose might well have been screwing her at the fund-raising office, but he'd not be able to see her now that she spent her days at home. Even *he* wouldn't dare assail Padhraig McCarthy's fortress.

That security, however, vanished with the thought that Lally might still be in the vicinity and that Deirdre might be sneaking out to illicit trysts when he himself was at work. Three late September mornings on the way to his office he parked down a side road in case she might be waiting for him to leave before racing off to her lover. The third morning his vigilance was rewarded when, fifteen minutes after he pulled in, she flew by in her red Toyota. He followed her into Clyard. She pulled into a parking spot on Main Street and went straight to a telephone kiosk. Ten minutes she spent there while he watched and seethed and horribly imagined. Lally, without a doubt. Why else would she drive all the way to Clyard to make a phone call? When she left the kiosk she got into her car again and headed back towards home, passing right by him as she went.

No point in confronting her: she'd simply deny. She had got awfully cocky lately, ever since she told him she'd walk out if he did a thing to Lally. More than likely Lally *was* locked up but had access to a phone. That situation could be remedied. From his office he rang Tighmor. No, his Grace was not available; could anyone else be of assistance? Ah yes, of course; and what would it be in reference to? His Grace would know? Right so, she'd see that he got the message. Late that afternoon when he returned to his office after a round of inseminations, a message to contact his Grace awaited him. He rang. The archbishop's tone was snappish: "what is it this time, Padhraig?"

"It appears that my wife and Father Lally are in constant phone contact." If he had caught her once she was most likely doing it all the time.

"Indeed. And what do you want me to do about it?"

Donnellan better watch that short temper of his or he'd very soon be in deep trouble with Padhraig McCarthy. "I suggest you contact Father Lally's superiors and have them take the phone away from him."

There was a long pause before the archbishop replied. "I wish it were that simple, Padhraig." The man's tone suddenly conciliatory. "Unfortunately, I have just been informed by the superior that Father Lally has refused to go to his post at the Congregation's Mother House as ordered. However, I have also been assured that he remains in Dublin, so there is no likelihood that he will establish any physical contact with your wife." Another lengthy pause. "As regards the matter of phone calls, I'm afraid you'll just have to rein in your wife if you want to prevent them from taking place."

"I'm going straight to the Gardai, that's what I'm doing," Padhraig hurled into the receiver before slamming it back in its cradle. But he didn't. Instead, he drove home at a speed that would have gotten himself in trouble with the guardians of the law had they spotted him. Deirdre was in the kitchen making dinner. Of the children only Gemma was around, sitting at the kitchen table writing. "We have to talk," he said abruptly to his wife.

"Shoot." She continued peeling a carrot without so much as looking at him.

"Not here." With a tremendous effort he restrained himself from striking her there and then. "Upstairs."

"Can't you see I'm busy," she said sharply. "You'll be looking for your dinner in half an hour, and God help everyone if it's a minute late."

"Upstairs. Now!"

She looked at him then, wiped her hands on a towel, and followed him. "Keep an eye on the potatoes," she called back to Gemma as she was going out the door.

"In here." He held open their bedroom door. She shrugged

and walked in. He shut the door.

"We're being very masterful this evening, aren't we?" Her sarcasm suddenly blinded his reason, blotted out the stinging recriminations he had prepared on the drive home. All that mattered now was punishment, battering her sinful body into submission. He pushed her forcefully down onto the bed. "How dare you," she yelled and tried to get up. He tugged at her sandals and threw them on the floor, slapped her hard across the face and pushed her down again, unzipped her skirt and pulled it off, grabbed her blouse and tore it open. "Stop it this minute, Padhraig," she commanded as he started to pull down her underwear. But she went limp and silent while he raped her, her head turned sideways and her eyes closed tight. Neither did she move when he finished and raised himself up. She was still prone when he left the room.

She rang in the morning. Ignatius was still asleep when Aoife brought him a portable phone. "I'm in Clyard." Her voice was strained. "I'm driving up to Dublin. Can you meet me at Eavan's about two o'clock?"

"Of course. Are you all right?"

"I'll tell you everything when I see you." She gave him her sister's address on Terenure Road West and rang off in a hurry. He worried about her while he washed and dressed. There was no doubting the distress in her tone. So what had Padhraig done to her this time?

Aoife volunteered the loan of her car. "'Twould take you forever to get to Terenure by bus," she said. "You'd have to go into town and out again." He accepted.

Eavan had a detached house with parking in the driveway.

Deirdre's car was near the front door. She herself, watching from the step, came slowly down the path and into his arms when he stepped out of the car. "Let me look at you." He held her from him. The darkness of her left cheekbone leaped out in ugly contrast to her pastel skin-tones. Not even an uncustomary application of rouge could hide the welt. "He hit you?" The savagery in his voice surprised even himself: he had not expected physical violence.

She hid her wounded face deep in his shoulder. "He did worse than that, I'm afraid. But it's over now. I'm not going back." He held her tight until the gentle pulse of sobbing ceased. "Let's go inside," she said then. The house was dim: dark wooden panels and heavy drapes restricted the light of a sunny day. "Eavan is at work, but Gemma is here with me." They found her daughter in the kitchen at the end of the hall, sitting at the table sipping a mineral through a straw and leafing listlessly through a magazine. "Father Lally is here," Deirdre told her, with an effort at cheerfulness.

"Hello, Father." Gemma smiled briefly, waved a languid hand, but made no effort to get up.

"Father and I have some things to talk about, pet. We'll sit in the front parlor. You'll be able to amuse yourself for a while?" The mother's tone was solicitous.

"I'll be fine." The girl waved weakly again and returned to leafing pages.

"She's still in shock, poor girl." Deirdre shut the parlor door. "She was downstairs listening when he ..." She choked, coughed, tried to smile reassuringly through the tears.

"Tell me about it."

She sat stiffly in a mushy leather-covered chair and told him briefly of the rape. "I feel so humiliated, as if I had been dragged through shit and left lying on the road for everyone to stare at. I just had to leave."

"Absolutely," he said. "You didn't have any choice." He wanted to hug her but felt she didn't want to be touched at that moment.

She searched his eyes. "You realize of course that this may precipitate his going to the ..." She shook her head. "He's just such a horrible man when you go against him. I wish I could say he won't do it, but ..."

"We'll take our chances on that." Though he didn't want to think at this moment what the consequences would be for himself. "The important thing is that you're safe now."

"I'm going to find a flat for Gem and me." She bowed her head. "For you, too, if you'll stay with us."

"Flats are terribly expensive in Dublin these days. At least until you get a job." Afraid to address that invitation. The answer to his fantasies, emotional and erotic. But did he dare accept? And why not? Hadn't he spoken to his God and let Him know his new-found belief in the moral rectitude of such behavior? Ah, but it was different when you actually faced the reality, wasn't it? We're all so brave till we face the fire. Was his faith in his rationalization strong enough to overcome a lifetime of faith in the strictures of Mother Church?

"Money isn't a problem for the moment," she told him. "Thanks to Gem."

"Oh!" He absolutely must not put off an answer any longer.

"Listen to this." She tried to smile, but her eyes remained sad. "I don't know what your ethical code will make of it but it's perfectly all right by mine."

"Sounds intriguing. Shall I don my moral theologian's hat?"

"She knew where Padhraig hid his money. Gem is a sneak;

she loves rummaging in other people's belongings. Many's the time I've had to yell at her for going through my drawers. Fortunately, she went through her father's stuff as well."

"I'm surprised he'd keep his money in the house?"

"I was, too. But I remember him telling me one time that farmers sometimes paid him in cash; something to do with their taxes. And our man, probably to hide it from the tax lads, too, has been keeping this money in a jar – literally in a jampot. At the bottom of a case full of instruments and things that he always carries with him on the job. I wouldn't be found dead going through the stuff – God knows where those instruments have been – but Gem checked it out and came across the loot."

"And you have it?" Wouldn't there be some sort of twisted justice in living off money that Padhraig McCarthy had cheated the tax man out of?

"He always leaves his bag in the hall when he comes home so he can grab it on the way out the door in the morning. So last night after he went to bed Gem sneaked down and took the money from the jar. It smelled of pigs but there was more than three thousand punt in it. Would you believe?" Her laugh was harsh, vindictive. "Then this morning we were terrified that he'd find it missing, but he grabbed the bag and left in a hurry without saying a word."

They discussed housing, about which he knew just a little from the *To Let* advertisements he had been perusing in the *Independent* and *Times*. Flats were hard to find, he said, so she might be better off renting a house, though these were running six hundred and up per month. But he held off on saying anything about sharing her dwelling; though he wanted desperately to say yes, each time it reached the tip of his tongue he pulled back. Until now he had merely sinned, but by moving in he'd be living in sin. There was a sort of finality to the act: if celibacy was the symbol of priesthood, co-habitation was its formal renunciation. However, he soon felt himself closing in on the Rubicon bridge, feeling the momentum in his tightened muscles and the rush of blood to his cheeks when he thought about it.

"I'm coming with you," he blurted, catching himself off guard before he had time to retreat.

She looked at him and the love in her sad eyes confirmed his choice. "Thank you," she said. "I was counting on that."

She couldn't stay more than a night or two in Eavan's house, she told him then: even though to stall Padhraig she had left a note saying she and Gem were visiting Eavan, after a day or two he'd guess she was gone for good and might come up and try to bring them back. In which case there'd be a terrible rumpus: Eavan might go for him with a poker – she couldn't stand the sight of her brother-in-law – and they'd probably have to end up calling the Gardai before someone got killed.

A gentle tap on the door preceded Gemma's entrance. She stepped in and walked briskly to her mother with just a side glance at the priest. All legs and arms in a green mini-skirt and purple tank top. "I just thought of something, Mammy." She looked again at Ignatius, as though wondering if he were trustworthy.

"Father Lally knows what's going on," Deirdre told her firmly.

"It just crossed my mind that Daddy probably gives change to people from the ... the jampot, you know, and if that's the case he might have missed the money already." Her eyebrows bobbed nervously up and down as she spoke.

"Shit!" Her mother screwed up her face and nibbled her

thumb. "You're right. I should have thought of that before." She looked across at Ignatius. "In which case we'll need somewhere else to stay in a hurry. He may even be on his way up right now."

"I might be able to find you a place for a few nights," said he who was living on the goodwill of others. "I'll ask Dominick and Aoife if you can stay with them. I can go back to Veronica's until we find our own place."

He felt the girl's unspoken question before her mother answered it. "Father Lally will be staying with us when we find a house. He's homeless, too, at the moment."

"Oh!" Then Gemma said gamely, "It'll be nice to have you with us, Father."

Aoife was out when he rang, so he tried Dominick. "Certainly. We might even be able to accommodate you all," his friend threw in, though unconvincingly.

"Not at all." Their third bedroom was Dom's home office and the fourth was Aoife's studio. "I'll ask Veronica."

"Can't wait to get back there, huh?" Dominick's chuckle was lecherous. "What have you got anyway, Lally, that I don't have – that has the women falling all over you?"

After Deirdre had rung Eavan they re-packed their suitcases and followed Ignatius back to Mount Merrion. "Dominick told me all about your situation." Aoife was out the door to greet them. "I hope you don't mind sharing a room." Her tone was apologetic.

After dinner Ignatius rang Veronica. Of course he'd be welcome. With just the slightest tinge of excitement in her voice to made him feel uncomfortable. But where else could he go? He used Aoife's parting hug to justify embracing Deirdre and Gemma briefly before Dominick whisked him off. They stopped at a pub en route.

"Could she charge him with rape?" The thought had been on Ignatius's mind since Deirdre told him what happened.

"She certainly can and I hope she will. Two pints," Dominick told the young man who came to take their order. "They abolished the marital exemption in relation to rape back in 1990. That was a terrible law altogether; it actually allowed a husband to rape his wife."

"So you'll bring it up with her then?" McCarthy convicted of raping his wife would hardly be credible accusing a priest of raping his daughter.

"I will indeed. I was just waiting for the right moment to discuss the matter with her."

They were silent then till the drinks arrived. "Slainte!" Ignatius toasted. "By the way, when Deirdre finds a house I'm thinking of moving in with her," he added casually.

"Grand. We'll be sorry to see you go of course." He drank deep of his pint. "You've become one of the family, you know."

Ignatius put down his glass and hugged his body with folded arms. "I feel that moving in with Deirdre is tantamount to walking out on my priesthood. And a great part of me doesn't want to leave. Sometimes I'm horrified that I could even think about quitting."

"I understand," Dominic said; "having gone through it myself."

"A couple of months ago I was in charge of the formation of novices. So how could I have got from there to here in such a short time?"

"Life is full of surprises." McElligott chugged his stout. "Sometimes it's a hoor."

"Tell me, what was going through *your* head, leading up to

your getting out?"

Dominick sat back and gazed at the ceiling. "You want to know the thought that was uppermost in my mind? The uselessness of it all. The feeling that what I was doing as a priest was serving no worthwhile purpose to man or beast. That was when I realized I had lost the faith."

"And you had no feelings of guilt about it? I mean, was God nudging you not to do it, or anything like that?"

There was melancholy in Dominick's smile. "God had long before that taken a holiday, Ignatius. I hadn't felt His presence for years. And He never came back, either then or since. So I've learned to live without Him."

"He has left me, too." Ignatius felt he was going to cry as he made the admission. "If He's there at all – and now I'm beginning to wonder – He seems to be *telling* me to get out. In fact it looks like He's throwing me out."

They were sitting side by side on the sofa, sipping tea from mugs.. Veronica's smile was warm as she turned her head and surveyed him. He said, "It'll only be for a few days till we find a house."

"We?" Pupil contraction and heightened cheek color bespoke more than idle curiosity. But when he told her of his intention to move in with Deirdre and Gemma all she said was, "so you've given up?" Without a sign of emotion.

"I don't know yet." Liar! He had definitely decided.

"Maybe I can talk to you then?" The eyes turned dark. "I mean talk seriously, not the polite nonsense that usually passes for conversation."

"By all means." Was this her *cri de coeur,* the response to which might make his priestly mission seem still worthwhile?

"I'd like to talk about God," she said somberly.

"Okay." So close to him that he could sense the warmth of her body. "Though I'm not sure how much help I can give you; God and I are on the outs at the moment."

She laughed, a delicious tinkle that sparked an urge in him to reach out and touch her. "Welcome to the club, Father. He and I have been squabbling for years. Which I've never really minded because I love a good argument. The problem is that lately I've begun to wonder – and this is what I want to talk to you about – I wonder if I'm really just talking to myself when I think I'm conversing with Him?"

"An interesting question." Suddenly he wanted her, with a ferocity he could barely suppress. Was this what they called base animal lust? He liked Veronica of course, but had never experienced any of the erotic feeling for her that drew him to Deirdre. Yet ...

"In the convent we talked a lot about the presence of God, and I thought at times I could actually touch Him there at my side. Especially during Holy Hour when I'd feel warm and mushy and want to reach out and put my arms around Jesus and bury my face in His bosom. Did you ever have that feeling?"

"The spiritual consolations of the illuminative way," he pronounced. "Just a short time ago I discoursed on the very subject with my novices." Sexual consolation from her was what he needed at this moment. "But it seems somewhat meaningless now."

"Thank you for saying that, Father." When she patted his arm it was as if a giant brush of goose-down had flitted across his body.

"Call me Ignatius," he croaked.

"Thank you, Ignatius. I always hated titles." She moved to the end of the sofa and sat cross-legged, with her legs under her dress, facing him. "But back to God. Do you think there really is a God? Because I'm not sure any more."

He nodded as one who knew what she meant. "I always took for granted that God *is*, that He made us and owns us, that we are beholden to Him and owe him worship. I had my first conversation with Him when I was seven; I remember it still. And over the years He was always there for me, whether I was good or bad. Until recently. He left me two months ago."

"But you still believe in Him, don't you?" Her tone hinting that she might prefer a negative answer.

"I honestly don't know. He grows dimmer to me with each passing day. So I'm learning to live without Him."

"Oh God!" She covered her face with her hands. "That's exactly the way I've been feeling." She uncovered and looked at him. "But I was hoping you might have something positive to say. Because I don't think I can live without God."

This last was a wail of anguish, to which he could offer no relief. After which they gradually descended to saws and aphorisms – no atheists in foxholes, the death of God, validity of all religions, if God didn't exist we'd have to invent him, the weakness of God after Auschwitz, God does not play dice – till the lust in Ignatius gave slow way to tiredness and his eyes began to droop and Veronica said reluctantly maybe it was time they went to bed.

INQUISITION

Although Padhraig McCarthy soon discovered that the money in his pot was gone it wasn't because he had been looking for change. Every evening on arrival home, after he shut off the engine and removed the key and before he opened the car door, he'd undo the clasp on his instrument case, push his hand to the bottom and feel for the comfort of his secret cache. Deirdre was right in thinking that he kept it there to save on taxes. But the taxes were only a part of his reason. The son of a well-to-do farmer and never in his life lacking for things material, Padhraig, nevertheless, was obsessed from childhood by a need to hoard his money. Even at boarding school, to which he was sent off at the beginning of each term with a comfortable allowance by a father who wanted his son to look as good as the best at Saint Fursa's, he spent with the utmost care and was known to bring home again most of what he had been given. For Deirdre, it was a major cross in their marriage to be always having to wheedle money out of him. Eventually, through persistence and formal budgeting – after a few major flare-ups she had developed the practice of typing up each month's needs in advance, and then presenting him with a detailed report of how the money was actually spent – she was able to get what was necessary to take care of the children and household expenses. But for her own personal needs – clothes, accessories, spending money and the like – she could never get anything like an adequate allowance. Hence the job at the fund-raising office, of which pittance pay she obstinately and successfully refused to make accounting to her husband.

When Padhraig's probing fingers failed to make contact with the contents of the jampot on this particular evening his immediate reaction was that he must have left the money somewhere. Which was a terrible shock to his system, for was anyone ever honest when it came to lost money found? But it took only a moment's reflection to conclude that he hadn't removed the money from the jar all day. Who, then, could have taken it? Whoever it was could have done so for one purpose only. Which thought produced an audible groan of despair from deep in his gullet. Further reflection on the day's events, however, led him to the firm conviction that no one had any opportunity to delve a dishonest hand into his case. From which he logically inferred that the jampot money had to be missing when he set out on his journey this morning. Which inference, since he had verified the money's presence when he returned home last evening, forced the conclusion that it had been removed while his case was sitting in the hallway at the foot of the stairs. If that were so – and it must be so – then the nefarious deed had been done between the time he arrived home last night and the time he left this morning. And since during that time all external doors and windows of the house had been locked – he was a stickler for security and always checked them before retiring for the night – the money had to have been removed by a member of his family.

Gemma, the rummager, was his primary suspect as he steamed full throttle through the hall door. Though never hitherto known to pilfer, her habit of searching through other people's belongings made her the most likely candidate. "Gem," he bawled as he dropped his money-less case at the foot of the stairs. "I want to talk to you. Immediately," he added stentoriously when his command was greeted with silence.

The kitchen door opened. Fiona emerged. "They're gone, Daddy." Languorously, with barely concealed satisfaction.

"Who's gone?" he snapped. His daughter's air of quiet possession, grown ever more cloying since the event, was beginning to get on his nerves.

"Mammy and Gem. Mammy left a note saying they're gone to visit Aunt Eavan." Fiona's tone implied that she, for one, had doubts about the truth of that note.

"What! Gem is supposed to be in school."

Fiona's shoulders shot up in a dramatic shrug. "When I got up they were gone and the note was on the table." She herself was starting University in Limerick next week. "They took the car, too. Mammy never takes the car to Dublin."

"Where's Cathal?" His son might be able to shed light on what Padhraig already feared was criminal behavior on the part of his wife and younger daughter.

"In his room, playing with his computer; where else?" She lowered her voice to a whisper. "He mitched from school today. He said he heard Mammy tell Gem they'd be off as soon as he left to get the bus. So he hid down the road until he saw the car pass and then came home again." She raised a pleading hand. "Please don't tell him I told you."

He looked at his watch: only half six: he had come home

early this evening. "I'm going to Dublin now," he told his daughter. "I'll be late getting home, so don't wait up."

"But Daddy, I cooked dinner for –"

"I'll grab a bite on the way." At the door he turned. "In case your mother rings don't let on where I'm going."

With the improved roads he could now make the hundred and three miles to the outskirts of Dublin in a bit over two hours. Add another fifteen minutes from the Naas Road and he'd be at his sister-in-law's by nine o'clock. By God, he'd give them something to remember. They'd be out of that bloody house and on the road before they knew what hit them. He'd have them back home by midnight. And then he'd see who took his money. She'd get more than he gave her last night, that was for sure. Gemma'd get a few wallops, too, especially if it was she who did the stealing. But no visible marks, mind you, in case they called the Gardai. Domestic violence they called it nowadays when a man disciplined his family. Fucking codology, but you had to play their game to stay out of trouble. So you hit them where it hurt but left no marks; that was the established wisdom in these politically correct times.

Rush hour traffic was over by the time he reached the Naas Road. Beyond Rathcoole he picked up the N81. Further along he turned right onto Greenhills Road which took him down through Kimmage to Terenure Road West. The car in front of Eavan's house was not Deirdre's; she had probably parked on the street. He pulled into the driveway, got out quietly and rang the bell. Surprise was on his side; he'd have them running before they recovered from the shock of his appearance.

Eavan answered the door. "Padhraig!" Surprised, though not shocked. "What are you doing here? And at this time of night?"

"Can I come in?" Be on top of them before they knew it.

"Of course! By all means. If you came ten minutes later I'd have been in bed." She had on a long pink robe.

He stepped inside and she closed the door. "Where's Deirdre?" Calm but firm; showing her he was not about to take any nonsense.

"Deirdre?" Her expression displayed astonishment. "Deirdre's not here, Padhraig. Why would you think she was?" Then a cloud of worry crossed her face. "*Should* she be here? Oh my God, I hope nothing has ... When was she supposed to arrive?"

He wanted to yell at her quit trying to cod me. But her so obviously genuine puzzlement stopped him cold. "She didn't ring you to say she was coming?"

"When I talked to her last week she said she might be up sometime soon. But that's the last I heard from her."

Could he believe her? She didn't like him, that he knew. So it was more than possible she was lying. What was certain, however, was that she read his face. "If you don't believe me go ahead and search the house." With a wild wave of her arm around the hall. The old semi-hostile Eavan who never had any time for him.

"Why wouldn't I believe you?" Don't let her know you're suspicious or upset. "It's just that she left a note this morning saying she was coming up to visit you. She took Gemma with her, and that girl is supposed to be in school. She wasn't doing too well last year, you know."

The phone on the hall table rang. Eavan picked it up. "Hello." He was watching her. Knotted brow followed by sudden smile. "Well hello, Tom; it's so nice to hear from you." A listening pause, then "Tom, can I ring you back in just a short while. My brother-in-law is here at the moment. Right so. 'Bye." She put the phone down and smiled at him. "Sorry for the interruption. So you were saying that you came up to take Gemma back?"

"Right. Only now I'm wondering where they can be?"

"Well, I can't possibly imagine." Her expression of worry was patently fake. "But you know Deirdre: she can take care of herself."

He wanted to throttle the information out of her then. Damned well she knew where they were. Without doubt somewhere with fucking Lally. Oh indeed! Fucking Lally, that's what she was doing all right. He'd kill them both when he caught up with them.

"Does she have any other friends in Dublin that she might stay with?" Though he knew the question was futile.

"Well of course she has lots of old girl friends. After all, she was a Dublin girl herself before you dragged her off to the back of beyond. But she always comes here on her visits, so I don't have any idea who else she might stay with."

Shit fuck damn blast! He'd better go. Behind that sphinx face was a woman laughing at him. He felt like planting his fist in her puss as she opened the door for him – and without so much as an offer of a bite to eat or a bed for the night. Nothing for it but to go back home. He drove angrily, maniacally, cursing slow drivers, passing where he could, tailgating when he could not, ignoring the hunger that was gnawing at him. Back on the dual carriageway he settled down to a fast drive and a slow burn as he contemplated his next move.

Ignatius was shaving in the morning when Deirdre rang with the news of her husband's visit to Eavan. "We'll have to assume that he's going to go ahead with his threat," he lamented, and sat on the couch, the left side of his face still unshaven.

"I'm so sorry," she said. "I really should have stayed."

"No way!" he dissented. "You must not be made pay for your husband's hatred of me. Anyway, it's something I have to face sooner or later, so it might as well be now." But the coward in him wanted to vomit those pseudo-brave words. He was not at all ready to have his life destroyed. Though in the past two months it had been turned upside down, made awkward, stressful, distressing, he *had*, nevertheless, remained a free man. Now he was about to be mangled in the machinery of the law: his liberty taken away, control of his life removed. He'd be held up to public odium as a sexual molester and condemned to a punishment he didn't deserve. This last aspect was actually the worst: the unbearable pain of unfairness seared his soul more than all other horrible prospects. They had no right, for he had done no wrong to merit such fierce reprisal. His inmost being revolted, against the law and against Padhraig McCarthy. In all his hitherto life he had never seriously considered harming anyone. He knew theoretically that he was capable of it – as all of us are, he admitted – given condign provocation. But not till this moment did he actually harbor in his mind an unqualified desire to end the life of a fellow human being. If McCarthy were here this minute and he, Ignatius Lally, had the means, he would without doubt take the bleddy bugger's life.

He had barely finished breakfast when Aoife rang. Would he come for dinner this evening? Deirdre and Gemma would be there of course. Would he ever? That would be lovely, Aoife said; Dominick would pick him up at Veronica's on his way home, at about six. Then she let him have the bad news: she had just received a phone call from Father Kennedy. Did she know where he might contact Father Lally? No, she did not. Well, would she tell Father Lally that Monsignor Fogarty from the Archbishop of Dublin's office wished to speak with him as soon as possible. He left a number for Father Lally to ring. "I thought I should let you know," Aoife ended apologetically.

He debated whether he should respond: was it just another ploy on Kennedy's part? Or was the AB from Tighmor pulling strings with his Dublin counterpart? At first he decided not to, then on impulse rang, overcome by a reaction to an inner suggestion of cowardice. Also perhaps by pleasant memories of Monsignor Fogarty. Professor emeritus of metaphysics at UCD, the Fog had been a University institution unto himself. Large and genial, with a magnificent bald head that was known to his philosophy students as the Noble Dome, he initiated generation after generation of priests-in-the-making into the mysteries of epistemology, cosmology and ontology. He knew each cleric by name and if in later years they met he could instantly recall both name and years of study.

Father Lally, was it? The voice at the other end was female, sweet, and cheerful as the sunny day outside. Monsignor would like to meet with him as soon as possible. He was available at two o'clock today if Father Lally had the time to spare? He had? Wasn't that grand altogether. Did he know where the office was? He didn't? Well here were the directions. Lovely. They'd expect him then at two.

He had to take several buses. Monsignor opened the door himself, beaming delight. Much older than he remembered him, greatly wrinkled, slightly shrunken, still sprightly on his feet, still recognizably the Fog; and still proud possessor of that noble dome. His office was as ordered as the philosopher's mind. Two walls of books neatly stacked, gleaming desk top bare but for the ubiquitous computer monitor and mouse, and a pad of paper; an array of photographs on a long credenza. He sat Ignatius in one of the visitors' chairs and himself in the other, eschewing the high-back seat behind the desk. "Twenty-five years, if my memory serves me right?" Eyebrows raised in childlike expectation of approval.

"On the button." Ignatius could only smile, despite his apprehension about the purpose of the meeting. There had always been a quality about the Fog that incited one to smile. Not *at* him of course, but with him: he seemed to carry around in his person not only humor but the secret to humor, such that as long as you were in his presence you, too, might share in this extraordinary gift.

"You were one of my best philosophers, Ignatius." Monsignor smiled faintly, as if remembering with pride some extraordinary intellectual achievement by his erstwhile student. "I had hoped you might have been allowed to do at least your MA and then go on to study theology in Rome. You'd have made a brilliant professor." He nodded his head and pursed his lips as if to reinforce the rightness of his judgment.

"I joined up to become a missionary," Ignatius pointed out. "Though I would have enjoyed teaching philosophy." He was surprised at the level of regret in this statement.

"I'll let you in on a little secret: you were one of only three of my boys that I ever tipped to become bishops." Again the soft smile playing about the lips and the friendly eyes caressing the student. "The other two did actually don the purple."

"I'm sorry I let you down."

"Oh you didn't let me down, Ignatius, not at all. Two out of three is not bad guessing." The smile was roguish. "But, like Marlon Brando in that film about the waterfront, you could have been a contender." Then, suddenly serious, he added, "anyway, the episcopacy is a very heavy burden; especially in today's world." The weight of sadness in the final phrase contrasted darkly with the previous banter.

"They've been taking a lot of heat from the media these past few years."

"Indeed." The Fog's head was bent, his eyes lowered, as if he were meditating on the perfidy of the modern world. "Not only the media, mind you: many priests seem to have forgotten the obedience they owe their Superiors." Eyes suddenly raised, gaze firm, in the manner of the professor making an important point in a philosophical discussion.

Was this another ploy of Kennedy's, who himself of course had sat at the feet of the Fog? "It's the era of personal responsibility, Monsignor," he said. "The younger people today, including priests and religious, are more and more taking charge of their own lives, and are willing to take the blame or praise before God and man for the decisions they make."

"Ah yes." The Fog sighed and the little smile returned. "The young, with their impetuosity, and very often indeed their idealism, are ever a source of worry and disturbance to the older generation." He gazed at Ignatius, his expression almost puckish. "And where do you fall yourself, Ignatius, in this generational dichotomy?"

In metaphysics tutorials the Fog would sometimes unravel an abstruse theory with a few simple questions that led a student to see the fallacy of his own reasoning. Ignatius had the feeling at this moment that he was being led into just such a trap. So be it: he would state his views and see where they led. Though for many years he had instinctively tended to favor personal responsibility over blind obedience, he had never, until his conversations with JJ, given the matter serious conscious thought. So it was as if now he was hearing the voice of another respond that "I myself am firmly with the younger generation, Monsignor. I believe we must each be held accountable for our acts. The horrors of this century have shown us all too well the folly of blind obedience."

He had to hand it to the Fog: not the slightest hint of discomfort at what must have been, to his profoundly traditional perspective, an unequivocally heretical viewpoint; and coming from a man he had once believed to be *episcopabilis*. "Indeed, Ignatius. And there are many who would agree with you. Including even some bishops." He paused. The expression dropped into meditation mode. Eventually, eyes on the floor and with the tone he would use to put forth a question in cosmology, he asked, "so, in this Journal of which you are the new assistant editor you will no doubt advocate freedom of thought over adherence to dogma?"

So that was it! But the new edition wouldn't be out till tomorrow; he and JJ had just finished sticking on the mailing addresses yesterday. So how had the Fog already come to know his new title?

Monsignor seemed to divine his thoughts. "We, too, have our canaries, Ignatius, just as they had on the waterfront. I've always been very fond of that film." He paused again to change expression. "In my old age his Grace has placed on me the burden of seeing to the purity of doctrine being taught in the diocese. So I thought it might be just as well to chat with you about your new position."

"I understand."

"Would you like to tell me a little bit about it." An avuncular plea for a very special favor. Whereupon Ignatius did explain to him, in very general terms, what JJ had in mind for the Journal. Nothing the Fog wouldn't have known already of course from perusing previous editions; after all, it must have been he who had threatened JJ with excommunication.

"We believe," he concluded, "that it is time to not only *allow* people to think actively and questioningly about their religious faith and what it means to them, but to positively encourage them to do so. Even," he added defiantly, "if that means challenging authority or dogma."

The Fog remained silent after he finished, head down, legs crossed, arms folded. The only sign of life he exhibited was the slow rhythmic raising and lowering of his free-floating shoe. "You're embarking on a slippery slope, Ignatius," he pronounced suddenly, straightening in his chair and uncrossing his legs slowly and with apparent discomfort. "I understand what you're saying and I do appreciate the concerns that are driving you and your friend in the direction you're taking. Nevertheless, you and your friend and your followers are implicitly rejecting the Church's *magisterium* – her infallible teaching authority – thereby becoming just another protestant sect."

What could he say? Infallibility was *the* stumbling block for Catholics in the pursuit of truth. It stifled discussion, the search for answers, honest disagreement, everything that was conducive to finding the real God. So he murmured platitudes about changing times, an educated laity, the danger of repressing opinions, the necessity of dialogue.

Monsignor listened, hand to forehead, as if hearing a confession. He stayed that way till Ignatius had run out of words. But when he looked up there was a bleakness in the soft eyes that Ignatius had never seen there before. "It's my duty to tell you, Father," he said ever so gently, "that if you continue to be associated with this Journal and continue to publish along the lines you have told me just now, you stand a very good chance of being formally excommunicated by the Holy See. Such cases have happened, even in the recent past." He nodded his head several times, in sadness and in affirmation of his solemn words.

"I hear you," Ignatius responded. But he said nothing further on the subject. The Fog chatted some more about former students he had recently met, and then about his own impending retirement. His jovial tone was back, as if all he had just said had been blown away on the wind. And he said not a word about Padhraig McCarthy's accusation.

ULTIMATUM

Physical weariness kept Padhraig McCarthy asleep till eight, an extremely late hour for a man who habitually left the house at seven. Even after waking he was slow to rise: for most of an hour he lay there on his back, simmering, stewing, coming to a slow boil over the events of the previous day. That his wife was with the hated Lally he had no doubt whatever: why else would she walk out on him like that? Right then! So accept the fact that she had left him for the fucking renegade priest, and decide what to do that would be most effective for himself and most punishing for the pair of them.

His first desire was to kill: slowly, excruciatingly, listening to them screaming to be put out of their misery. Only their agonizing deaths could excise the pain they had inflicted on him. He let himself savor their torments: Lally hanging upside down, disemboweled like the pigs his father used to slaughter; Deirdre stretched taut, naked, on a rack, her face contorted as he had seen her in childbirth. There was relief in playing and replaying these grim scenarios, assuagement in visualizing the extremity of their fates, even an erotic thrill in contemplating their final convulsions.

He'd like to do it to them, too, he told himself savagely, though he knew he wouldn't. Not because he was squeamish but because he himself was not going to suffer for their punishment. Whatever he did – and he *would* do something drastic – must be legal, leaving him free to enjoy the comeuppance they so richly deserved.

He didn't want to do anything public. The frame-up of Lally he had since regretted, not for its effect on the priest, but for the risk it had posed for himself. However, try as he did – in bed and on his feet, through a solitary breakfast and a solitary walk through the fields behind the house – he failed to come up with a plan for revenge that left himself completely clear of danger. In the end, desperate for action and bereft of ideas, he cancelled his appointments for the remainder of the day and drove to Tighmor to see the archbishop.

His Grace was out at the moment, the woman who answered the door said. He'd be back about two or thereabouts if – who was it? Dr. Padhraig McCarthy – would care to wait. And what was the nature of his business, so she could inform Dr. Donnellan? Private? Ah yes, of course. And his Grace would recognize who he was when she gave him the name? He would. Well, that was grand. No trouble at all then. If he'd care to sit in the parlor or go away and come back at two she'd see what she could do when his Grace returned.

He left and drove uptown, found a place to park, passed a bookshop and went in and began to browse, then felt hungry and went in search of a pub. Over a pint and a sandwich he hashed and re-hashed his approach and at two o'clock sharp he was back at the episcopal palace. Yes, his Grace had returned and yes, he would see Dr. McCarthy immediately. New respect in the woman's tone for a man who could command an immediate audience.

"Padhraig!" But though Donnellan's handshake was cordial, behind the amiable smile lurked a wariness that McCarthy found disconcerting. "I trust all is well with you and yours?"

"Things are not so good, your Grace." He had planned his approach: today he would be sorrowful, not angry: the plaint of an upright man who has been grievously wronged.

"Have a seat and tell me all about it." The archbishop sat behind his desk.

"Father Lally and my wife have now run off together and they've taken my youngest daughter with them."

Hard to tell what was going on in Donnellan's mind. He picked up a pencil and tapped the rubber end against the desk in a steady rhythmic motion. "You're sure of this, Padhraig?" He asked eventually, bleakly, without looking up.

"Absolutely." Shaded nuances of doubt would only give Donnellan an out.

"Ah dear God!" Followed by a sigh of extraordinary length and feeling. "As if we didn't have enough trouble on our hands already."

Sympathy was a luxury Padhraig McCarthy could not spare at this time. "I'm here to let you know that unless Lally is locked up in a monastery within twenty-four hours and my wife and daughter are back home, I'm going to the Guards to file charges of rape and sodomy against the blackguard." He pounded the episcopal desk to show the depth of his emotion and the firmness of his resolve.

Dr. Donnellan pressed joined fingers to his lips and stared hard at his desk. Then, having apparently received inspiration, he leaned forward and looked McCarthy square in the eyes. "Your behavior, Padhraig, in these most trying circumstances has been steadfastly that of a fine Catholic gentleman. Your patience has been heroic, your forbearance extreme. And now, in the light of this new development, it is understandable that you should be angry beyond measure. I, too, am angry for you. However, you need have no fear: justice will be done, and it will be done swiftly. Father Lally will receive his ultimatum, and if he doesn't accept it then the full force of the law will descend on him like a ton of bricks. You have my word for this, Padhraig." His Grace leaned back, nodding his head in reinforcement.

"Thank you very much, your Grace," said Padhraig McCarthy. "Twenty-four hours."

Dr. Donnellan's nodding slowed to a halt. His lips pursed. His eyes took on the glassy stare of a man doing heavy sums. "As regards the actual time frame," he said eventually. "I think we may need a little more latitude. It'll take a while to –"

Padhraig McCarthy stood abruptly. "Twenty-four hours, your Grace. If I don't hear from you that Lally is locked up by" – he looked at his watch – "a quarter past two tomorrow, I'm going to the Guards." He held out a hand which the archbishop barely touched, then strode purposefully out the door.

With the Fog's sober warning echoing in his brain, Ignatius walked from Drumcondra to O'Connell Street. From the Quays he took a bus to Ballsbridge and stretched out on Veronica's sofa waiting for Dominick. *You obviously don't give a damn, Lord, do you? Letting things go from bad to worse on me. Prosecution by the State, excommunication by the Church; You're really out to destroy me, body and soul, aren't you?*

His Lord neither yea'd nor nay'd, maintaining His perfect silence.

Dominick arrived before Veronica came home. Ignatius left

her a note promising not to be too late, confused, as he wrote, by feelings of lust for her that jangled with his longing for Deirdre.

"Aoife tells me you had a call from the AB?" Dom drove patiently through the frustrating stop-and-go traffic.

Ignatius described his meeting with the Fog. "He threatened me with excommunication," he concluded.

"Cripes! Coming from the Fog that's not to be taken lightly, I suppose."

"I wasn't even aware they still *did* that kind of thing," Ignatius half wailed. He had been under the impression that though the penalty remained in the Code the practice had fallen by the wayside; like capital punishment in civilized countries, which it resembled.

"Yes, they still do it. I've read of several cases in the *Times* over the past few years. Priests who blessed unions of homosexuals, or spoke out for freedom of choice regarding abortion. Things like that." They were stopped at a light. Dom glanced quizzically at him. "Would it bother you?"

"Yes." His vehemence surprised himself. "Despite all that has happened, Dom, I'm still a priest and I want to stay a priest. And, God help me, I continue to have faith in the institutional Church, despite all its warts and punks. Infallibility, no; the one and only true, I doubt; but a vehicle for salvation I still believe it to be."

"In that case you'd better tread carefully, lad. Ah! at last." The traffic speeded up somewhat.

Dom kissed Aoife the moment he stepped in the door. Ignatius had a sweeping urge to do the same to Deirdre who stood behind her but he refrained, even after Aoife kissed him on the cheek. Mrs. McCarthy, however, had no such reticence: she wrapped her arms around him and pressed her lips on his, firmly and for longer than a greeting kiss required. Even Gemma, taking her mother's cue, offered him a light but exquisite brush of her soft mouth.

They had finished the pork chops and Aoife was dishing up the sherry trifle when the phone rang. Dom's voice boomed from the hall. "I have no idea where he is, Brian." A long silence. "Sure Brian, I'll do that if he contacts us. That was Kennedy," he announced on return. "Your husband," he nodded to Deirdre, "went to see *his* AB in Tighmor today and gave you," he nodded to Ignatius, "exactly twenty-four hours, starting at a quarter past two this afternoon, to get thee to a monastery. Or else ..." Dominick made a slashing motion of hand across windpipe.

"Damn him anyway," Deirdre said softly.

"Please, let's go on with this lovely sweet," Ignatius urged. "We can talk afterwards."

"A man after me own heart," Dom bellowed. "Nothing stops the gobbling of a sherry trifle."

"Everyone go sit in the parlor now," Aoife commanded after the last dessert dish had been scraped and the last tea-cup drained. "I'll take care of the clean-up."

"I'll help you, Mrs. McElligott," Gemma offered.

"He made that very same threat before but he didn't carry it out," Dominick noted as he poured drinks at the parlor sideboard. "What's your take on this one, Deirdre?" He asked as he handed her a brandy.

"It's different." Sitting next to Ignatius on the sofa, her hand sympathetically rubbing his shoulder. "He held off before because I threatened to leave him if he did anything. Now he's raving mad because I did leave."

"So you think he might go through with it?"

She nodded slowly, her hand moving gently across Ignatius's back. "I'm sure he's in a terrible rage right now. Padhraig can't stand to lose anything that belongs to him. And I'm his property, you see." Her smile was bitter.

They sipped in silence. "Well I'm going to fight it," Ignatius shouted suddenly, to his own surprise though the conviction had been growing inside him since Deirdre's arrival. He no longer had to worry about destroying her family: it was already in ruins.

"Good man." Deirdre leaned into him in a hug. "You owe it to yourself."

"*Togha fir*," Dominick shouted. "I'll defend you to the death." And for the next couple of hours they discussed options and plotted strategies and considered contingencies. Later, they had tea and cake, and made a plan to meet again next evening. Then Dominick drove Ignatius back to Ballsbridge.

Veronica was less enthusiastic when he told her his decision. "Even if you get off they'll have dragged your name through the mud, and the stigma will be there forever. If it were me I'd skip the country while the going is good."

That thought *had* crossed his mind in less optimistic moments. "But by the time I'd be able to leave they'd be on the look out for me. And then I'd really look guilty."

"I can get you a fake American passport through the underground." Perkily, sitting on the other end of the sofa, knees tucked up beneath her robe. "And one of the people in the play I'm in is a really great make-up artist. Your own mother wouldn't recognize you when he's finished."

His own mother! The poor woman would die of shame when the media got wind of it all. Was there no way to stop the catastrophe? "I'm wondering if it would be worth while trying to reason with McCarthy myself?" A wild thought that had burgeoned on the drive back with Dominick, but in a state so inchoate that he hadn't dared to bring it up with his friend. "After all, we were at school together. And the old school scarf, you know..."

"Might be worth trying," Veronica admitted dubiously. "But if it doesn't work, remember I can always get you the passport."

He stayed awake for hours debating with himself. He should go see the bugger; no, he shouldn't; dammit, he ought to try at least; McCarthy might physically assault him; he'd never forgive himself if he didn't give it a shot; what did he have to lose anyway?

Veronica's alarm woke him. He was up like a shot, still half asleep, forgetting where he was until he, naked, almost collided with her, naked, at the bathroom door. They both laughed – what else was there to do. But then she impulsively put her arms around him in a skin-to-skin hug and murmured in his ear, "you're such a sweet man, Ignatius; if you were free I'd marry you." She laughed again after closing the bathroom door, but called out, "I never let anyone see me going pee-pee."

He dressed and decided to stay in his room until she left for work. He read his breviary, trying hard to attend to the prayers, despite an involuntary ear that listened for her movements and an imagination that refused to let go of her nakedness. Eventually he heard the click of heels and waited to hear her go down the stairs. But she stopped at his door and knocked. "Ignatius?" She stepped in; "I'm going to leave you my car in case you do decide to go see that awful fellow." She held out a key. "I can take the bus."

"You're wonderful," he said. "Thank you very much."

Her closing of his door coincided with the voice of his God. *What are you up to, Ignatius,* He said. *I let you have one woman and now you want two?*

Oh Lord, You're back! Do I ever need You? What a mess I'm in. Where have You been all this time? Never mind: it's enough that You're here now. Listen! What should –

Just go and see him. Like a father admonishing a timid son. *Talk to him about Me. You've nothing to lose. And if you convert him it might make up to Me for some of your own bad behavior.*

He made a quick breakfast, grabbed the key to Veronica's car, and drove down Serpentine Avenue at a dangerous speed.

Padhraig McCarthy didn't sleep well after an evening spent in front of the telly with the sound turned low so he'd hear the phone in the hall. He had several morning appointments he could not forego, so he woke Fiona at seven and told her to stay right by the phone while he was gone – the archbishop didn't have his cell phone number. On his return shortly after eleven she informed him wearily that no one had rung; she went off to her room with the air of a martyr, muttering that she was now behind time getting her things ready for the university. He was making himself a cup of tea when the front door bell rang.

Lally! The sheer unmitigated gall of the fucker. McCarthy had an instant urge to slam the door in his face. "What the bloody hell are you doing here?" Barely managing to control the rage that was heating up fast at the sight of his nemesis.

"I'd like to talk with you, Padhraig."

Lally's subdued tone of near defeat fired him up like a major intoxicant. "I'll bet you bloody would." With all the disdain of the strong for the weak. "But we've nothing to talk about. You got my message, I presume?"

"*You* know, Padhraig, and I know, and God knows, that

there isn't an iota of truth in the charges you have leveled against me. If –"

"Of course they're true. And I can prove that they're true. And I will. And you'll bloody well rot in jail for the rest of your life. And you'll bloody well rot in hell for all eternity. That you will, my lad." An extraordinary sense of power building up inside him at the capacity of his words to destroy his enemy.

"I'll tell you this much, Padhraig: if you persist in pressing these ridiculous charges, I'll fight them in court and I'll win and I'll prove that you made them up out of malice, and then it's you who'll wind up in –"

"Get the hell off my doorstep right now before I throw you off." What insolence! Threatening him in his own house.

Lally didn't move. "I know you're a man of faith, Padhraig. You were President of the Children of Mary at Saint Fursa's, for God's sake. You were even expected to go on for the priesthood at one stage. So please! In the name of God and for the salvation of your own immortal soul give up this mad vendetta. And for the record, I did *not* try to steal your wife from you, as apparently you seem to think. Furthermore, though I regard it as highly unnecessary, I'll make you a promise that as soon as you retract I will make it a point of honor never to speak to her again."

The bugger stood there, arms akimbo, oozing piety, obviously expecting Padhraig McCarthy to fall on his knees in abject repentance. Well, Padhraig McCarthy'd show him. "I'm going back into my office now," he said, slowly and deliberately, matching the tone of the man before him, "and I'm going to take out of its cabinet the shotgun that I keep for shooting vermin. And I'm going to load a pair of cartridges into the breech. And I'm going to bring it back out here and I'm going to shoot some vermin if it's still standing on my doorstep." He turned abruptly and walked back down the hall leaving the front door open. At the parlor door he paused. A car engine started, revved, roared, receded into the distance. He continued down the hall with a smile on his face.

The smile soon vanished when he sat to think. Fucking Lally was not going into a monastery, was going to defy him, was going to call his bluff. Well, he'd soon find out who was bluffing. No need now to wait till a quarter past two. "Fiona," he bawled, standing at the bottom of the stairs.

"I'm busy, Daddy," she shouted from above.

"I want to talk to you right now," he bellowed.

"Can't it wait?" she wailed. "I'm in the middle of things."

"Now." Stentorian.

A minute later she trod slowly, huffily, down the stairs. "Can't I ever have a minute to myself?" Standing next to him with folded arms.

"Change your clothes; we're going to see the Guards." She was wearing jeans and a dirty sweat shirt.

"What for?" No sign of a move to obey his order.

"Just do as I say. We're finally going to press charges against the man who raped you."

"Daddy!" The wide open eyes of abhorrence. "That was just a bluff. You said we would never ..."

"The bugger has called our bluff. Now we *have* to go through with it."

"But Daddy! This is ridiculous. You know you can't do that. It'd be" – arms waving in all directions as she sought the right word – "totally stupid."

"It would be stupid of us not to do it. Now go and get ready." At times she'd try the patience of a saint.

"You're starkers, Daddy, you know that?" Her expression one of horror. "I always knew you had a screw loose, but now you've really gone over the brink." And not a stir out of her to obey his instruction.

"Fiona, before I lose my temper will you go and change your clothes. We're leaving in five minutes."

"I'm not going to do it, Daddy." The color rising in her cheeks and his own fierce temper reflected in her eyes. "Do you think I'm going to ruin my chances at the Uni by getting involved in your mad lie that could only end up getting me sent to jail? Because if you think that you better think again."

"Change your clothes!" This time he issued a full-throated roar.

"I won't," she shouted defiantly.

He hit her then, a stinging slap across the face, as he had done to her mother a few days ago. She staggered back, hit the banister, the mat slid from under her, she crashed to the floor, her head striking the ceramic tile with a sickening crunch. She lay there, eyes open, perfectly still, in a pose he had often seen when she'd sun herself on the patio outside the back door. The only difference was the trickle of blood that oozed from under the back of her head, stark red against the white floor. "Fiona!" Sudden fear rippled through him. "Are you all right, sugar? I didn't mean to ..." He dropped to his knees beside her, tried to lift her head, felt the blood on his fingers, felt for her pulse at the neck. There was none. Put his hand by her heart. There was no beat.

CRUCIFIXION

Ignatius drove away in a hurry. Not till he was heading back towards Clyard did he feel safe from Padhraig McCarthy who was, he felt, quite capable of carrying out his threat. As he approached the entrance to the novitiate, he felt a desperate urge to visit. There was a peace and grace about this place from which he might draw strength for the upcoming struggle. He slowed and was about to turn in when he saw the auctioneer's sign atop the left pillar and remembered that the place was being sold. Like himself, its past was being trampled, its future in doubt. He continued on, drove through the town, and a few miles later picked up the Dublin road. Thirty miles north he spotted the familiar sign for his old alma mater and on impulse turned left into the narrow road that led to the village of Clarion, a mile beyond which lay Saint Fursa's College. He hadn't been back since he left in 1970. The village looked more spruce than he remembered: houses and shops were brightly painted and the single street had a clean swept look. Lawlor's pub evoked memories; it also reminded him that he was hungry. He stopped and went in. The interior, though dim as he remembered it, was now a modern lounge, unlike the sawdust-floor men-only bar of his school-days. A family of four – tourists, most likely – sat at one table eating hamburgers and chips, a young couple at another, their rucksacks beside them on the floor. He picked a small table in a corner where he could observe and recall.

January 7, 1970: they had returned from Christmas holidays that afternoon. The College, as always on opening days, was chaotic: boys straggling in, dragging suitcases and boxes, cars coming and going, parents roaming the corridors, priests on the prowl keeping an eye on things. But as there was no real supervision Padhraig McCarthy, Brendan Shine, and Ignatius Lally decided, with three hours to kill before supper, that they'd walk into Clarion. Against the rules, but who'd notice on this particular day? A cold, dry evening, already getting dark; they walked briskly to stay warm. McCarthy it was who suggested Lawlor's as they were passing the public house. Ignatius still remembered the shock on poor Brendan's face – he was killed a year later in a car accident – at the suggestion. A fierce pious lad, even by the standards of those days: known as Saint Brendan because of his penchant for visiting the chapel during recreation. ''Twouldn't be right to go into a pub,' he said now, having already expressed mild guilt at taking the unauthorized walk. But Ignatius, himself known to be pious and touted as a sure thing for the priesthood, had agreed with McCarthy, leaving Brendan no alternative but to join them or walk back alone to the College. Friendship won out and Shine went reluctantly in, then suffered the humiliation of ordering a lemonade while Ignatius and McCarthy each had a Guinness.

They were good friends in those days, McCarthy and himself; with Shine they had been a regular threesome at recreation since their first year at Saint Fursa's. So what went wrong? The rugby contretemps later that year of course: Tommy the Tiger's tactless behavior coupled with McCarthy's unforgiving nature. But was it really possible that he had concocted the rape allegation just to get back at Ignatius for something that hadn't been his fault in the first place? Or was he consumed with jealousy over Deirdre's obvious attraction to his former friend? Whatever the cause, it had to have hardened into a terrible hate for him to commit such a vicious act. The expression on his face this morning said no softening of attitude was likely. If Ignatius Lally wanted to protect himself he was going to have to fight. Maybe this was meant to be the scrap they never had at Saint Fursa's? There was a custom at the College for settling rows between boys: on Saturday evenings after supper and chapel a makeshift boxing ring was set up in the gymnasium where squabblers could settle their differences under Queensbury Rules and the watchful eye of Mr. "Bunkum" Farragher, the physical education teacher. After The Tiger had given Ignatius McCarthy's out-half position on the senior rugby team, the latter had truculently challenged him to prove in the ring which of them was the better man. Ignatius had declined, though more from fear of winning than of losing: McCarthy would never live down another defeat. But his unwillingness to box had brought about the final breakdown of friendship between them. So now, twenty-nine years later, he must undertake to fight in a bigger and more public arena the battle he had then refused.

He lunched on a sandwich and a glass of beer and drove out to the College. The side view of the chapel from the long curved driveway, the clean cut-stone buildings that housed classrooms and dormitories, the large-windowed sports pavilion presiding serenely over the level playing fields: from the outside nothing seemed to have changed. At the moment the pitches were deserted, the silence palpable. The boys would still be in class. He parked Veronica's car and strolled the grounds and smelled the cut-grass air, and remembered times when his world was young and God was his very best friend. *Are you still with me, Lord?* he asked plaintively; they hadn't talked since that brief morning colloquy.

His God was no longer there. *You can't be gone again! What have I done now to offend? And just when I need you most.* But His Lord's silence was loud in the soft autumn breeze, His absence as pressing as a rugby scrum. *So why did you come back at all, then? Just to lead me astray, telling me to go see that maniac? I'd never have gone if You hadn't been so definite. Raising my hopes, then dashing them down. Or did my visit have some effect on McCarthy, after all? Maybe when I left remorse set in? Perhaps he remembered our days here at Saint Fursa's and decided he couldn't go through with his mad revenge? Was that your purpose, Lord?*

It was almost half three when he drove out the main gates again. Boys had begun to trot out of the pavilion onto the fields, clad in the familiar green and white horizontal stripes, kicking rugby balls or striking *sliotars* with limber hurleys. He had considered stopping in to visit with whoever he might find among the priests – if indeed the laity had not taken over the running of the place as they had in so many of the colleges – but refrained out of embarrassment of having to explain his current predicament. Soon enough they'd be reading about him in the newspapers, hearing his name on the radio, seeing his face on the telly. *Oh God! What have You done to me at all?*

He had the car radio on for company as he headed back to Dublin. Which was how he came to hear the five o'clock news. *A teenage girl was murdered earlier today near the town of Clyard in County Tipperary. Gardai have not yet released the name of the victim pending notification of the girl's mother who is believed to be in Dublin. But they are said to be looking for a Catholic priest in connection with the killing. The girl was due to start University in Limerick this coming week.*

The name of Clyard registered immediately, but it took another few seconds before the possible relation of the tragedy to himself seeped through. It couldn't have any connection, of course. How could it? He hadn't even seen Fiona while he was there. Pure coincidence, fueled by his over-stimulated imagination after his run-in with Padhraig. *Mother believed to be in Dublin.* Any number of mothers could be gone to Dublin. *Looking for a Catholic priest*; the coincidences were multiplying, but that was all they were. It just couldn't be. Anyway, Fiona, for all the wrong she had done him, could not have been murdered. And Deirdre could not sustain another calamity. Nevertheless, a dull weight hung around his mid-section for the remainder of the journey.

Which Veronica's face did nothing to lighten. Still dressed in her power suit – ominous in itself – her expression mingled mistrust and fear with an awful sorrow. "What on God's earth happened?" Keeping herself at a distance, without the hug she had got into the habit of giving on his every arrival.

"What happened what?" But he knew then that Fiona McCarthy was dead and that he himself was somehow implicated.

Veronica backed into the parlor before him as if fearing a knife in the ribs, the words tumbling out of her as she went. "The Gardai were at Dominick's this afternoon. They told your friend Deirdre that her daughter, Fiona, had been murdered this morning. And they said they wanted to question you about it."

"Holy Christ! Has the world gone mad entirely?" He collapsed on the sofa and covered his face with his hands. "Am I stuck in a nightmare, Lord? When will I wake up and find myself back in Shankill in the midst of my novices?"

Veronica's frightened voice confirmed that it was no wretched dream. "You didn't do it, Ignatius, did you?" But her tone suggested just a shadow of doubt.

He uncovered his face and stared at her. "Of course not – how could you even think it? Why would I do a horrible thing like that? I didn't even see the girl today." And he told her in a torrent of words what had happened, in the hopeless hope that explaining might somehow exculpate him from the guilt that the mere unfounded charge had laid upon him. When he finished she came and sat beside him and put an arm around his shoulder.

"I believe you," she said with stark simplicity.

"What did the Gardai say? When did it happen? How?"

"All I know is what I heard from Aoife; she called just after I got in from work. She doesn't believe you did it either, of course, but she wanted you to be forewarned that the Gardai are looking to question you. They didn't say much, apparently: they really came to find Deirdre who, fortunately, was there at the time. She's in a terrible state of shock, the poor woman. Naturally. She rang home immediately and got a hold of her husband. He said that you came by at about twelve o'clock and had an argument with himself and Fiona – is that her name, Fiona? – and that you suddenly lashed out in a fit of temper and hit her across the face and knocked her down and she cracked her head on the floor and died on the spot."

"I never even saw her. He wouldn't let me in the door. Threatened to shoot me if I didn't leave." Blathering in hope it might relieve the pain. "Where's Deirdre now?"

"Aoife said she had left with her other daughter. They were heading down home."

"Oh God! What do I do now?" But his God gave him no help.

"Dominick will contact you, Aoife said, but you're not to ring them, just in case ... In the meantime," Veronica got to her feet, "I'm going to make us some dinner."

They were finishing the dishes when McElligott arrived. "I'm getting to be an expert at shaking a tail," he said, straining for the lighthearted touch. "Drove into town, parked the car, walked around the shops, hid in a doorway, took the bus to the end of Serpentine, stood in another doorway for five minutes, and listened for footsteps all the way down the street."

"I'll put the kettle on for tea," Veronica said.

"I'd prefer a whiskey if you have it." Ignatius joined him. He had never been drunk in his life but at this moment it seemed like a good idea. "*Firinne*!" Dom raised his glass in a toast. "Here's to the triumph of truth." He sipped and put down his drink and looked earnestly at Ignatius. "I have no doubt in my own mind, of course, but just for the record tell me you didn't do it."

"Of course he didn't do it," Veronica half shouted, with all the ferocity of a mother whose child has been impugned.

"I didn't do it," Ignatius said bleakly.

"But you did go down there this morning?"

"Yes. I talked to Padhraig, but I never even saw Fiona."

"Deirdre," Dom said, "even in her distress – and the poor woman was almost out of her mind, as you can well imagine – had no doubt whatever that it was Padhraig himself who did it. The way he described you as hitting Fiona was exactly the way he had hit herself a few days ago. 'Ignatius could never do a thing like that,' she said over and over." Dom sipped again, this time more deeply. "I thought you'd want to know how she felt."

"Then it shouldn't be too hard for the Gardai to figure it out, either," Veronica said.

"I have no idea what evidence the Gardai will find, or may have already found." Dominick's tone was as sober as a preacher's discussing sin. "But unless there's some forensic evidence linking Padhraig, or unless there was an eyewitness to the event, it'll be your word against his, Ignatius. And the worst part is that his previous lies about you may actually provide him with a motive against you: you went down there to talk them out of exposing you; you argued with them; they refused to retract; you got angry and struck Fiona and killed her and then took off. All very plausible to a jury if the original charge were true."

He wanted to scream, lash out, hurl his glass against the wall: anything to vent the pounding frustration that beat like heavy metal inside his head. Instead, he asked Dom, as calmly as he could, "if I were your client how would you defend me?"

"Sure there *has* to be a way for the truth to get through!" Veronica beat a fierce tattoo with both her platform heels against the unoffending carpet.

"We'd go looking for evidence to prove your innocence, of course." McElligott's neutral tone devoid of either hope or despair. "Which brings us to the vital question: what are *you* going to do?" Looking into his empty glass like a man who had no expectation of a refill.

"What I'm hearing you say is that if I went to trial I'd probably be found guilty of murder." Knowing that the anger in his voice was directed at Dominick and realizing that it was unfair, but unable to control its direction at this moment. "So what do you recommend?"

"That's not possible," Veronica wailed. "Can't be, can't be."

Head shaking wildly.

Dominick said, "I can only be helpful to you, Ignatius, if I abstract from our friendship for the moment and think of you simply as a client." He gazed suppliantly into his glass. "So, if you were a stranger who came to me with this case I'd be very much inclined to suggest you plead guilty to a charge of involuntary manslaughter and take the consequences." He raised a hand to silence Veronica's scream. "Even if I believed you to be entirely innocent, which I do of course." He tried to suck an imaginary drop from the empty glass. "But when justice cannot be achieved one must settle for the best terms one can get." He looked sorrowfully at his friend. "I know this sounds absolutely awful, Ignatius, and it is, but I don't know what else to advise. Unless some solid evidence comes to light against McCarthy."

"Well, *my* advice still stands, Ignatius: go on the lam." Veronica stood. "Who wants to get drunk? There's still half the Jameson left." They all had refills.

"So," Ignatius waved a weaving glass at Dominick, "what you're telling me is that I should go to the Gardai, give myself up, plead guilty to killing Fiona, albeit accidentally, and go quietly to jail. Which would also imply admitting I raped the girl as well, wouldn't it?" He glared at Dom. "And that should add another ten years to my sentence. Is that what you want me to do?" He gulped all of his whiskey and almost choked.

"We wouldn't admit to the rape," Dominick said dully. "And in the absence of the only witness, you'd most likely not be charged with it. Although there are no guarantees there either."

"What would *you* do if you were in my position?" How often he'd been asked that question by penitents seeking to justify their past misdeeds.

McElligott slugged his whiskey, too. "To be honest," he said, very slowly and deliberately, "I have to agree with Veronica: if I thought I'd get away with it I'd disappear." He looked at Ignatius with infinite pity. "That's what I'd do. The law is a terrible thing to have close in around you. I've been to Mountjoy and I could only wish it on my very worst enemies."

Ignatius slugged again. "I'll have to think about it." The whiskey was going to his head. Tomorrow he'd decide.

"Is he going to be safe here?" Veronica, too, had finished her drink. "I mean ..."

"I'd say you're all right for the moment." Dom looked at his watch and stood. "I better be getting home. But don't put off your decision for too long." He was heading for the door when he turned. "Did McCarthy spot your car today?"

"I don't think so. I parked on the road out of sight of the house: I didn't want him to see me coming."

"You're safe then, I'd say. Anyway, if they knew where you are they'd have been here long ago." At the front door he shook Ignatius's hand, then impulsively wrapped his arms around him in a great bear hug. "Good luck, old pal. If there's anything at all I can do ..." On the threshold he swung around. "But remember, this meeting never took place: I could be disbarred for it, you know."

"Jesus! I need another drink," Veronica said after she closed the door. In the parlor she poured them both more Jameson. They drank in silence. Ignatius was feeling quite light-headed now and, though he remained aware of his awful predicament, it didn't seem quite so terrible at the moment. Veronica stood abruptly and kicked off her platforms. Still standing, she finished her third generous glass of whiskey. "I think I better go to bed now, Ignatius, before I collapse completely."

"Me, too." His head was fuzzy and his body lead. They clutched each other for support going up the narrow stairs.

He had his hand on his door knob when she grabbed him by the arm. "No! No! I can't let you stay by yourself tonight, poor lamb. You're coming into Mammy's bed and sleeping with Mammy." He had neither the energy nor the will to resist, and barely managed to undress and fall into her big brass bed before sleep took him down in a sliding tackle.

He woke to a bursting bladder and a throbbing head, but with no immediate memory of where he was. Daylight seeped through a curtained window. A door slammed somewhere below, a car engine whined into life. As he slid out of bed a hand grabbed his arm. "Where are you off to, Ignatius?" Veronica's sleepy voice brought back recollection of last night's events.

"To the bathroom." He had to get there in a hurry.

"Well, come right back, do you hear?" She released his arm.

After relieving himself he washed his hands and drank a glass of water. Wakefulness brought his predicament crashing down on him like a rugby pack on an unfortunate out-half. And to top it off he had spent the night in Veronica's bed. He was heading towards the visitor's room when she called out again. "This way, Ignatius: my room, where you were." He told himself that he was too miserable to argue with her at the moment, and shuffled back to her bed. She immediately got out on the far side. "Don't go away, I have to brush my teeth." She was long enough in the bathroom for him to have come to his senses and taken evasive action, but he was still in her bed when she returned, naked, and pushed her way gently in on his side. She snuggled her head into his shoulder, draped an arm over his middle, a leg across his thigh, and murmured into his ear, "do you think, Ignatius, you might do me an enormous favor?"

Blood and hormones and whatever else were rising at this point to gale force. No different at all from the passion he had felt for Deirdre; so was love only lust in disguise? "What's that?" he crackled through a throat of mucus.

"Remember I told you that I never had complete sex with a man?"

He waited for her to say more but her silence constrained him to answer. "I seem to remember you saying something of the sort."

"Well, it's true. Really. I've never let a man get ... inside me. You know what I mean?"

"Yes." Her hand with widespread fingers was stroking his belly, the pinkie grazing his hairline, just a quiver away from his tumescence.

"Because of my brother, you know." She grabbed hold of it then, gently but firmly, and moved him around as if changing gears. "I told you all about that, didn't I?"

"You did indeed. Very understandable, of course." He only vaguely remembered her telling him something about a brother who sexually molested her.

"But, you know, I've been thinking recently." She let go in order to wrap cool delicate fingers about his scrotum. "I can't go through my entire life without shaking off this fear. Do you know what I mean?" The sensation was exquisite.

"I do indeed." How long was he going to be able to hold out?

"So I made a decision last week." The hand moved lower, gently pushing his legs apart. "I'm going to find myself a nice man, I said, and I'm going to have complete sex with him. It's the only sane thing for a woman to do, isn't it?" she ended, as vivaciously as if she were discussing the buying of a gorgeous frock. The rush when her fingertip touched his anus was entirely new to his repertoire of pleasure.

"A good decision, I'd say. In the end everybody needs sex, I suppose."

"Even priests, Father, don't you think?" But without waiting for an answer she swept the blankets aside, rolled over on top, and had him inside her before he knew what was happening.

When it was done and over with and she had smothered him in hugs from the sheer thrill of accomplishment and gone off to shower and get ready for work, allowing she was dead late already but wasn't it so well worth it, he lay there unable or unwilling to move. It wasn't his God he was worrying about, nor the guilt of carnal sin, nor the remorse of yielding to the flesh, nor even remotely the fear of divine retribution. What was sticking in his craw, diluting remembered pleasure, paralyzing his power to share this woman's first post-coital joy, was the singular thought of Deirdre McCarthy. Ludicrous of course, wasn't it? As well as incongruous, illogical, inconsistent, or any other word in the dictionary that could possibly describe the feeling of guilt for being unfaithful *to* the woman you were unfaithful *with* in the first place. Infidelity squared, perhaps? But the guilt was there, nevertheless. They had made a pact, Deirdre and himself, albeit never put into words, that they would be true to each other. And as that commitment was more satisfying to him than ever was his vow of celibacy, so its shattering was the more piercing of his inmost being.

He admitted, in fairness, that it was not Veronica's fault. So that when she, dressed and ready to leave, sat on the bed and kissed him soundly, he responded as if she were his only love. "I'll bring back the make-up lad," she said when leaving. "And I'll arrange for your passport as well." She was half-way down the stairs when she came clopping back up again. "On the other hand I don't know if I should let you go at all," she said, smiling gleefully from the doorway.

DEATH

The three hour drive to Clyard that afternoon were the longest and worst of Deirdre McCarthy's life. Somewhere between Newbridge and Kildare she passed Ignatius Lally returning to Dublin, though neither was aware of that odd fact. Gemma periodically sniffled and cried, forcing her mother to remain dry-eyed and controlled. But Deirdre's mind was too numb for controlled reflection. Images coming and going of Fiona, her first-born, beautiful baby: infant smile showing tiny first tooth; Fiona crawling, walking, running, talking; at two holding baby Gemma in her small fat arms; Fiona leaving home for her first day at school; first communion in her white dress and veil ... Young people ought not die; *how could You, God?* Was He punishing her for her lapse from faith? Her adulteries? Who knew? *For who shall know the mind of the Lord?* Indeed.

"Do you think she's really dead, Mammy?" Gemma's tone a melange of hope and desperation.

The naive faith of the younger daughter that her mother might somehow undo the tragedy brought about the release of Deirdre's tears. "I think we have to believe what the Garda told us, love," she said between sobs. The bloody brute! Of course it was her husband who had killed their daughter. A new advanced phase in his policy of control, this physical lashing out, though she had long feared it would come to that. Behind his never ceasing demands – occasionally latent, most often quite patent, and at times even sinister – for absolute obedience from wife and children lay that ultimate threat of violence which, though never spoken, had hovered like a dark cloud over their lives. On occasion he *had* actually slapped Gemma and Cathal, though not in her presence, but he had never until a few days ago laid a hand in anger on his wife. The latter act was something he could do but once: she had promised herself many times over the years, especially when smarting from his acerbic tongue or the fury of his silence, that if ever he struck her she'd leave him on the spot; though she had never contemplated the possibility of his raping her. Anyway, she had kept her promise. But now she must wonder if by leaving she had somehow contributed to Fiona's death: her presence had been the children's buffer before the onslaught of his anger. Would he have fatally struck his favorite child if his wife had been there to bear the brunt? Now she'd have to get Cathal away from him: he too was in danger. For though he used his son as a foil to jeer at Gemma, whom he had come to dislike because she saw through his domineering ways, Deirdre had a sense that he didn't care too much for Cathal either. The boy lacked those aggressive masculine traits on the field of hurling and football that his father so admired: many times out of hearing of the girls she had heard him berate her youngest for being a funk. Which accomplished no end at all except to put Cathal into sulks, for above all others in the world he worshiped his Dad and sought at every turn to gain his favor.

Oh, Fiona, what has he done to you? Her daughter's

treachery forgiven by death. Should she face him down and accuse him of murder? She wanted to scream his crime for all the world to hear: he must be put away for what he had done to their daughter. And for his horrible offenses against her dearest Ignatius. *Prudence, Deirdre, prudence. Hold back for the sake of those already hurt and those he might yet injure if given the chance. Say nothing till you have the evidence; accusation would only put him on guard and ruin any chance that he might let something slip.*

She warned Gemma to say nothing either, and when they reached home just before seven and several cars were in front of the house they entered as grief-stricken family but not as accusers. Padhraig's mother and two of his sisters were there and a half-dozen neighbors, all sitting in the parlor with drinks in their fists, speaking in the restrained hushed tones becoming to mourners. The women embraced them and the men shook hands and all watched Padhraig manfully shed tears while he hugged in silence his tragically diminished family. Deirdre felt more than saw the numbness in Cathal, and was surprised by the vehemence with which he clutched her in that embrace of family solidarity instigated by his father.

An awful tragedy altogether, the neighbors averred. Who would ever have thought such a thing could happen in a place like this? And to such a fine upstanding family as the McCarthys, too? But the law was going to find the blackguard who did the foul deed and bring him to justice for sure even if God help us he wore the garb of a priest. What was happening to the country anyway that the clergy had sunk so low? Time was and not so long ago either when the worst that could be said of the man of God was that maybe the creature was a bit fond of the bottle. But not any more faith there seemed to be nothing they'd not stoop to nowadays as they worked their way through the commandments of God like a drunk going through a half-barrel of porter.

Deirdre seethed and held her peace and waited for the comforters to take themselves home. Which they were in no hurry to do as long as Padhraig kept plying them with booze which in turn stoked the fires of gossip that ranged from clergy to politicians to the business practices of the rich and mighty to the crass lack of shame by the media and back to the sins of God's anointed. When the clock in the hall struck ten she stood, emotionally exhausted, and announced that she simply had to go to bed but that of course they were all welcome to stay as long as they wished. They straggled off then, the reluctance in their steps as outspoken as the sympathy from their tongues.

Padhraig closed the door on the last one out and was heading silently up the stairs when she called out to him. "Where is she?" It was the first time she had directly addressed him since arriving home.

Stopping on the third step up he answered without turning. "At the Regional; they're doing a post mortem tomorrow morning." He continued up the stairs.

Mingled grief and anger overwhelmed her, the anger alone almost forcing her to scream *murderer* at him then and there. Instead, she stopped him again with a question. "Have you made any arrangements?"

"Let's talk about it in the morning. We can't do anything till after the post mortem." His tone suggested *he* might break down at the very next word.

She returned to the parlor where Gemma and Cathal still sat in stony silence and put her arm around her son. "How are you, dear?"

"Awful," he croaked. But he made no attempt to shake off her embrace, as he had done so often in the recent past.

"Were you still at school when it happened?" she asked gently. It was then he pushed her arm aside and scooted out the door and up the stairs with his heavy tramp, without so much as a word out of him.

"What was that all about?" Gemma, red-eyed, asked. "He looked like he –" But Deirdre silenced her with a finger to her own lips. They went to bed without another word.

While they were at breakfast Padhraig rang the hospital for information and the undertaker about the funeral. The familiar tone barking into the hall phone made her marvel that she had lived so long with this obnoxious man. Women were stupid, weren't they? Putting up with so much – for peace and family and financial security, they told themselves – instead of asserting their rights to be treated as equal human beings. No more. If she had had any doubts about the rightness of her leaving, listening to him now bullying the people at the other end of the fiber optic removed the last vestige.

"They'll probably release her late this afternoon," he said studiously, standing in the kitchen doorway, looking at the floor. "Aidan will take care of the funeral arrangements." Aidan McCarthy, his cousin, was the only undertaker in Clyard.

"I'm going to the hospital this morning to see her." Wondering as she spoke why she bothered to tell him; no doubt a remnant of the long-standing habit of accounting for her every move.

"Why would you want to do that?" The half savage tone of his question made both Cathal and Gemma look up from their cereal.

"Because I want to," she retorted coldly and went on with her breakfast.

"They won't let you see her," he half-shouted. "They'll be doing the post mortem."

"Then I'll have to take my chances, won't I," she said sharply.

He took in quick air then, a familiar precursor to a spate of bellowed abuse. But instead he turned and strode down the hall and out the front door, slamming it after him.

"Can I come with you, Mammy?" Gemma asked plaintively.

"Yes." She wasn't about to leave her alone with her father. "You can come, too, Cathal, if you want."

"I'm going to spend the day in my room," Cathal growled and forthwith departed upstairs.

When they found parking in the hospital grounds Deirdre suggested that her daughter might not want to come inside. "I want to see her, Mammy," Gemma said very firmly.

Yes of course they'd be able to see her. But they'd have to wait till the post mortem was completed, which would be in about an hour. In the event they waited more than two hours in the open lounge by the reception area, browsing magazines, watching the coming and going of patients and visitors and the endless crisscrossing of the space by staff. Deirdre kept an eye on the clock over the front desk and after an hour and a half had gone by asked the receptionist for an update on their waiting period. The latter didn’t know anything more. Eventually a white-coated woman approached and offered condolences that sounded sincere and led them down a stairway and along a series of corridors to a small room with double doors. In the middle of the room was a single table, shrouded in a blue cloth.

"You don't have to look," the woman said gently to Gemma, before she pulled back the shroud.

"I want to." Deirdre felt the steel in her daughter's voice and it gave her courage to withstand the shock herself.

Fiona's head was swathed in bandages, which highlighted her face with startling clarity. Like an alabaster relief on a virgin's tomb, peaceful and beautiful, but no longer her daughter. *Oh God, Fiona! What has happened to us at all?* Gemma was clutching her hand and she felt the shaking sobs of her living child.

They left quickly, drove through the Glen, stopped at a pub for tea and sandwiches, and a few miles further on found a secluded spot to sit by the bank of the Suir. Quiet dark barely-rippling waters, stately swans, occasional row-boats passing with peaceful splashing of oars, helped restore calm to her nerves. Gemma held her hand, they rarely spoke. But in the stillness her guilt returned: if she had only stayed ... thinking she was doing the right thing ... focusing on herself alone ... if she had but given a little consideration to ... Stop it! How would Ignatius view it? He had become her behavior model these past few months, and he had told her a few days ago she had done the right thing. She had to talk to him, see him, hold him. Holy Mother! How she hated Padhraig for what he had done. There had to be justice somewhere. But was there?

"Let's go home," she said to Gemma. "I have things to do." She'd ring Father Lally – the name by which she now called out to him in her mind – as soon as she got in, whether Padhraig was in the house or not. Padhraig wasn't, but neither was Ignatius at Veronica's. She rang Aoife, but no one answered there either. She cooked dinner, and when Padhraig failed to come home by six she and the children ate. Then, while Gemma and Cathal washed up, she rang Eavan. "When will I see you?" She desperately needed the company of this sister who had always been her closest friend.

"The best I can do, unfortunately, is tomorrow afternoon. There are things I absolutely must do at work in the morning." She arrived just after three, as they were getting ready to go to Aidan McCarthy's Funeral Home. In the car on the way she leaned over and whispered in Deirdre's ear, "I have news for you from someone; tell you about it when we have a chance to talk."

It had to be about Ignatius: who else? And there was an upbeat nuance in Eavan's whisper that suggested it wasn't more bad news. Which hope kept her from sinking beneath the weight of good will that emanated from friends and relatives who all evening long paraded into the funeral home and embraced and condoled and viewed and prayed and shook unbelieving heads. The place mercifully closed at nine and they all went home, it having been decided earlier not to remove the remains to the church till morning.

After the children had gone to bed and Padhraig had departed for his room with a mumbled goodnight, the sisters remained in the parlor with glasses of wine. "So what's this news you have for me?" Deirdre asked, with a mixture of apprehension and impatience.

Eavan moved over and sat beside her. "Put on the telly first so no one can hear us."

Deirdre found the remote and tuned to a talk program. "Is it about Ignatius?" she whispered fiercely.

"Who else? He wants to see you." Eavan raised her hand to stop her sister from speaking. "Just listen now and I'll tell you all about it. I got on the bus this morning as usual to go to work. And for once I got an inside seat – mostly the bus is crowded by the time I get on and I'm lucky to get any seat at all. Anyway, this fellow with a beard and dark glasses and a raincoat plopped down next to me. I didn't recognize him – I hardly ever get to sit with anybody I know in the morning rush – so I ignored him and took out the *Times*. And he never said a word. When I got off at Westmoreland Street he got off too, and as I was heading for the bridge he was walking alongside me. 'Hello, Eavan,' he said all of a sudden. 'Do I know you?' I asked; I was a bit suspicious, mind you: you get a lot of strange characters around Dublin these days. 'Ignatius Lally,' he said. 'Deirdre's friend. Remember me? Never mind the camouflage.' And he gave me this big smile from the undergrowth."

"I must say the whole thing gave me a bit of a shock. I knew you didn't believe he did it and I liked him myself the time we met. But I just had to hear him say it. So I asked him: 'you didn't do it, did you?'"

"'No, I didn't.' And there was something about the way he said it that made me believe him."

"He has that way about him," Deirdre said. "But anyway, go on."

"'I have to see Deirdre,' he said. 'When is the funeral?'"

"So I told him and he said he'd meet you in the grounds of the novitiate about half an hour after the funeral was over. He said to be sure to let you know that. And then he turned around and disappeared."

"His majesty has decreed there will be no reception after the funeral," Deirdre flicked a thumb in the direction of the ceiling, "so I'll be able to drop in on the way back. If you and I go in separate cars maybe you can take the children home for me?"

The clouds darkened on Eavan's usually placid face. "God

forgive me – I know he's your husband and all that – but if I had a shred of evidence I'd turn the bastard in this minute."

"So would I," Deirdre managed before bursting into tears.

In the morning the mourners followed the hearse on foot from funeral home to church, where Fiona's coffin was placed on a catafalque in the nave, and a mass of the resurrection was celebrated, in which priest and people prayed for the repose of Fiona's immortal soul, and priest and servers filled the air with smoky incense, and the priest praised the virtues of this pure young maiden untimely plucked with her life spread out before her but though God's ways were certainly mysterious just as certainly they were not without plan and that plan in the end was the best for all concerned. They followed the hearse once more on foot to the new section of Clyard's burial ground where the priest once more called heaven's pure angels to receive the pure soul of Fiona McCarthy into eternal rest. They cried when the coffin was lowered and the clay thumped on the wood and then they dispersed with slow sad steps through the cemetery gate and up the town to retrieve their cars and return to their homes.

Eavan took Gemma and Cathal for lunch at Ronan's, a slick new fast food place much frequented by the youth of Clyard. Padhraig was nowhere in sight when Deirdre got into her car and drove through town. She checked her rear view mirror to make sure she was not being followed before turning in the novitiate gates. The grass had overgrown along the driveway, the hedges near the house needed trimming, the building itself wore an air of desolation. She pulled up by the main door and waited. A few seconds later a sharp tap on glass took her by surprise and there he was, peering in the passenger window in beard, dark glasses, and raincoat – as described by Eavan – and topped with a soft tweed hat. Then he opened the door and slipped in beside her. "I'm so glad you could make it," he said.

They held each other for quite a long time across the raised drive shaft, murmuring and touching and kissing. Eventually she straightened, removed his hat and glasses, and said, "let me get a good look at you. Is it really yourself?"

"Good disguise, eh?"

"Your own mother wouldn't know you."

"She didn't, as a matter of fact." The sound he made was part chuckle and all sigh of regret. "We got together yesterday in a room at the back of Flannery's grocery in Drumnamwika. Paddy Flannery is one of her oldest friends; she told me once she almost married him before my father came along; and often regretted afterwards that she didn't, she said."

"What are you going to do?" She forced the question, though she was terrified of the answer.

He faced the windscreen and stared at the facade of the former house of novices. "I'm going away," he said soberly. "But I'm not going to tell you any more so you won't be forced to lie or get yourself into trouble on account of knowing." He turned to her. "I love you very much, Deirdre."

Which brought on another bout of embracing and kissing and desperate groping, until he backed off and said, "I have to be going." He kissed her one more time and then put on glasses and hat, opened the door, and swung his legs out. Half in, half out, he turned and spoke very slowly. "Listen now: you'll be hearing very strange things about me in the next couple of days. Don't believe any of them. Just remember that I'll be all right, and I'll get in touch with you whenever I think it's safe to do so." Then he was gone, in a slow trot around the gable of the building till he disappeared from sight behind the shrubbery.

She spent the rest of the day in a trance-like state: putting off Eavan's questions with an "I'll tell you later," weeping every time she remembered Fiona, mechanically making dinner which she didn't eat, and studiously staying out of Padhraig's company. Not that this last was hard to do: he was in and out several times throughout afternoon and evening and when he finally came to stay he went straight to his room. Eavan was a great comfort, staying with her through the evening and sleeping with her at night. When she had to leave in the morning Deirdre cried again, even though they had agreed that Deirdre and the children would return to Dublin after the inquest and stay with Eavan until they found a place of their own.

The inquest was scheduled for eleven o'clock at the courthouse. She took Gemma in her car, leaving Padhraig to go by himself. Cathal declined her invitation to join them, but just as they were backing down the driveway he came racing out and jumped into the back seat. He offered no explanation for his change of mind and none was asked. In the courthouse Padhraig sat with his family, stoically keeping up appearances. When called he gave evidence that Father Ignatius Lally, a Catholic priest who had in the past been a friend of the family, had come to the house to remonstrate with Fiona regarding some serious charges his daughter had made against him. Padhraig replied, when questioned by the coroner, that he was under advisement from his solicitor not to discuss the nature of those charges in the present hearing. He went on to state that Father Lally had become enraged when Fiona refused to retract her charges and in sudden anger had lashed out at her with a vicious slap across the face. His daughter had staggered back, lost her balance, and fell to the floor, striking her head a sickening wallop on the tile. Padhraig paused at this juncture to recover his composure and wipe his eyes. Later, he bowed his head and covered his face as the coroner declared the cause of death to be massive hemorrhaging of the brain produced by a severe blow to the back of the head. Which injury was consistent with the deceased falling heavily backwards and striking her head on a hard tile floor. No evidence to the contrary being submitted, the jury returned a verdict that death had occurred as a result of the deceased being struck by the said Father Lally and her resultant fall.

Once outside the courthouse Deirdre walked away from her husband. Her children followed her down the street to her car. They cleared the town in sullen silence. Her brain was dead, she couldn't think, couldn't focus, scarcely knew where she was going. Even when Cathal said in a loud voice from the back seat, "it was daddy killed her," it took several moments for the words to register.

"What?" Gemma screamed.

"I said Daddy killed Fiona." A kind of surly satisfaction in the boy's repeated statement.

"What are you saying, Cathal?" Deirdre pulled the car off the road by an iron gate, shifted down to neutral and put on the hand brake. "What in God's name did you say?" She swung around in her seat to get a look at him.

"I *saw* him hit her." Belligerently, as if expecting not to be believed.

"You saw Daddy hit Fiona?"

"Yes." The boy was shouting now. "He slapped her across the face just like he said the priest did, and then she went flying back against the banister and the mat slipped from under her feet and she crashed backwards onto the floor. I saw the whole thing, so I did. It was awful. She lay there without a stir out of her. And then Daddy knelt down and started shaking her and trying to get her to move and yelling and crying. And when he stood up again I sneaked back into my room so he wouldn't see me."

"But weren't you in school that day, Cathal?" Though she had never known the boy, for all his other faults, to lie.

He reddened. "Supposed to be, yeah, but anyway I didn't go that day. Or the day before, either."

"You realize what you're saying?" Staring hard at him, heart pounding as if it would explode through her ribs.

"I realize, yes." Still belligerent. Staring right back at her.

"And where exactly were you when you saw all this?" If he really did see it ... Oh God! Ignatius, my love, come back!

"You know the way the rail on the landing runs along as far as my room?" Explication instantly dissolving the tone of defiance. "Well, I was lying flat on the floor so I could peep over the top and they couldn't see me. Because Daddy didn't know I wasn't at school. I saw the priest as well when Daddy was arguing with him," he added gratuitously.

"Really?" Now here was something that could be verified. "Where was *he* standing?"

"I saw him out my window. He was in front of the door and Daddy was yelling at him like a madman and then he said he was going to get the shotgun and shoot him if he didn't go away." The boy's momentary grin at that recollection was more like a snarl. "Boy! You never saw anyone run so fast. It was kind of funny."

It was also a corroboration of what Ignatius had told her. She checked for traffic and turned the car around towards Clyard. The sergeant at the station expressed his condolences again. A stocky man with deep-set eyes and chubby cheeks, he had been to the house twice before the funeral to ask them questions. "We don't have any word yet on the whereabouts of ..." He let the sentence trail, as if embarrassed to actually name the priest.

"Well I have some new information for you." Then she choked: *Oh God, you are indeed without mercy, forcing a woman to indict her husband for killing her daughter.* "Cathal here has something to tell you."

She was too distraught to admire her son then, but afterwards she did. The lad never flinched: not when the sergeant ushered them into a small bleak room with just a table and four chairs; nor when a Garda placed a tape recorder on the table and a microphone in front of him; nor when the sergeant asked him in a cold harsh voice to tell his story exactly as he remembered it. He repeated almost exactly what he had told them in the car, then answered a barrage of questions put by the sergeant and the garda. As to why he didn't speak up before, he said he didn't want his father to know he hadn't gone to school. As to why he spoke up now, he said he hated his father for what he had done to his sister and he hated him even more for the way he had lied at the inquest. "You should never blame others for what you did yourself," he ended, with all the truculence of a schoolboy berating a classmate for cowardice.

"This changes things a bit," the sergeant said mildly after the tape recorder had been turned off. "If you'll all stay here for a few minutes I'll need to speak with my superior." Both he and the garda left and closed the door behind them.

"What are they going to do now, Mammy?" Gemma asked. Cathal, silent, stared unblinkingly at the wall.

"We'll have to wait and see." *You are absolutely horrible, God. Ignatius, my dear, come back, wherever you are. I so need you right now this minute.*

The sergeant was gone a long time, or so it seemed. When he returned he closed the door and sat next to Cathal. "The situation is this now: a car has just gone out to bring Dr. McCarthy in for questioning. Of course there's no need for you to meet him unless you want to. And I'd strongly recommend that you stay somewhere other than in your own home for the time being, just to be on the safe side. But let us know where we can contact you."

"We're going to Dublin," Deirdre said. She gave him Eavan's phone number. "I presume we can go back to our house to get some things?"

"Why wouldn't you? We'll be able to hold him for the rest of the day anyway." The sergeant stood. "That'll give you plenty of time. But don't leave here now till I get word they're on the way in."

Which word took an agonizing half hour to come through. The patrol car passed them, blue light flashing, just by the novitiate gates. No one spoke a word for the entire journey. "Pack one suitcase each with what you'll need for the next couple of weeks," she told her children. After she had packed her own she rang Aoife on impulse. "Have you heard anything from Ignatius?"

There was a silence before Aoife answered, "not from him, but there was something on the news just a few minutes ago." The starkness of her tone raised the hairs on Deirdre's nape. "Oh dear goddess!" Aoife paused again. "I don't know how to tell you this."

"Go ahead." *You'll be hearing some very strange things about me*, he had said.

"Ignatius borrowed Veronica's car a couple of days ago and it was found abandoned this morning down by the Cliffs of Moher."

"Oh God!" But she wasn't sure if the ejaculation was for Aoife's benefit or her own. *Remember I'll be all right,* he had promised.

"They found a note in the driver's seat. It was in Ignatius's handwriting. All it said was, *SORRY, VERONICA*."

"Did they find Ignatius?" She had to force the question, for despite his warning she was terrified of the possible answer.

Harsh breathing at the other end came from a woman in deep distress. "No. But they found his clothes on an overhanging ledge. Oh Deirdre!" This last was a wail of utter despair.

LIMBO

Getting through immigration had been his worst fear, even though the supplier of his American passport assured him he'd have no problem. Veronica was instrumental in securing that document for him; Dominick paid for it. The process was illuminating.

Ignatius had expected to be taken skulking through back alleys to a basement flat in a seedy neighborhood; instead, she rang the door-bell of a smart-looking Georgian house in Merrion Square and escorted him, bearded and hair-dyed, up a flight of stairs to a small business office. The sign on the door said ***COLLECTORS' DOLLS: EXPORTS AND IMPORTS***, and the heavy-set man behind the desk was dressed in a business suit. Veronica presented him with an envelope. The man perused the contents briefly: a single sheet of paper and two passport photos of Ignatius taken by the make-up artist after he had finished work on Ignatius's face.

"He's a priest," Veronica said. "They told me you'd be able to find a match."

"Maybe." The man took keys from a drawer, opened a filing cabinet to the side of the desk, and rummaged among the files. Eventually he extracted a thick manila folder. "Let's see what we've got here. A prolonged inspection preceded what sounded like a *huh* of satisfaction. He looked up at Ignatius. "How'd you like to be Father Colm O'Leary? Born 1949 in Kenmare, County Kerry, emigrated to America as a priest, became an American citizen, died in 1997 in a road accident in Kerry."

"The immigration people won't have a record of his death?" He had no idea how those things worked.

"Not at all. He was an American citizen, came over on holidays, got himself killed, and was buried in Kerry. As far as the American authorities are concerned he hasn't returned yet to the States. When we slap your photos on his passport you'll become Father O'Leary."

"Brilliant," Veronica said. "How long will it take?"

The man waved pudgy hands. "Getting the pictures on is the tricky part; it'll probably take a couple of hours, so if you'll come back about eleven we'll have it ready for you." In the event it was after one o'clock before they had the passport in hand.

All the reassurance in the world couldn't quiet the butterflies in Ignatius Lally's stomach as he presented himself to the immigration woman at Shannon airport. However, all she did was glance at him, glance at the picture, find a clean page, stamp it, and hand the passport back to him. It wasn't until he was seated by the departure gate that he realized his hands were shaking. It wasn't just the passport: at this first moment of relative calm his body was demanding relief from the stresses of the past few days. He closed his eyes and remained in a stupor until it was time to board. When the plane took off and he began to relax, the discomfort of his false beard pressed in on him again. He'd been wearing it on and off for the past four days and his skin was getting increasingly tender and irritated. But he daren't get rid of it until he reached New York.

"Go and stay with your uncle," Mammy told him at their clandestine meeting in Drumnamwika. Ignatius wasn't enthusiastic, but he didn't have many options. He had met uncle Sean several times in his youth when the judge, Mammy's older brother, had grandly descended on the farm as the wealthy American tourist, and he hadn't particularly liked the man. So when JJ at their last brief meeting suggested he might be able to stay for a short time with Rosemarie in upstate New York he jumped at the offer.

"I'll ring her tonight so, and she'll be expecting you."

He hoped JJ hadn't yet informed her of his reported demise: to protect them from legal problems he had told only selected friends about his planned fake suicide, though he did advise the others not to worry if they heard strange stories about him. He had to tell Dom, as well as Mammy and Dan.

At JFK when the customs man asked him to open his suitcase he was briefly terrified, but the search was cursory. After customs, he removed the beard in a rest room and rang Rosemarie. Yes, she was expecting him. How to get to Hillsview? By rental car would be easiest. "It's rather awkward to get here by train or bus from the airport." She gave him detailed directions. At the rental counter he realized that if he used his credit card he could be traced. So he converted the five hundred punt that Dan had stuffed in his pocket after driving him down to Shannon from the Cliffs of Moher, and took a taxi. He had another five hundred or so in his wallet that Dominick and JJ had given him.

Over the Whitestone Bridge to the Hutchinson Parkway to Interstate 684 to Interstate 84 west to the Taconic Parkway north to Hillsview Road. Then take the fourth right for one point one miles and he'd see the sign for WIT. *Women In Training*,

Rosemarie had explained in answer to his question; they decided not to call it a seminary because the latter had a common derivation with semen.

The entrance had high concrete pillars that had once been white but now had tie-dyed stains of green and brown, and an iron gate that was rusty and open. The winding gravel driveway led to a long one-story brick-front building with a white pillared porch guarding the front door. He paid the taxi driver, tipped him generously, retrieved his suitcase, and rang the door-bell. The woman who answered was tall, angular, with a mop of shoulder-length brown hair lightly streaked with gray. She was dressed in tee-shirt, shorts and sandals.

"I'm Colm O'Leary and I came to see Rosemarie Scanlon," he told her. "She's expecting me."

The woman looked puzzled. "Rosemarie said she was expecting a priest by the name of Ignatius Lally."

"Same person." In answer to her raised eyebrows he added, "it's a long story."

"You'd better come in," she said. "I'm Sorcha. An old friend of Rosemarie's from Dublin. I'll get her for you."

She was delighted to see him, Rosemarie said. JJ had been cryptic in explaining why he was coming, but no doubt Ignatius would fill them in on the details. However, as she was the cook this week, she'd have to wait until after supper to hear everything. "I must get back to the kitchen now, but maybe the boss can show you around." Nodding at Sorcha, who shook her head.

"We have no bosses here" she said. “They elected me moderator for the time being. But I *will* show you around."

The place was built as a retirement home for nuns forty years ago, she told him as they strolled through various rooms and halls and out into the grounds at the back of the house. Sorcha's face captured his attention: dark eyes that combined luster and intensity, a mouth feminine in shape and softness that yet bespoke the authority of a leader. Down the yard a young woman in a long summer dress bent over a straggly flower patch. Maria," Sorcha said, "I'd like you to meet an Irish priest. Father Lally – I think." Maria Bertonelli."

Maria dropped her gardening tool and pushed back her long black hair. "Pleased to meet you." She offered her clay-soiled hand.

"Maria and I are engaged," Sorcha said nonchalantly. "We're getting married after ordination."

As he let go the woman's hand he wanted to wave his arms and cackle like a clocking hen. Lally in Wonderland! Staid, traditional, Novice Master transported to a world in which God had disappeared and he himself was a sex maniac and murderer set down among women who were about to be ordained and then marry each other. Stranger still, the two of them were looking at him as if expecting his approval of this surreal moral landscape. "Well, that's certainly –" He stopped, searching for an appropriate expression, and ending lamely with "different."

"I think we shocked the poor man," Sorcha told Maria.

What could he say? "Just give me some time to absorb it. You are, after all, abolishing a few taboos here."

"Three," Maria shot back. Petite and pretty, with Mediterranean skin and features. "Women priests, non-celibate priests, and lesbian marriage."

"Which is an awful lot for a mere man to cope with in one day," Sorcha added. Her expression was sympathetic.

"When we told the bishop, even he was a bit shocked." Maria giggled, like a girl disclosing her first date.

"But he has agreed to perform our marriage ceremony anyway," Sorcha said.

"Do you think I might have a drink?" He was parched, and also too tired to ask more about this bishop.

"I'm so sorry. I've been remiss as a host." Sorcha led him back to the patio grouping of plastic chairs and wooden benches. "We have lemonade and maybe even some white wine."

"Wine, if you have it." And he had thought himself liberal!

"I'll get it." Maria headed for the door. "You Irish people sit there and talk."

"I'll have a glass, too," Sorcha called after her.

"So how do you reconcile all this with ordination?" Was even the most liberal Catholicism broad enough to embrace such departure from the orthodox?

"Christianity is the religion of Christ." Sorcha sprawled, ankle on knee so that the angle of her shorts revealed thigh all the way to her backside. "At least it was until it was all fucked up by celibate bureaucrats and power-mad popes and bishops." She glanced at him, as if to see how he took that, then stared down the yard. "Those of us who are serious about the religion of Christ, which is nothing more or less than to love one another, can either abandon the whole screwball mess and seek Christ on our own, or we can try to reform the institution from within. The people in this house believe our mission is to stay and reform."

"And you believe this is how God wants you to go about it?" *Speak to me, Lord! Please! I don't know what to say to this woman.*

"We believe that Christ was God's messenger; whether he was God or not, we don't know or care, but his message was clear and simple: love one another. And love includes sexual love. So as long as we don't hurt anyone in the process we can sexually love whoever we wish. *Dilige et quod vis fac*, Augustine said. The pity is he didn't stick to that thought instead of getting all hung up on sex."

"So if I understand you," he said, "your aim is to have Christianity focus on its most basic tenet. And to accomplish that you feel it necessary to abolish both celibacy and Christian marriage."

"No, no!" She wagged a reproving finger. "We only want to abolish the *requirements* of celibacy for ordination and heterosexuality for marriage."

"And you believe God would approve of that?"

"Show me where He said He didn't."

"What about ordaining women. Christ only ordained men." Hypocrite! He no longer believed that argument himself.

She chortled. "You'd have to be an eejit or a pope to try to sustain that dumb premise. Because to be logical you'd have to conclude that only Jewish fishermen or tax collectors were eligible to be ordained."

Maria emerged with the drinks, and Ignatius was so thirsty he felt like gulping the wine. At least Dominick and his group had withdrawn when they could no longer tolerate the rules of the institution, but these women wanted to stay though their views were even more heterodox. *But are they wrong*, *Lord*? was the refrain that jangled in his brain. The past couple of months had so weakened his hold on orthodoxy that he was no longer quite sure where he stood.

He met the other ordinandi at supper. Kelly was a local woman, a chubby youthful-looking mother of three grown children. She was here with the blessing of her husband with whom she spent most of her weekends. Jasmine, who was ethnically Chinese and a former Air-Force pilot, was recovering from a bout of pneumonia. Her black boyfriend had supported her until he found out that she was actually going to be ordained. Now he was having difficulty accepting the fact, so she was thinking of dumping him. Gina, who reminded Ignatius a lot of Terezinha, had abandoned a tenure track at a state university. She described herself as a lesbian in search of a partner. "I'd like to find one before I start my ministry," she said.

After the meal Rosemarie took him for a walk out the quiet country road. "I had a ring from JJ a while ago," she told him. "He said it was reported on the news that you had committed suicide. What's going on?"

He filled her in on his most recent escapades. "I couldn't let him know I was going to be officially dead – for his own protection."

"I don't believe all this!" She shook her head in bewilderment. "So what are you going to do now?"

"Stay dead. And try to find a new life here. But I'm too tired to talk about it now." The length and stress of the day suddenly unplugged the drain on his energies. "I'm feeling totally wiped out. Jet lag, I suppose."

"You can have the bishop's room for tonight," she told him. "We'll discuss your future tomorrow."

He slept well and woke at six. But he stayed in bed, listening to the silence, until a door slammed and footsteps sounded in the hall. The bishop's room had its own bathroom so he was able to perform the morning ablutions without venturing forth into this house of women. When he did step out the Air-Force pilot was passing, in a long white dressing gown, wiping her hair with a towel as she went. "You'll find breakfast in the dining room," she told him,"unless the cook slept in."

Rosemarie and Sorcha were at a table, eating and talking. "Help yourself," they told him. On a sideboard were various cereals, cut-up fruit, orange juice, coffee, bread, and a toaster. He joined them with a bowl of cereal and a glass of juice. "We were just talking about you," Sorcha said. "Rosemarie was telling me all about your predicament."

"Ridiculous, isn't it?" For reasons he could not fathom he was feeling light-hearted, while recognizing that at any moment the reality of his plight could plunge him into despair.

"Do you have any idea what you want to do next?" Sorcha's question, put between bites of fruit, had the casualness of a prepared probe.

"Other than have breakfast," he said flippantly, "not a clue."

"Does your visa allow you to work?" Rosemarie's inflection suggested she feared it did not.

"I have an American passport."

"Oh!" they chorused.

"That certainly makes things a lot easier," Rosemarie added.

"We could use a chaplain," Sorcha said offhandedly. "I don't know if you'd be interested? It's not exactly an orthodox Catholic institution, as you may have gathered."

"Tell me about it." His life was getting weirder and weirder, so being chaplain to a women's seminary seemed scarcely outrageous any more.

They told him about the workings of this feminist house of priestly formation, so different from the CWM seminary of either his own time or the present as to make comparison pointless.

"We've been studying for the past three years," Sorcha said, "although we didn't have any prospect of ordination until Bishop Paul came along a few months ago."

"That was when I decided to join them," Rosemarie put in.

“Who is this Bishop Paul?” Ignatius asked.

“He was a bishop in Brazil; you’ll meet him soon and he’ll tell you all about himself.”

He still didn't know what to make of their enterprise. "So what kind of studies are you doing?"

"The mass and sacramental liturgies, of course,” Sorcha said. “Then public speaking and pastoral counseling. We're not delving much into dogmatic or moral theology, and we're only looking at the bits of canon law that suit our purpose. You see, we're focusing on how best we can serve in hospitals, hospices, battered women's shelters, homeless shelters - any place where the poor, the downtrodden, or the helpless are to be found. That's the kind of work we believe that Jesus Himself would be doing if He were here today."

"What would you expect from a chaplain?" He desperately needed some way to make a living.

"The mass of course," Sorcha said promptly. "Though not confession - we're into direct confession between ourselves and God. But we could benefit from your experiences as a pastor. I think you'd be able to make up the rest of your duties as you went along." She paused. "There's just one problem: we don't have any money to pay you. In fact, in our present state of penury we couldn't even afford to keep you here if you were to work for nothing."

Shit! "I don't have any resources myself,” he told them. “And I need to find a job that'll support me." *You're really dragging me to the bottom, aren't you, God?*

"However," Sorcha continued evenly, "Bishop Paul told us that if we should find someone willing to serve as our chaplain he might be able to get us some funding for the post. So if you're interested I'll ring him and see what he has to offer."

"I'm interested." The real question was whether he could retain his sanity. But then, an insane chaplain in an insane world should be a perfect fit.

"Right. Lovely. I'll ring the bishop then."

He spent the morning walking, initially in the garden, then on the road. The exercise invigorated him, till he actually laughed aloud at his ridiculous situation; though whether the laughter was hysterical or merely tension-reducing, he couldn't tell. When he returned Sorcha was waiting for him. "I've got something for you. Let's go sit in the back and I'll tell you all about it."

He could wind up homeless, he told himself as he followed her around the side of the building.

"Here's what the bishop told me." She settled into one of the plastic chairs. "There's a foundation in New York called the *James Murray Foundation for the Promotion of Socially Conscious Catholicism*. James Murray, the founder, was a Catholic of Irish descent who amassed millions in stock-market transactions that he realized at the end of his life were of 'dubious ethicalness' – as the bishop put it. So before he passed on he tried to make sure of his eternal reward by establishing the well of James Murray's remorse, a Foundation to promote the ethical values that he had so flagrantly abused in his own days of greed."

"Like any respectable Irish business man," Ignatius put in.

Sorcha smiled. "Anyway, his son Malcolm runs the Foundation now. From which he takes an enormous salary, the bishop said, as he decides who is worthy of his father's largesse for propagating progressive Catholic tenets; such as liberation theology, the just wage, ethical investment, women's rights, freedom of reproductive choice, etcetera. Apparently if you convince him you've a mission with a progressive Catholic tag on it he'll drown you in dollars."

"How do I meet this magnanimous distributor of largesse?" Feeling giddy at the thought that something good might be about to happen to him.

"The bishop said he'd ring him and get you an appointment."

Which he did, Sorcha informed him later that same day; and for next day at that. She drove him to the railway station in the morning. It wasn't his first visit to New York: as Superior of the Brazilian mission he had once spent a month in the Big Apple raising funds to finance a health insurance program for himself and his confreres.

He was Father Colm O'Leary and he had an appointment with Mr. Malcolm Murray, he told the receptionist on the fortieth floor, a pretty young woman in a power suit who sat behind an L-shaped desk laden with computer equipment.

"I'll see if he's available." She struck some keys, glanced at a screen, tapped an impatient black-nailed finger on the desk while awaiting a response, struck some more keys, frowned, hit a single key with just a touch of asperity, then smiled and looked up at Ignatius. "He'll be with you in exactly three minutes and thirty seconds. You may take a seat while you're waiting."

The reception area was spacious, the chairs luxurious, the array of magazines on the coffee table enticing. But he needed to collect his thoughts again for the forthcoming interview. The key words for Mr. Murray were *progressive* and *feminist*, Sorcha had told him. And what words could better describe his putative new post? He just needed to focus his mind on the introduction, always the most important element when one wanted to make a good impression. He didn't have much time; "He'll see you now," the receptionist called. She stepped out from behind the desk, swinging her long model-thin legs in tights beneath an extremely short skirt as she led the way to the great man's lair.

Lanky-tall, was Ignatius's first impression as Malcolm Murray strode forward to greet him across acres of deep pile carpet. Slicked black hair, shiny forehead and sensuous lips suggested he could be a man of thirty, though closer inspection revealed the lines and droops of the forty-plus. "So good of you to come, Father." His smile was expansive. Then the thin nose twitched and sniffed and the smile gave way to a frown. "You smoke cigars?"

"No. I've never smoked in my life."

"Good." The frown deepened. "I can't stand smokers." The nose sniffed again. "But I detect cigar smoke somewhere."

"Could be the taxi I came up in. It reeked of tobacco."

"The gall of those people." The Foundation magnate stamped his foot into the rich pile. He swung around and strode back to his desk. "Stacey!" He pressed a button on a console.

"Yes, Mr. Murray."

"Get onto the Commissioner and complain that people are still smoking in taxis."

"Yes, Mr. Murray."

The Foundation chief smiled at Ignatius. "I'm so sorry, Father. Come and sit down. Stacey will bring us coffee in just a minute." He led the way to a grouping of armchairs facing a full-length window that offered a view of two other glass-walled skyscrapers. "Decaf, of course. I can't abide caffeine." He hitched up his trouser legs and wiggled in his chair to get comfortable. "Now, let's see. You're a friend of Bishop Paul. Am I right?"

"You are indeed. The bishop –"

"Don't tell me. It'll all come back. The bishop has a seminary for women who wish to be ordained as Catholic priests, and you have presented yourself for the post of chaplain there. Am I right?"

"You certainly are."

"I'm a member of Mensa, you see. Photographic memory, that sort of thing. I can recite much of Shakespeare by heart."

"That's impressive!"

"I've actually written a book of crossword puzzles based on his works. Published by Random House." The deprecatory hand-wave suggested it was a mere trifle. "I've also had a couple of my crosswords published in the New York Times."

"Brilliant," Ignatius pronounced.

Malcolm Murray smiled in modest embarrassment. "That's all beside the point, of course." Stacy came in then with a silver tray that she placed on the coffee table. Mr. Murray poured. "Tell me now about your proposed new job, Father. I find the whole idea of a women's seminary and of ordaining women to be very, shall I say, intriguing."

What was he to say? He knew nothing about his proposed new job, or about WIT. But, *impress the man and you'll get the money,* Sorcha had emphasized. So he said, "those ladies are taking a giant step forward for women in the church, blazing a trail into the twenty-first century. The time has come to break down the final barriers to women's equality in the church of God by ordaining them to the priesthood. And whatever will help them achieve that end is extremely worthwhile."

"Indeed. Just so. Very laudable." Mr Murray's head nodded vigorously. "But tell me, Father, how will the post of chaplain help them accomplish that purpose?"

"The chaplain will attend to their own spiritual needs. The basis of their ministry, which is to attend to the material and spiritual welfare of the sick and the downtrodden, will be found in their deep spiritual lives of prayer and sacraments and union with God that –"

"I'm an atheist myself." Malcolm Murray interrupted. "And I like to think I do some good works, too." His eyes challenged Ignatius.

"Indeed!" Christ Almighty! That was a critical piece of information that Sorcha had failed to give him. "I somehow thought that ..." So his entire bloody case went out the window, didn't it? She *had* said the fellow wasn't an institutional church man, that he thought the clergy and hierarchy were seriously insensitive to the real needs of their people. But an atheist!

"Don't feel too bad, Father: a lot of people have been fooled before." Mr. Murray's grin had the gleeful quality of a small boy who has just uttered his first obscenity in the presence of adults. "Of course I do go to church – family; keeping up appearances, that sort of thing." He looked embarrassed,

"Our differing beliefs about God needn't form a barrier to creating a better world for the materially deprived."

"Just so! Just so indeed." Mr. Murray seemed pleased with his response. "We're concerned about improving people's lot in *this* world, aren't we? My father, you see, established the Foundation as his own personal insurance policy for heaven. Of course, I myself don't feel the need for that, since I don't believe in heaven. However, I do believe in helping my fellow human beings." His finger caressed a pimple on his forehead. "But above all, I feel myself ethically bound to carry out my father's wishes. Socially enlightened Catholicism is what he stipulated should be promoted by his Foundation, and by golly that's what the Foundation's money will be spent doing."

"These women are certainly socially enlightened," Ignatius said.

"Your request will have to go to our Board of course," Mr. Murray told him, standing to indicate the interview was over. "For that you'll need to fill out the formal application that Stacy will give you on the way out. But, since *I* make the decisions, I can tell you now that you will get some funding. However," the Foundation Head's smile was tinged with malice, "we'll review your chaplaincy at the end of a year and decide whether or not to continue our support."

Ignatius felt like crying in the elevator on the way down.

RESURRECTION

On his return to WIT a smiling Rosemarie met him at the front door. A surprising sight because, while she had pitied his plight after initial doubts, their relationship had never exceeded the politeness of casual acquaintance. "Great news, Ignatius; I'm so happy for you; they've arrested McCarthy; you're in the clear." The phrases tumbling out of her like water pitching through rapids.

He caught the gist of it, but recent experience warned *don't get your hopes up, Lally.* So he paused a moment before replying, and then all he said was "tell me slowly what it's all about."

“Come on into the kitchen and I’ll tell you all.” She led the way. They sat at the table. Her eyes were brilliant. "JJ rang about an hour ago and told me the news. Apparently the son saw McCarthy hit his sister and told his mother and she went to the guards and they arrested the fellow and charged him with murder."

"That poor woman! What she's going through." Afraid to focus on the effect for himself. But a wave of emotion hit him then, bringing tears to his eyes.

"And do you know!” Rosemarie’s eyes opened wide. “I had to convince JJ that you were still alive? Despite what you had said to them they were in a panic when they heard the reports of your suicide."

"I wonder if I *am* still alive?"

"It's marvelous, Ignatius. Gobsmacking great! Now you can get your life back together again." The woman was bursting with enthusiasm. "Do you think you'll –? Ah, but it's too soon yet to ask you where you're going from here, isn't it?"

"You're absolutely sure of all this?" He was still stunned.

"Oh yes, No doubt at all. JJ was quite emphatic that you're no longer a suspect. How could you be?"

"And the other thing? Any word on that?" Of course a man charged with murdering his daughter was hardly likely to accuse him of having raped that daughter. But you never could tell, especially with Padraig.

"He said nothing about it. But I can't imagine the brute making accusations against you now. And by the way," she lowered her voice though there was no one else around, "we don't have to tell the people here anything about this since they don't know why you came in the first place; I only told them you needed time to rethink your life."

And he certainly needed to do just that, was his thought as he escaped to his room. But he lay on the bed unable to think or feel, like an out-half overcome with exhaustion the moment the match was over. And when he eventually got up and stretched and shook himself in an attempt to restore energy to listless limbs his mind still refused to focus. He removed his shoes, dropped onto the bed again, and slept.

He woke to darkness, scrunched up like a baby in its mother's womb. His limbs were stiff, his body cold, and for a time he had no memory of where he was. Gradually the recollection of

Rosemarie's smile and words drifted into his consciousness like the onset of an evening mist. But he couldn't cope with them yet. He rolled off the bed, removed his clothes, slid under the sheets and went back to sleep.

He woke to the morning sun in the window and the sound of footsteps passing his door. Rising, he washed and dressed, feeling ravenous. Sorcha was alone in the dining room. He filled his plate and sat with her. "We missed you at dinner." She was munching on an apple. "Rosemarie said you were probably exhausted, so we didn't disturb you."

"I was." He was eating too fast, in danger of choking. "I was very tired."

"And how did your visit go with the great Mr. Murray?" She smiled. "The bishop says he's rather an odd character."

"He's that all right, I'd say. However, he promised me some funds." But did it matter any more? He had to go somewhere to think.

"Isn't that wonderful. We're looking forward to having you as chaplain." She went on to talk about the future of WIT, bubbling with plans and enthusiasm. He nodded and agreed and waited for a chance to leave. And took it when Maria joined them.

He ought to be peeved beyond measure at the timing of his nemesis' fall, he told himself as he strode down the road. Just one day earlier and his tattered reputation would have been restored; he'd have had the pleasure of seeing Kennedy grovel and the archbishop wriggle, and have basked in the glory of vindicated victim. Instead, he was officially, publicly, dead; he could never set foot in Ireland again as Ignatius Lally. And his immediate prospects here in the United States were tenuous, not to mention the long-term outlook; they were as murky as Liffey water.

So he good reason to be furious. Yet he didn't feel the anger. A sense of wild elation and an urge to laugh out loud were his dominant emotions. Perhaps he was so overcome with relief that he couldn't focus on the past injustice that had destroyed his future? But that explanation proved unconvincing when he reflected on that past injustice and failed to provoke even a semblance of outrage. Perhaps it was his forgiving nature? He laughed outright at that suggestion; Ignatius Lally was not a saint, and sanctity of a high degree would be required to forgive what Padhraig McCarthy had done to him.

So unless he was a masochist who rejoiced in pain, which he had never hitherto been, his lack of anger could only be explained by lack of injury to cause that anger. Yet, he *had* indubitably been hurt. And was still hurt, and would continue to be hurt, by what McCarthy had done.

Or would he? A startling thought instantly pricked at the undercurrent of his elation. Did he like where he was now? Did he look forward to his future options? If he did, then deep in his psyche must be an outlook on life so new and so radical that it had not yet crashed into consciousness. An outlook that was willing to shake off his previous life, as a snake casts off its last year's skin. In the space of a few months he had mutated from a priest whose life was in order to a priest whose life had been shattered, and if he wasn't feeling devastated at such a change then might it not be reasonably inferred that he had not been satisfied with the life he had been living?

So what part had he not been pleased with? He'd been a happy man, hadn't he? Master of Novices was a challenging and deeply satisfying post that carried with it the respect of his peers and a comfortable closeness to his God. Celibacy, the obvious answer, was a vocation-long problem that he had, despite his Terezinha lapse, learned to live with. There *was* Deirdre McCarthy, of course, but prior to the awful accusation his relationship with her had not exceeded the bounds of clerical propriety, nor had it seemed likely to do so in the future. But perhaps that was true only prior to their passionate love-making and the resurrection of his resentment over the loss of Terezinha? So for the loins of Deirdre McCarthy was he willing to lay aside his life as a priest? And yet he had promised his Lord that if He, his God, would return, then he, Ignatius, would leave his Deirdre and cleave to Him alone. Even now he was willing to put off contacting her until he had resolved his puzzling embrace of an altered life.

That resolve was put to the test immediately on his return to the house when he was assailed by a fierce desire to hear her voice. But he had to know where he was going and what he was doing before he talked to her again. So he retreated to his room and shut the door and spent the rest of the morning reading a mystery novel in an attempt to clear his head.

It seemed to work. By lunch-time he was composed enough to engage in the meal-time conversation. By early afternoon he was rational enough to commit not to think any more on the subject till his grant money was approved and he was in a position to decide on the future. In the late afternoon he went for a stroll along a trail in the woods behind the garden. The low autumn sun shafted pinpoints of light between the trees, the foliage resplended in orange and yellow and red, and just a whiff of cool breeze foretasted the winter to come. He wasn't intentionally thinking of anything when the Notion arrived. *You'd be talking with Himself about all this beauty and what-not in the old days, wouldn't you?* it introduced itself casually.

For sure, he acknowledged. *I would indeed.*

And thanking Him for it all.

Shouldn't I be thanking Him now, too, even if He is ignoring me?

Well, that's an interesting question, isn't it? I mean, you've been getting on pretty well without Him lately, haven't you?

Indeed I haven't. Life without Him has been a misery.

Really now, Ignatius? Think about it for a bit. You used never do anything without consulting Him: always getting His opinion and blessing and approval before you'd so much as decide on a piss. And now look at you! Standing on your own two feet like a rooster flapping his wings on a wall, and making the most audacious choices of your entire life without even a nod in His direction. I'd say that's getting along pretty well without Him, wouldn't you?

So what are you trying to tell me?

Just that I don't think you're unhappy any more without His presence.

I'll be the judge of whether I'm unhappy or not.

Arrah, weren't you like a child learning to walk? You knew how to stand on your own but you were afraid to let go of Him until He let go of you first. Now you can get around quite well by yourself, thanks very much. And what I'm suggesting to you is that that's what He wanted you to do in the first place – walk independently and pick your own paths in life without bugging Him all the time for answers to your problems.

So you want me to be a free thinker? Is that what you want?

Sort of, I suppose. For example, you've known for a long time that the Church is wrong on a lot of things, so why continue to act as if you believed it wasn't? Isn't that dishonest? Do you think that's what He expects of you? Stand up for what you believe, man!

Like the women here at WIT are doing, I suppose? And Bishop Paul? I don't know if I can do that. I do actually agree with what they're doing, but if I openly sided with them then I, too, would be a schismatic and a heretic. And I'm not sure I'm ready for that yet.

Yet? And why not? The Journal you worked on with JJ was heretical in the eyes of the Church, wasn't it? The Fog certainly thought it was. And besides – listen to this – if you did join up with these WIT women you'd be able to marry Deirdre and still remain a priest. Now there's an idea for you!

Why do I think you're the real reason I wasn't upset when the truth came out too late?

"Oh I am! I am! The Notion smirked.

He hurried back to the house and rang Deirdre, though it was past ten, Irish time.

The trial and conviction of Dr. Padhraig McCarthy for the manslaughter of his eldest daughter, Fiona, was a feast for the media and a nightmare for his family. The horrific story of a respected veterinarian who had violated his own daughter (two of her classmates testified that Fiona had told them her father had shagged her), accused a pious Catholic priest of raping her, killed her in a fit of rage because she refused to testify against the same priest, and then crowned all his previous crimes by attempting to pin the blame for her death on the selfsame innocent man of God, could not but provide entertainment for the masses when professionally and graphically presented on television, radio and a vast variety of print media. In the new Global Village world the story even transcended the borders of Ireland, making headlines as far away as San Francisco and Hong Kong, and bringing lucrative contract offers to Deirdre McCarthy from Hollywood, Bollywood, the BBC, the cream of New York publishing houses, and many other institutions of international entertainment. All of which offers were refused by the felon's privacy-obsessed wife.

In this tragedy of classical Greek proportions the incident that plumbed the deepest feelings of sorrow among the masses of the world was without doubt the suicide of Father Ignatius Lally. Was ever a man more unjustly destroyed? the media wailed. Never mind that he was not exactly a paragon of celibate observance: a diligent digger of muck from a world-renowned magazine had unearthed his *affaire de coeur* with one Terezinha Gomez in the heartland of Brazil fifteen years earlier. Nevertheless, the media wept, a terrible injustice had been perpetrated against a man whose only sin had been to love not wisely but too well. Which raised again, the editorials ran, the question as to why clerical celibacy was still ... The judge, too, drew heavily on the tragic death of Father Lally when sentencing the felonious veterinarian to the maximum jail term permitted by law for the crimes of manslaughter, incest, and buggery.

Like most media events, the affair had but brief time and interest limits; it was blown away in early December by the crescendo of excitement that surrounded the approaching Millennium. By Christmas it was a faded memory in print and video archives.

The last three months of the second millennium, CE, was the period in her life that Deirdre McCarthy would most like to forget. There were times when she feared she was going into a state of permanent forgetfulness. Days of daze, nightly nightmares, media madness, courtroom chatter, all combined to overstretch the tolerance of her tortured mind and threatened to shut it down. She believed that were it not for her sister she'd not have survived the ravages caused to her mental health by the circus that surrounded the trial and conviction of her husband. Eavan was a brick: a shoulder to cry on, a solver of problems, a giver of advice, a family therapist. And not least was her role as teacher substitute for the children: Deirdre hadn't dared to send them to school while the horrible drama was unfolding, so Eavan set them homework and encouraged them to study as a relief from the misery in which they, too, were immersed. It was a particularly stressful time for Cathal. The boy's statement to the Gardai had resulted in his father's arrest, but Padhraig McCarthy had maintained his innocence through the commencement of the trial. Only when the jury had been selected and his own lawyer had strongly suggested he plead guilty in the face of overwhelming evidence did he confess his guilt, thereby sparing his son the tragic duty of testifying in court against him.

The case ended a few week before Christmas, but the joy of that season by-passed the McCarthys. Eavan did her best, but neither Christmas mass nor Christmas gifts could produce even a semblance of cheer. The cessation of publicity brought Deirdre its own cruel aftermath of revulsion, depression, and even suicidal thoughts. She now had time to grieve for the daughter she'd lost, the husband she'd once loved, the children whose lives would be forever scarred, and the priest she had loved and lost. But her grief, which nature intended to heal the mind, was so intermixed with bitterness that it had little chance of success. Nature had not caused this tragedy, and nature could not effect the cure. She hated

Padhraig for what he had done; and even death could not quench her anger at Fiona's perfidy.

Hardest of all to deal with were her ambiguous feelings towards Ignatius Lally. She had feared the worst from the findings on Moher, even though he had forewarned her not to worry. However, her relief when he rang a week later, safe in America, was soon drowned in the theatrics of criminal prosecution. His occasional calls thereafter, though welcome, were never well timed; anyway, events so forced her to focus on daily survival that her emotions could not cope with eros. Ignatius was banished to the periphery of her thoughts with the promise that he'd be recalled when the crisis was over. But now, sorting through the debris of the tragedy and finding him waiting, she could not bring herself to restore him to his former place. Why that was so, she could not say. He had done no wrong. On the contrary, he was the victim, or one of the victims; Padhraig had destroyed *his* life even more than hers. And he had been so patient, so willing to suffer his own destruction rather than risk the ruin of her life. It wasn't his fault that her husband was psychotic.

And yet. What? She agonized over that *what*. If Ignatius Lally had never entered her life her daughter would still be alive, her husband would not have committed those horrific crimes, her family would still be together in Clyard. But who had brought Ignatius Lally into her life? Was it Ignatius Lally? No. Was it Deirdre McCarthy? Yes indeed. Wasn't it *her* dinner invitations that had aroused the jealousy of her mad husband? Wasn't it *her* obvious adoration of the man Padhraig hated that drove him to do what he did? So it was *her* passion that had set off the chain of events that had dragged herself and her family down this sorrowful road. Then why think of apportioning even the slightest tittle of blame to Ignatius Lally? She could not, of course, and she would not.

And yet. He wasn't responsible but he *was* the occasion. That's what he was, the innocent occasion; he was analogous to one of those Italian women you read about, whose beauty distracts male drivers in Rome and causes them to crash. So did she want him back in her life to remind her by his presence of the disaster her infatuation had wrought? On Christmas day after dinner she walked alone down Terenure Road in the rain, having declined her sister's invitation of company, and she thought about all this and concluded she could never look Ignatius Lally in the face again. And when later that evening he rang she thanked him for saying he loved her, but didn't reciprocate. And when he asked if she had plans, now that the trial was over, she said she was far from thinking about anything like that yet. Later still in the evening it struck her that his enquiries might be merely his way of ensuring she was all right before he said goodbye to her and went on with his new priestly life in America. But that thought did not provide her with the comfort it ought to have if she no longer wished him to be part of her life.

Despite what she told him, she had to make immediate decisions about her future. Padraig's lawyers had sucked whatever he had in savings. The money that Gemma had found in the jampot was spent, and they were living in Eavan's house at Eavan's expense. She must pick up the pieces and face the fates that had ruined her life and go looking for a job. Which she did. She had scarcely begun the search when serendipity found one for her, as if to show that not all the fates were cruel. Two days after Christmas she was on her way into Eason's bookshop to enquire about job openings.

"Deirdre", she heard her name called as she walked in the door.

She scanned the crowd and found the gaunt-faced man smiling at her by the magazine section. "Father Kennedy!" She knew him, but not terribly well: he used to drop into the office for a brief chat on his infrequent visits to the novitiate.

"I was thinking about you the other day." He held out a cordial hand. "Could I entice you to Bewleys for a cup of tea? I have something I'd like to discuss with you."

She acquiesced, though not without a worry that it might be something unpleasant to do with Ignatius. Furthermore, she bore this man a grudge for the way he had treated Ignatius.

"We were terribly sorry to lose you when the office was moved to Dublin." Father Kennedy bit into an eclair. "However, we were fortunate to find a very competent young man to fill your shoes."

"I'm glad to hear that." What was he trying to do? Show her how dispensable she was? Anger stirred within her: next thing he'd be blaming her for the whole Ignatius injustice.

"But now," the priest paused to finish chewing, "the young man is leaving us for a more lucrative job. And since I knew you were currently living in Dublin it crossed my mind that perhaps you'd be interested in having your old job back?"

"*To survive up here you're going to need a lot more money than those fellows in Clyard were paying you*," Eavan had advised her. "I'd need a lot more money than you were paying me in Clyard," she now told Father Kennedy.

"But you would be interested in the job?"

"Only if the money is right," she said firmly. "I have two children to support and a much higher cost of living to cope with."

"I understand." And apparently he did. Else he needed her desperately. Anyway, he doubled her previous salary and invited her to start work at the beginning of the New Year.

The media blitz surrounding the prosecution of Padhraig McCarthy ought to have proved a boon for a Catholic clergy under siege for years because of alleged sexual abuse by some of its members. Here was a case to give pause to those who saw clerical pederasty everywhere: an innocent priest sent to his death through a viciously false accusation. Might not many other allegations be found equally untrue if properly investigated? The media regrettably failed to discuss this point of view. In the opinion of Brian Kennedy, Superior General of the Congregation of World Missionaries, their response was as mean-spirited as if poor Father Lally had been actually guilty. A national editorial even asked why Father Kennedy, who knew of those base charges from day one, didn't reveal them? Had he done so, it pointed out with perfect hindsight vision, the charge could have been challenged and disproved on the spot, and the life and reputation of the unfortunate priest would have been spared. It was, the editorial continued, another case of clerical cover-up, and again their failure to be open and honest had militated against the innocent, who this time happened to be one of their own.

A leading provincial editor, more reflective and less strident, wondered what might have happened had not Father Lally's superiors, as well as the archbishop of Tighmor, immediately jumped to the conclusion that the priest was guilty as charged? The presumption of innocence must always be maintained until all the evidence is in, the editor noted. In particular, it behooved the superiors of a religious congregation not to abandon a member who was faced with a catastrophe such as that which confronted the late Father Lally.

As if all this unwarranted criticism were not enough to depress a saint, Brian Kennedy had also to deal with a lambasting from his own conscience. His instincts had told him the man was innocent, he censured himself with pitiless candor. "We helped drive him to it," he confessed pathetically to Father Mullen.

"Arrah, I don't buy that at all, Brian." And the reddening of Mullen's face was a sure sign that the man's defensive quills were being raised. "We did the right thing according to the information we had at the time." But Kennedy closeted himself with his conscience and scourged himself with recriminations and prayed to his God for forgiveness and wondered if there was any possible way he could make up for the wrong he had done.

Such was the state of his mind the day he spotted Deirdre McCarthy in Eason's. He did indeed need someone to run the fund-raising office, and he had indeed thought of Mrs. McCarthy for the job. But not till they met did he think of her as a reparation receptacle for his sin against Ignatius Lally. He had rejected the media insinuations that his dead confrere might have had an affair with Mrs. McCarthy – *de mortuis nil nisi bonum* – but he had no doubt that theirs had been a beautiful, while completely appropriate, friendship. Hiring the job-needy woman and doubling her salary went some small way towards assuaging his guilt.

A week after Deirdre commenced work at the fund-raising office in the Mother House, Mullen collared him coming out of supper and said brusquely, "I need to talk to you, Brian." They left the compound and took to the sidewalk of a nearby housing development. "I heard something today that'll raise the hair on your head." There was a dour satisfaction in Mullen's tone that said the news could not be good.

"I don't need any more bad news today, Dermot." He had just gotten a letter from the Namibia mission superior telling him that Father Cormac Heron had been charged with sexually molesting one of his mass servers.

"I was talking to my Garda friend this afternoon and he let drop a casual remark that I thought you should know about." Mullen as usual teasing out his information.

"Who's being arrested this time?" God! He couldn't take any more of this.

"Nobody, thanks be to God. We were discussing the McCarthy case and he said, 'do you know, the detectives in that case don't believe Lally committed suicide at all.'"

"What?" Kennedy stopped dead and stared at his confrere. "Don't tell me he was murdered, too?"

"No! No! In fact they think he's still alive. They believe that knowing he was being hunted for the murder of the McCarthy girl, he faked the suicide and skipped the country." Mullen's crooked grin challenged refutation.

"God help me, I think I'm going out of my mind." Kennedy closed his eyes and stood perfectly still. "They really believe he's still alive?" In a dreamy tone, as if he were trying to communicate with the dead.

"That's what my friend said. He did add that they have no interest in investigating the matter because no obvious law has been broken, other than maybe public mischief or something minor like that. Anyway, they've enough to do besides delving any more into the McCarthy case."

Kennedy's eyes remained closed. "If he's still alive we must contact him. A terrible injustice has been done to that man and it has to be righted."

Mullen's snort resembled a pig requesting supper. "If you turn over that stone, Brian, you're liable to find a lot more things underneath than you want to see. My advice would be to leave the matter alone, like the police have done."

But Brian Kennedy was not prepared to leave the matter alone. He let his imagination run wild overnight on the tantalizing possibility. In the morning he went to see Deirdre McCarthy in her office. Things were going well, she told him; her predecessor had done a good job. "You miss Father Lally, I suppose," he said.

"I do; he was always very helpful." But her reaction to the question gave him no helpful clue.

"Did you know there's a rumor going round that he may not be dead after all."

A fleeting expression of fear flitting across her face was immediately repressed. "You're joking? She said."

But in that instant Kennedy knew that she knew. Her response was too casual for one who had believed her dear friend dead but had suddenly been given hope that he might be still with the living.

"You *know* he's alive, don't you?"

"I don't know what you're talking about, Father." But too late the eyes opened wide and the look on her face expressed utter surprise.

"Listen!" He eased himself into the visitor's chair. "A terrible injustice was done to Father Lally. Everybody knows that and everybody tut-tuts. But I was a party to that injustice. And it's no salve to my conscience now for me to say that I thought I was doing the right thing at the time. Since the report of his death and the discovery of the truth my conscience has given me no peace. So

I have to make reparation to Father Lally, now that I know he's alive. But I can't do it till I know where he is. And it's my belief that you can help me there."

She swivelled her chair till her back was to him. Her hands covered her face. He heard the quiet sobs and sat waiting in silence. Eventually she swung back and stared at him, red-eyed. "I still don't know what you're talking about, but it seems to me that if Father Lally were still alive and had disappeared then he wouldn't want anyone to know where he is. And if anyone did know I'm sure he'd want that person to keep his whereabouts a secret. Wouldn't you think so, Father?"

He nodded his head and waved his hand to indicate she might be right or she might be wrong. "Up to a point, yes. However, if there were someone who wanted to do him a great deal of good and that person didn't know where he was, I'm sure Father Lally would want the person who knew to tell him. Don't you think?"

She showed him her back again for a bit and when she returned she said, "I'll have to give the matter some thought, Father." With that he had to be satisfied for the time being.

ASCENSION

As if God, or malevolent fate, had only so much misery to expend on those hurt by Padhraig McCarthy, the agony months of Deirdre were paralleled by a period of recovery and relative tranquility for Ignatius. The Murray Foundation formally committed to fund his chaplaincy with thirty thousand dollars a year for three years, beginning in January, 2000. For the three-month interim, Sorcha agreed to let him stay on in the bishop's room on payment of two hundred dollars a month, a sum he could just afford from the money he had brought from Ireland. And when Bishop Paul presented him with a used but serviceable car he felt that he was on the road to starting a new life.

The bishop himself was responsible for much of Ignatius's renewed hope for the future. Dom Paulo Da Silva Ferreira, to give him his full title, was celebrating his eightieth birthday the day Ignatius paid him his first visit. "*Seja bem-vindo, padre.*" He hobbled down the driveway, hand outstretched, a slightly stooped, grey-haired, man with tired eyes and dark wrinkled skin. "Sorcha has been telling me what a wonderful priest you are." He took both of Ignatius's hands between his and pressed them firmly. "Coming from her that's no mean compliment," he added, the smile turning mischievous. And that was the start of a friendship between the two men that in a few months became as firm as though nourished by a lifetime of commitment. Dom Paulo had been Bishop of Campo Florida in the south of Brazil from 1960 until 1975 when, having fallen in love with an American nun and concluding that such human love was a gift of God too precious to be rejected, he resigned his bishopric. "A decision I have never regretted," he told Ignatius when he introduced his wife, Kathleen.

His intention had been, on resignation, to remain in Brazil and seek employment as a layman. The Brazilian hierarchy and the Vatican bureaucracy had other plans for him. "'You must leave the country if you are to have a hope of getting a dispensation,' I was told in no uncertain terms. So I came to America with the love of my life and applied for laicization. But after three years of waiting and getting the run-around we got married without the church's blessing."

In the meantime he had been approached by a group of Catholics who were disenchanted with the institutional Church but who were devoted to the liturgy and the practice of brotherly love. "They asked me if I would serve as their pastor, and how could I refuse? I felt that through them God was calling me to a new ministry." The group grew in numbers over the years and begot other groups, so that now - more than twenty years later - they totaled several thousand, scattered across New York, New Jersey, and Connecticut. Bishop Paul, as he preferred to be called, had eventually found the task of ministering to the spiritual needs of this growing congregation more than he could cope with alone, so over the past ten years he had trained and ordained five young men to assist him.

"And now we're going to add some women priests." The accompanying half-smile suggested knowledge from sources unknown to others. "This good lady here" – he nodded at his petite wife, still a pretty woman with long black hair and a trim figure – "has sensitized me to the feminist mode of thinking."

"So what's your status now vis a vis the Church?" Ignatius asked him during one of his early visits.

"Well, they ignored me for a while; later on they threatened to excommunicate me if I continued to say mass in public. But they didn't actually do anything until the first ordination. Then they formally excommunicated me."

"So how do you feel about that?" Would Ignatius Lally dare step outside that Body which was entering the third millennium of its existence with the firm conviction that outside Itself there was no salvation.

"*I* am the Church." The bishop said this with the easy simplicity of a man in tune with his own convictions. "The Church is the people of God and I am of the people of God. No legal bureaucracy can deprive me of that. And the people who need my ministry are no less the people of God." He followed up that justification by offering Ignatius a small additional salary if he would serve two recently formed congregations in western Connecticut. "These are genuine followers of Christ and they need our spiritual help."

Ignatius made a snap decision to accept and then fretted all the way back to WIT. *If you would only talk to me, Lord, and give me some guidance*; but *I suppose this is another of your ploys to make me think and act for myself. All right, so be it. But on your head let it be if you don't like my choice.*

"He's not well at all," Rosemarie said when he told her

about his visit with Bishop Paul. "We're praying he'll survive long enough to ordain us at Easter."

"Why don't you ask him to move up the date?"

There was a sour quality to her laugh. "We did, believe me, the last time he was here. Very delicately, of course, but we got the message across. He wouldn't hear about it. 'I'll ordain you at Easter, as I promised,' he told us. 'To change that schedule now would be like giving Almighty God a vote of no confidence.' Of course it's our belief that he wouldn't ordain us at all if it weren't for his wife."

"Maybe *she* can get him to change the date?"

"We've debated asking her, but we're concerned that if we put too much pressure on him he might back out of the whole thing."

When Ignatius arrived on his next visit the bishop was taking his afternoon nap. "I'll make us a cup of tea while we're waiting," Kathleen said. So he sat in the kitchen while she put on the kettle and got out the cups. "I'm worried about him," she said. "He's not well at all. It's his heart," she added while taking the tea bags out of their envelopes.

When they were sipping tea in the living room Ignatius said casually, "the women at WIT are concerned that he may not be well enough to ordain them at Easter."

"Indeed." Kathleen looked past him out the window; there was profound sadness in her eyes. "I worry about that, too."

"Could he be persuaded to move up the date, do you think?"

"I wish." Her smile only deepened the melancholy of her expression. "We're dealing here, unfortunately, with a prime example of *machismo Brasileiro*. He still has serious misgivings about ordaining women at all, you see. Not from a theological standpoint – that doesn't bother him in the least – but because he hasn't learned to accept yet that women can ever be more than second class citizens. He only agreed to do it after a lot of persuasion."

Ignatius had to smile at the casual tone of this last statement. "How did you manage it, if you don't mind my asking?"

Her face brightened. She lowered her voice. "I gave him to understand that he'd be facing a cheerless old age without feminine comfort if he denied me this request." And she chortled softly, as if once again savoring her victory.

"But you don't think you can persuade him to move up the ordinations?"

"He's terribly superstitious about changing dates. But I'm working on him," she added. A piece of hopeful information that he related to the women of WIT on his return.

At the beginning of January, when the first installment of the Murray funds arrived he rented a furnished house a few miles down the road from WIT. He had in mind not only his own comfort but also that of Deirdre and her children, feeling sure that once the dust of tragedy had settled she'd want to come and live with him. This hope was not dampened by her evasive replies to his queries about her plans for the future; she needed more time to recover from her gruesome ordeal. But whenever she was ready she'd find him ready, too. For, by accepting to work with Bishop Paul he had made the choice of cutting himself off from the institutional church and thereby freeing himself from his vow of celibacy. *And if you don't like it, Lord,* he told his God at the time, *You'd better let me know soon, because I'm acting independently now and taking responsibility for my decisions, like You told me to.*

His Lord gave no indication whatever, of approval or

otherwise.

On a chilly Friday evening in late January he returned from visiting his congregation in Lichfield to find a Toyota Camry sitting in his driveway. As he pulled in two men stepped out of the car. He felt certain he was hallucinating when his brain said they looked awfully like archbishop Donnellan and Brian Kennedy.

"Ignatius!" The man he imagined to be Kennedy bounded towards him like a fawn to its mother. "It's so great to see you. The moment we heard that ... Ah, gee!" He stood before Ignatius, smiling in deepest embarrassment. "I just don't know what to say. I ... You look great in that beard. Doesn't he, your Grace?"

The Donnellan apparition stepped forward with cordially outreaching hand. "Father Lally, it's good to see you. You gave us a terrible fright." Ignatius mechanically grasped the extended glove. "And I'm so pleased ..." The bishop image then shivered violently. "I wonder if we could go inside. I find this American winter chill almost unbearable."

He let them in. The house was warm. He hung their coats in the small closet and led them into the living room. "How did you find me?" Still unsure that he wasn't imagining the entire scene.

The two men sat. Donnellan rubbed his hands vigorously. "Mrs. McCarthy finally agreed to tell me when I told her we had some very good news for you." Kennedy focused his eyes on the floor. "We always had our doubts of course that you had ..."

"Can't say I blame you at all for what you did, Father," Donnellan affirmed stoutly. "Not one blessed bit. We were all too hasty in condemning you and we all owe you a tremendous apology. And that's why Father Kennedy and I are here today." He shivered again. "Do you think we might possibly have a cup of tea, or anything hot; I'm chilled to the bone. If it's not too much trouble,

Father."

Pouring water into the kettle and turning on the electric stove, locating mugs and tea bags, provided the distraction he needed to absorb the extraordinary fact of his visitors' presence. But with absorption came anger that heated in tune with the water on the stove. By the time he returned to the living room his temper was as scalding as the tea.

"That's much better," Donnellan said as he sipped. "I needed something to warm my insides."

"So you came all the way over to apologize for the past?" But without waiting for an answer Ignatius continued, as if talking to himself, "I've often wondered what I'd say to the two of you if this situation ever arose."

"Not merely to apologize," Donnellan said expansively. "There is also the question of your future."

"I've imagined hanging your Grace upside down by your shoelaces, with your purple socks covering your chubby hairy calves and –"

"We have given the matter a great deal of thought," Kennedy, red-faced, cut in. "And we came up with a plan that we think you will find quite acceptable."

"Swinging to and fro from a tree branch, was where I placed you, and you pleading loudly for mercy. Only I couldn't decide if you'd be wearing suspenders on your socks. That bothered me a bit."

"Obviously you can hardly return to your Novice Master post." Donnellan pressed on. "So we –"

"As regards you, Brian, I don't really want to elaborate on what I had in mind for you. Suffice to say there was a reference in it to balls."

"His Grace has gone to great lengths to find you a suitable position," Kennedy persisted. "One that won't expose your – what shall we call it? faked suicide? – to the world. After all, if that *were* revealed you'd be in serious trouble with the authorities – misrepresentation of a crime or something of the sort."

Ignatius stared from one to the other, the anger still inside him. "And of course both of *you* would be in major do-do as well when it came to light that you, too, had wrongly accused me of rape and buggery."

"The media has already raked us over the coals for that," Donnellan said, and sighed. "But we did what we did to save holy Mother Church from further embarrassment. I'm sure at this point you are able to appreciate what an awkward predicament we were in."

"At this point," Ignatius said, suddenly weary, the anger draining out of him, "I don't give a damn. I no longer even want to string the two of you up by shoelaces or gonads or anything else."

"All right then!" Kennedy almost shouted. "So now we can start moving forward again. As we were saying, we have come up with a plan that will ensure you an excellent future. Would you like to tell him about it, your Grace?"

"Which doesn't mean of course that you both don't have serious penances to perform." Ignatius looked sternly from one to the other.

"One of my classmates from Maynooth is now the rector of a seminary in California," the archbishop said. "So I rang him and asked if he could find a position for an extremely worthy priest who through no fault of his own finds himself in a terribly awkward situation. Needless to say," he raised a hand to ward off an imagined objection, "I didn't go into the details, so as not to betray your secret. But I suggested to him that since as well as being a very brilliant theologian – which Father Kennedy has assured me is the case – you are also a missionary with long and varied experience, perhaps a post as professor of pastoral theology would be appropriate. He rang me back three days ago to say that, subject to the formalities of applying, the job is yours."

They both looked at him, tails wagging, awaiting his approval.

"I have a serious moral dilemma," Ignatius told them. "And since you're both distinguished moralists perhaps you can help me."

"What do you think of his Grace's offer?" Impatience in Kennedy's tone.

"It's all right, Father," the archbishop said. "Let Father Lally state his dilemma first."

"I saw a movie last week where two variations on a woman's life were shown. She raced to catch an elevator before the doors closed; in one variation she caught it, in the other she didn't. In the case where she did catch it she wound up being killed; in the case where she didn't she went on to enjoy a happy life. Afterwards, it struck me that if I had taken the variation in my life where I obeyed you, Brian, and had gone to the Mother House and accepted a lifetime of punishment for a crime I didn't commit, then Fiona McCarthy would not have been killed, Padhraig McCarthy would not be serving a life sentence in jail, and life for both of you would have been a lot less complicated."

"Ah now, Ignatius," Kennedy began, but Ignatius cut him off.

"So, morally speaking, and supposing I could have foreseen the consequences of my actions, which variation should

I have chosen?"

"Ah indeed! But fortunately, and praise be to God, we don't have the ability to see the future," Donnellan said. "So your dilemma is a purely hypothetical one."

"'Greater love than this no man hath,'" Ignatius quoted. "'than that a man lay down his life for his friends.' But He said nothing whatever about the man who would lay down his life for his enemies."

"But you *will* take this post, won't you, Ignatius?" Kennedy was leaning forward in his chair, elbows on knees, like a jockey urging his mount to the finishing post.

Ignatius, unblinking, stared back at him. "I won't, Brian, but thanks all the same. I have more important things to do with my life right now. Anyway, I'm planning to get married as soon as we get the paper work sorted out."

Deirdre was doing laundry after work when he rang. "It's me," he said.

"Well! I was getting worried about you. You haven't called for weeks." Despite her continued ambivalence about the future of their relationship, he was never far from her thoughts.

"Eleven days," he corrected. "My mother died," he added somberly.

"Oh, Ignatius! I'm so sorry. Had she been sick? I don't remember you telling me." She knew how very fond he was of the mother he called a harridan.

"No. Massive heart attack, they said. But that's the way she'd have liked to go: quickly."

"When did it happen?"

"She died on Saturday morning. We buried her today."

It took a few seconds for the implication to sink in. "We? Do you mean ...?"

"Yes. I'm ringing from Mullagh. I'm coming up to see you."

"Of course!" There was no ambivalence in her glandular reaction. "When?" Trying her best to keep calm.

"Tomorrow, if that'll suit. I need to get out of this place in a hurry."

He rang her at work next day, just after one o'clock.

"Where are you now?"

"At Dominick's."

"I'm going home sick right now." Yes, he had a rented car and would meet her at Eavan's in half an hour. *Now don't overdo it, Deirdre McCarthy*, she warned herself on the way. But of course she did: told ambivalence to take a hike the moment she saw him, raced into his arms, and said all the things she'd been holding back for the past several months.

"I missed you terribly, too," he responded when they eventually unclinched.

"You're the healthiest looking dead man I've seen all week," Dominick observed.

"Must be the cold winter air of God's own country," Ignatius reflected. "It does wonders for the skin." He had reluctantly torn himself away from Deirdre for a couple of hours to visit the group that Dom had summoned to his house in a hurry.

"Tell me," Veronica said, sitting snug against him on the sofa, "you went to your mother's funeral, right?"

"I did." Her loss had not fully sunk in yet, but he knew he was going to hurt for a long time to come.

"So didn't anyone recognize you? I mean, the beard is good

and all that, but ... I'd know you anywhere."

"I wore dark glasses and a hat, and I stayed in the background as much as possible. Dan introduced me as his cousin back from England."

"And you think that fooled them?" Turlough asked incredulously. "Sure down the country everyone knows everyone. They'd spot you a mile away."

"It didn't fool them one bit, not at all, but it gave them the message that they weren't to talk to strangers about my being there. One of the neighbors came up to Dan at the wake and said 'I'm sorry for your trouble.' And then he looked at me and he said, 'I know Father Ignatius is here, too, in spirit.'"

"The Journal sold over five hundred copies this time," JJ told him.

"And 'tis as dull as a bishop's piss," Turlough growled, "Not a serious discussion of atheism in the whole sad cycle of sermons."

"Which didn't prevent our old friend, the Fog, from threatening excommunication again if I didn't withdraw it." JJ took an emotional swig of whiskey. "I told him if he arrived in hell before me to keep my seat warm."

Ignatius told them about Bishop Paul and his fledgling church and his own new ministry. He also filled them in on the women in training to be priests, about which they were already aware through JJ and Rosemarie. When he mentioned the ordinandae's rejection of celibacy Veronica shouted "Yeah! Yeah! Yeah!" and put an arm around Ignatius's shoulder. "Will you marry me if I go out and join up?"

Which caused a general laugh. But later when he was leaving she hugged him tightly, kissed him on the lips and whispered in his ear, "come stay with me tonight; do please, just this one time." Her pleading eyes were fiercely tempting; only the promise of his night with Deirdre precluded any possibility that he might succumb.

Easter Sunday in the year 2000 was a watershed for the women of WIT. The ordinations were to be held inside a large tent that had been erected on the lawn behind the house by *Karen's Party Rentals* of Hillsview. The morning was mercifully sunny and mild, with just enough of a cool edge to make the less hardy keep their jackets on. The ceremony was scheduled to begin at eleven in deference to the distance most of the attendees had to travel. Delegates from Bishop Paul's scattered congregations had been invited to participate and, while a few arrived the day before and stayed overnight at local motels, the majority traveled from home that morning. Also present were some close relatives and friends of the ordinandae.

Promptly at eleven the liturgical procession – those about to be ordained, the priests of the congregation, and the mitered bishop – exited the front door, walked slowly in single file around the side of the house to the back of the tent and advanced solemnly up the aisle that was created by the congregation seated on Karen's white plastic chairs, to the flower-decorated altar on a wooden dais at the front of the tent. The ordinandae were attired in albs, maniples, and across-the-shoulder stoles, while priests and bishop wore full celebrant regalia. As they processed they sang that ancient and beautiful hymn to the Spirit of God:

Veni Creator Spiritus,
Mentes tuorum visita,
Imple superna gratia,
Quae tu creasti pectora ...

Before the mass began, one of the young priests stepped to the front of the altar and addressed the congregation. "My dear friends, it is my sad duty to inform you that Bishop Paul is not able to be here with us today. He is suffering from chest pains and is in the Westchester Medical Center for observation. Let us pray that Almighty God will spare him to us for many years to come."

He paused to let a ripple of sorrow sweep the congregation. "Yesterday however, Bishop Paul, out of his great concern for the future of our congregation, and in the presence of all of his priests, did in his hospital room ordain Father Ignatius Lally to the fullness of the priesthood as bishop."

The young priest paused again while a wave of audible surprise rolled through the congregation. "And lest there be doubt in anyone's mind regarding the validity of this ordination, I and my colleagues can testify that it was performed according to the traditional rite of consecration. The ordaining bishop is a legitimate successor of the Apostles and he used the accepted form of words and laying on of hands to transmit that succession validly to Bishop Lally." This time a burst of hand clapping emanated from the congregation.

The mass began, the new bishop and the priests con-celebrating. Rosemarie read the lessons, Sorcha the gospel, and Bishop Ignatius gave a stirring sermon on the beauty of the priesthood and the ground-breaking step the *ordinandae* were taking today in being admitted to this bastion of heavenly grace and power, and hitherto male exclusiveness.

Bishop Ignatius then pressed his episcopal hands on the head of each woman to be ordained and asked Almighty God to pour out on her His Holy Spirit. While he was performing this age-old rite Gemma McCarthy nudged her mother and whispered, "what do we have to call him now?"

"I expect *Father* will do fine," Deirdre whispered back.

"Why can't we call him Ignatius, like you do?" Cathal complained.

"Why don't you ask him yourself when we go home what he'd like to be called," the mother said.

Sitting just behind them and listening to the whispered conversation, the newest woman candidate for priestly ordination heaved a sigh. But even Veronica herself couldn't tell whether that sigh bespoke contentment or frustration.

And throughout the entire long ceremony, the God of Ignatius Lally maintained his eternal silence.

Also by Walter Keady

Celibates and Other Lovers

Mary McGreevy

The Altruist

The Dowry

The Agitator

Being and Becoming

Love, Justice, and Other Deceptions

Monica and Freddie